MW01631780

Watch What She Can Do

Watch What She Can Do

- a novel -

NICOLE BROOKS

Copyright © 2024 Nicole Brooks
First Erid Press Inc. Edition March 2024
All Rights Reserved

Print Book ISBN 978-1-7751554-9-2
eBook/.mobi ISBN 978-1-7383049-0-5
eBook/.epub ISBN 978-1-7383049-1-2

Print and eBook cover design by Nicole Brooks
Book design and proofreading by Nicole Brooks
Editing by www.michellemeadereads.com

Watch What She Can Do is a work of fiction. Names, characters, places, businesses, events, and incidents are either the product of the author's imagination or are used fictitiously. Any resemblance to actual persons or events is coincidental.

All rights reserved. No portion of this book may be reproduced, stored or transmitted in any form without permission from the publisher.

Other titles by Nicole Brooks:

Just Because We Can (2018)
Cake: a novel (2019)

For Jeremy
I’d call 911 for you

- 1 -

"REMEMBER WHEN WE first started dating and you said that you would never do my laundry?" Stan's voice, laced with humour, rose over the volume of the television.

I snapped my teeth together, my jaw muscle flexing, and set another pair of folded grey briefs on the pile. I'd never known someone to go through so much underwear in my life. It wasn't hard—seven days of the week, seven pairs of briefs. I eyed the pile, knowing there were double that, if not more. If Stan did his own laundry, that pile would be clipped back to a single, stiff-by-the-end-of-the-week pair in a heartbeat. *Gah.*

"You're so funny," I managed. His backhand gratitude had gotten old about thirty-six years ago. *Just say thank you*, I wanted to shout.

He released the footrest of his chair. A metallic *sproing* followed by a *clunk*—the sound of Stan's relaxation commencing. "C'mon, Willie. You don't have to be like that." He ripped open a bag of snacks.

"Like *what*?"

"Bitchy."

My head swam as a wave of vertigo came over me. I blinked hard before glancing at him. His affronted scowl was locked on the TV. I hadn't given him what he wanted—a chirpy, appreciative response. *Poor baby*. I reached for a shirt and imagined hurling it in his face and storming out the front door screaming the litany of things I'd never had the guts to say as I went. Instead, I pushed back the fantasy, folding the shirt with a sigh and adding it to the heap. I forced a grin. Two could play at this game. "Remember when you never used to complain about the food I made you?"

His scowl deepened as he stuffed a pork rind into his mouth—an apparent necessity since I hadn't put mayonnaise in his precious mashed potatoes, and he couldn't bear to eat them at supper earlier. I'd watched him push them around his plate, muttering, "It's not that hard to always have mayo in the fridge." Like it would be the end of him to have to eat them with sour cream instead. The way *I* liked them.

Another puffed fat curl disappeared into the abyss as he flipped the channel on the TV. Hockey to car show, back to hockey. A slight sheen glistened along his retreating hairline. He'd worked himself into a sweat gorging on those things.

I swallowed hard, fighting back the ugly thing that had lived inside of me for years, another version of me that was violent and destructive, one I barely had a handle on some days. I wanted to scratch his eyeballs out and scream and have him cower beneath me for all the times his way won over mine, for all the moments his opinion reigned supreme, for all the times he didn't hear what I was trying to say because his own voice was the loudest one in the room. Ignoring the twist in my stomach, I sniffed and collected my work, hoisting the laundry basket onto my hip. It would be safer for everyone if I just removed myself.

His eyes followed me, his features softening. "You sure take everything the wrong way lately."

I shot him a glare. I doubted that he ever considered that he *said* everything the wrong way.

He gave me his everyone-thinks-I'm-a-nice-guy grin—a lopsided smirk that somehow made him look ten years younger and the life of the party. "The laundry thing's a compliment. I'd be lost without you. In fact, I'm pretty sure I couldn't survive without you." He coughed and crunched another pork rind.

That right there. I gripped the handle of the basket. The fact that he *knew* this, could admit it, but carried on the same old way, was what burned me the most. I also knew there was a dark threat to his seemingly kind words. He'd told me he couldn't live without me the few times I'd walked out the front door when the kids were little, unable to carry the load of motherhood any longer. But even then, he'd wielded the line more as a weapon than a compliment. He'd said exactly what he knew I'd need to hear to keep me in this house—not because he appreciated what I did for him, but because it would be too much work to do any of it himself. So now, even if he didn't mean anything by it, I would not accept his feeble attempt at flattery. Not today. I was too tired. I continued past him, retreating.

"Here comes the silent treatment," he muttered after me.

You started it. Just once, he could ask how my day was and care for the answer. Or better yet, he could rise from his throne and gently put his hand over mine—insisting I sit before I collapsed—while he folded his own laundry. Why was I doing his laundry anyhow? He was retired, the kids were gone, I still worked. Why was this still my job? It's not like he mowed the lawn for me—I did that too. For years, the outside of the house was his, the inside, mine. But slowly his knees got worse and trudging around the yard behind a mower or shovel became too painful, so I'd picked up his slack. I froze for a second, wondering what he actually did around here beside make work for me. After being unable to think of a single thing, I forced my legs to move again.

Stan's coughs followed me to the bedroom. I sat heavily on the edge of the bed, tears already burning down my cheeks as exhaustion settled across my shoulders. How did I get here? At sixty-three, I should have been long past this feeling of grinding through each day. I was supposed to be travelling with girlfriends and reading novel after novel and running square-dancing clubs. But even with the kids gone, I was stuck in mother-mode to the biggest child of them all. It was like quicksand—once in, there was no getting out.

I searched for feelings of love toward him and came up empty. When had that happened? Surely there must be something or I would have left a long time ago. Wouldn't I? What kept me tethered to this place where I had raised three beautiful children, made a home for everyone, gave up all parts of myself for others' comfort? I sighed deeply. I didn't even know myself well enough to think of an answer.

Stan coughed harder and cleared his throat. And again. He'd been doing this since yesterday and it was starting to drive me nuts. How hard would it be to go get himself a pack of cough drops? But we both knew that unless I threw the medicine in his face, he wouldn't take any.

The cough was punctured by silence, then a wheeze. *Is he choking?* My heart thumped in panic, but the urge to jump up and run to him didn't come. Instead, I wiped my face, crept out of the room, and peeked around the corner to check on him. He was still stuffing food in his mouth, just stopping every few seconds to touch his chest and cough.

I went back to folding, dragging the idle chore out as long as possible. I didn't want to go back to the living room, where only Stan and a long, lonely evening waited for me, but *Jeopardy!* was about to start. Our nightly eight o'clock ritual. I needed to get it together before I faced that long hour with him.

As I neared the bottom of the basket, my nerves began to settle. Stan would so love that this task calmed me—further proof that I was built for domesticity. I jammed his underwear in the top drawer of the dresser. He *always* thought he knew what was best for me.

I put the laundry basket back in the corner of the bedroom and sat on the edge of the bed to check my phone. I'd felt it buzz a few times earlier from the pocket of my cardigan. I opened the text from Jonathan asking if I could pick up the kids after work tomorrow. I gripped the phone. He knew Fridays were my busiest day and I'd repeatedly asked him to find alternate arrangements if he needed me then. *It's for the kids,* I chided myself, letting my lower back round out to ease the ache there. I typed back a lackluster, *I guess so*, hoping he'd get the real message.

The second was from Roxanne asking if I had asked yet. I smiled at her commitment to me. Every so often, she'd asked if I had gotten permission from Stan to come visit her on Vancouver Island. Her requests had ramped up in the years since the kids had moved out. From my frozen existence here in Edmonton, I'd dreamed of the thaw of a beach retreat for years, and sure, I could have just packed up and left, but the fallout it would have caused was not worth it. Asking for what I truly wanted with Stan rarely was. It seemed pathetic in hindsight.

But maybe it was finally time. I steeled myself and typed out an all-caps yes. Surely by now I'd be able to go. If I pre-cooked all Stan's meals and made sure he had clean clothes to wear, gave the kids a heads up so they were available if he needed anything. I knew I had plenty of vacation banked at the store, so Ivan wouldn't be able to say no. *I deserve this.* I nodded minutely to myself. I really did.

My brain was flooded with days that would follow my declaration; Stan's harsh diatribes oscillating with the cold silences. I just knew it. My eyes misted up as I deleted the message. I needed to come at this properly. The luxurious wool coat I'd splurged on five years ago came to mind—the red had looked so striking against my black curls. But after a winter of Stan's grunting every time I put it on, I hid it in the back of the closet and went back to my old brown parka. Asking forgiveness instead of permission never worked with him.

I sat up straighter and formed a plan; I'd return to the living room in a better mood, laugh about how Stan's many charms had lured me into being his personal laundry elf, and he'd smile at his victory and then I'd pounce. It would probably end with me having to strip and do the deed, but a *yes* would be worth it.

My head swam with the thought of having a week to myself. And if he argued that it was a lavish expense, I'd bring up the fact that he'd just bought a five-hundred-dollar fishing pole without asking me first. With him being retired, technically I was the breadwinner here—*he* should be asking *me* for approval to buy and do things.

Once changed into my nightie, I moved my phone to the deep pocket on the side, scrunched my hair, pinched my cheeks, pasted on my non-bitchy face, and returned to the living room just as Alex Trebek's face loomed into view. Pulling a blanket over my legs, I sat in my chair. "The laundry elf's done," I said, my tone deceptively cheerful. The duplicity slithered from my lips, bringing a genuine smile to my face.

Relief and victory lifted his features. He was so pathetically simple—just *thinking* I was happy with the life he provided for me made him happy. He nodded to the TV, his blue eyes glittering. "Ready for me to kick your ass?" He loved nothing more than lording his imagined intelligence over mine.

"You better hope there's no medical categories tonight." My ten years as a nurse—even though long gone—came in handy once in a while.

I focused on the screen as the categories were revealed, suspicious that it was a rerun as some seemed familiar. *They probably recycle categories.* Stan answered the entire first round with fifteen correct to my three. He was beside himself with satisfaction.

The second round started, and Stan whooped. "*What women want*? Now that's a loaded category."

For men to stop telling us to smile, to let our hair go grey, a bed to ourselves, to eat chocolate ice cream without thinking about our waistlines, to be able to go out at night without fearing rape, male birth control… My mind reeled off answers. The last thought was for Annette, who'd argued intensely in its favour since her and Jonathan were deep into a vasectomy stand-off. The heated argument at Easter dinner had resulted in strong words over who was responsible for reproduction between a married couple. Back in the day, it had been one of Stan's friends who had finally been able to guilt him into doing it because the pill had been making me sick for years. It was a favour Stan lorded over me regularly, especially when he wanted something from me. He'd tut, "So, my going under the knife for you was for nothing?"

A contestant asked for What Women Want for two hundred. Stan rubbed his hands together, giving me a kind smile that caused my inner seething to falter. "Here's your chance, Willie. You've got this." Maybe his love for me was real and I was just a grumpy old lady. Surely there were bigger assholes in the world than him.

Alex's soothing voice started, "Some help around the house; would it kill you to get out the Bissell bagless cannister one of these every once in a while?"

"What is a vacuum cleaner," Stan boomed, unable to stop himself from trying to win. His eyes slid to me, gleeful he apparently beat me at my own game, missing the irony, and I scoffed at my desperate attempt to see the best in him.

One week away, that was all I wanted. That was how people survived the drudgery of life now—plowing through the days while looking forward to that one all-inclusive trip to Mexico in February. Why couldn't I be the same? I braced myself as the next question was uttered. "Time to exercise; perhaps a class in this discipline named for Joseph, who initially called it Contrology."

"What is Pilates," I muttered.

Stan shook his head. "What the hell" —he coughed wetly— "is Pilates?"

"Exercise. Something you should look into." I snapped my lips shut. *Be nice, remember the trip.*

The categories continued. Apparently, women wanted Levi's, Sleepytime tea, and time to do crossword puzzles. *No wonder I'm so miserable.* I'd set my goals too high. I didn't need vacations to visit my girlfriend—according to *Jeopardy!* I just needed to lower my standards and I'd be as happy as a clam.

Commercials came on. Some advertisement for a fancy Las Vegas car restoration company. *OK, now was my chance.* I took a quick breath and blurted, "Stan, can I go visit Roxanne?" I hated the pathetic grovelling in my voice.

A wince passed over his face and he touched his chest. "I don't know why you still talk to that crazy bitch."

Because she's my best friend? "You still talk to Dave." I held back the rest, *even after what he did to me.* The memory of Dave's greasy lips pressing to mine, his tongue excavating my mouth, hand gripping my breast while Stan threw back shots of whiskey across the bar still made me nauseous even twenty years later. When I'd told Stan, he'd just waved me away, as he did now.

"Dave's harmless. You need to get over that."

Tears burned behind my eyes. How did he always do this? Turned everything around on me? On a dime, me asking to go on a trip had changed into me having to get over being assaulted. I dabbed at the corner of my eye. It was useless.

Stan coughed, wheezed, and suddenly flung out his arm, sending the lamp crashing to the floor. I flinched and whipped my head around. He was clutching his chest, his fingers clawing at his rotten orange Oilers t-shirt. His eyes swung to me—electric blue and full of panic. The air in the room seemed to crash down, along with my stomach. *Heart attack.*

"Willie," he gasped. His hand kept working his chest as if trying to claw out the organ that was suddenly betraying him. I was frozen, unable to react or think as my body thrummed with electricity.

A wet gurgling emanated from his mouth, and the long-buried nurse in me finally moved me from my chair. I leapt in front of him and fell to the little square carpet at his feet, feeling the short fibres scrape my knees. "Stan?" I gripped the arms of his chair.

"Help," he choked out, both hands now clawing at his chest and neck.

My heart galloped as I leaned across his knees and grabbed the phone from the side table where the empty bag of pork rinds lay. "I'm calling 911," I said, my voice wobbling. I pushed the numbers, my fingers trembling so badly they hit *nine-two-two*. I choked and started over. *Six-one-one.* A low moan escaped me. *Focus! Nine-one—*

"Gah," Stan gargled, leaning forward just far enough to grab my arm.

"Stan, let go, I have to call," I whimpered as his grip on my forearm tightened. He continued to gargle and squeeze. Louder and tighter. "Ow, Stan! Please let go." He was going to snap my arm in half. I listed toward him to ease the crushing pain his death grip was inflicting. My vision swam before me as an old memory surfaced from the back of my brain—my father pinning my mother against a cupboard in the kitchen. He had been so mad.

I shook my head and balanced the receiver in my left hand and curled my thumb over the buttons—the right ones this time—attempting to call for help one-handed. Stan clenched impossibly harder, and the pain stilled my entire body—including my thumb, which hovered over the Call button.

I felt my mind detach from my body. Hovering above, I was staring down at the two of us, at his vicious grip, at my still thumb. I remembered my mother's terrified eyes swinging to little me, urging me with a look to go hide in my bedroom so I didn't have to watch. My breath came in shorter and shorter. A car revved on the TV and then backfired, making me jump.

I lifted my gaze and searched Stan's eyes. The blue had darkened. Steely.

"Will. Ee." His chest rose in staccato movements and fell heavily.

My mom wouldn't have called.

I could not call.

I sucked in a quick breath, my nostrils flaring. Spots danced before my eyes. My thumb flinched but did not press the button. Alone. I could finally be alone. A sob crept into my throat as tears burned behind my eyes. I saw myself folding laundry that was only mine. I saw myself having a bonfire in the backyard, Stan's new fishing pole jutting from the centre. I saw myself sleeping in the centre of my bed, never to be awoken by his nasal cacophony again. I saw myself never eating mayo in my mashed potatoes. I saw myself going to Vancouver Island without having to ask for permission.

His face was contorted in pain and then twisted up in anger. I watched him watching me, knowing that he knew what I was thinking. With obvious effort, his thin lips moved, forcing out a bitter, *"Cunt."* The word was as clear and sharp as a lightning bolt.

It sliced into me, and my whole body relaxed in defiance. As the receiver slipped from my hand and fell to the floor, a dark determination settled over me. If that was what he thought of me, then he could leave. The ugly thing that had lived inside me for years was ecstatic at finally being able to take over. I looked back up to him and lost myself in the lacklustre eyes of a man who, I suddenly suspected, had never truly loved me.

"WHAT HAVE I done?" The dismay in my voice was real, but was I imagining the reverence buried beneath? Stan's grip on my arm finally relaxed enough to pull myself free and I rocked back onto my ass with a thud. I tried to stand, but my muscles were jelly, so I scootched backward—not taking my eyes off him—until my back hit the far wall.

A contestant clapped loudly on the TV as he gave the right answer for final *Jeopardy!* The horrible, sticky clicking in Stan's throat had stopped. His face was frozen in a grotesque, tortured grimace—his bottom lip permanently stretched down, twisted, forever trying to pull in air. He was hideous.

I'd let my emotions get the best of me. For so many years I'd been careful with my anger, and for good reason if this was the result. My hands shook roughly, and a sharp pain tore through my chest. I gripped the front of my nightie, my fingers digging into my skin, feeling my heart thundering behind my ribs, breathing so shallow I feared I would pass out. He was gone. Whatever thoughts I'd had, whatever regret might come, it was too late. The glow of the TV played off his stilled features.

The old me had risen up and fought back. The person I was before marriage and children ground me down had re-emerged in a critical moment. I had taken control for the first time in a long time. A wicked part of me wanted to relish in the idea, but the treacherous thought ultimately revolted me. *This is not who I am.* My stomach tightened and I jerked forward and vomited down the front of my nightgown, filling the little lace eyelets with the white mush of the mashed potatoes I'd ruined earlier.

SECONDS, MINUTES, DAYS seemed to pass as my mind pulled up random memories: the first time I met Stan at Ezzy's and the desire ensued, when we found out I was pregnant with Tanya, how heartbroken he had been when his mother died, the dismal moment I realized he was never interested in giving me an orgasm, when I almost died of a ruptured ovarian cyst because Stan didn't believe the pain I was in, how Roxanne had lectured me about the importance of having high standards—which in her eyes, Stan did not meet. "There had to have been some good," I whispered to myself. I forced my thoughts back to the first time I'd met him and afterward how he'd escorted me home to my parents' house from the bar, leaving the softest, most gentle kiss on my cheek. I remembered how, after Tanya had been born, he'd held her so close to his body, tears rolling down his face—it had been the first time

I'd seen him cry.

I smiled a little, recalling how once he'd figured out my favourite treat—chocolate covered almonds—he showed up for every date with a box of them. My smile faded. He'd started giving me the side eye when I indulged in the same item years later, as if my waistline had become more important than my joy.

That was how it was with him. Every small, sweet thing he'd done in the beginning eventually soured, and when I told him years later how much of an asshole my father had been, Stan had crowed about never raising his voice or hand to me. But there were other ways to maintain control.

As I now watched his body intently for any sign of life, I wondered if he too had been holding something ugly back. Simply tolerating me so his needs could be met. What else explained the grip on my arm and that foul word? Maybe the real Stan had always been there, and it was just that the wool covering my eyes had grown thinner and thinner with every trip around the sun. Before I knew it, he was more like my father than I'd ever imagined, and I was forever stuck with that. Maybe we had started with love and had grown to hate each other over the years but kept up the ruse because that was what married people did—stayed together because on some level it worked—ignoring all the other crap that came with tolerating and abiding by someone else for decades. But I knew, on some deep level, Stan had benefited immensely more from this union than I ever did.

I shifted and the renewed stench of vomit made my stomach roll again. Was this somehow my fault? If I had said no the first time he'd brought a bag of laundry over to the little apartment I'd shared with Roxanne in university claiming his washer was broken, would we not be here now? If I had told him to find a laundromat, would I have not set in motion his ultimate plan for having a housekeeper, a babysitter, a mother-with-benefits?

"No," I said to the decaying air. Stan had to take some

responsibility for getting himself here, too. If he had treated me a little better, if he had shown me an ounce of this *love* everyone pinned for, I wouldn't have hesitated to call.

Breathing deeply and with focus, my jaw slowly relaxed. And then my tongue. And then my shoulders. Finally, my chest lifted in a long, slow inhale. I breathed out the heavy, black air that had filled my lungs for so many years, visualizing it latching on to Stan's departing soul. I didn't want it anymore.

- 2 -

I WASN'T SURE how much time had passed, but I knew I couldn't sit here all night. I had been lost in thoughts and questions for what seemed an eternity, and suddenly it dawned on me how guilty this made me look. A talk show host yammered from the TV about an up-and-coming graffiti artist in Toronto, and I pressed the heels of my palms into my eyes, trying desperately to clear my head and force myself to move. Crawling toward the phone, I grabbed it, then scurried back to my watchful position against the wall, scared my proximity to Stan's body would somehow rouse him just for revenge. I dialed 9-1-1, with accuracy this time. By the time I'd answered all the operators' questions and hung up, I was certain I was having my own heart attack. I'd called for help the last time Stan had a heart attack and had forgotten the intensity of their interrogations. I surely had tripped up somewhere and given clues as to my guilt. Had I said I'd called immediately or after trying to resuscitate him? Maybe I hadn't said anything. Did I tell them that I found him like this or witnessed it? For the life of me I couldn't remember.

I had to compose myself before scrolling through the recent calls until all three of the children were found, chastising myself for not knowing their numbers by heart. My voice was a hoarse whisper as I told them their father had died. The phone dropped again and I wrapped my arms around myself to control the fierce shaking that was taking me over. As I thought of the lie I was going to have to stand behind—the farce I would have to live for the rest of my days—little puddles of cold sweat accumulated in my armpits, beneath my breasts, and along the edges of my briefs. But hadn't I already been living a different kind of farce all these years? This was simply the other side of the same coin.

I finally looked at the old scroll clock on the mantel. I flinched as I saw that it was just before eleven. I'd sat for two hours? I forced myself to focus and run through the story. "We were watching TV, and I was about to go to bed when he knocked the lamp on the floor. By the time I assessed him and called, it was obviously too late." To my own ears, it seemed suddenly weak—that he just up and died. Which he did, but reinforcements couldn't hurt. I looked wildly around the room, begging myself to think clearly for a second.

Prep the scene. I knew that people didn't have a heart attack from one junk food binge, but it couldn't hurt. I heaved myself up and stumbled to the kitchen, my legs still weak, dumped two cans of beer down the sink, found a couple old Hot Rods, peeled them and disposed of the meat sticks deep in the garbage can. On second thought, I grabbed four more and did the same before returning to the living room to stage the scene. I leaned as far away from him as I could and reached forward, tucking several of the Hot Rod wrappers into the cracks of his chair—gagging as my hand touched his lukewarm leg. When my hand brushed several wrappers that were already there, I winced. His doctor had forbidden these after his last heart attack three years ago. I yanked my still-shaking hand back, silently condemning Stan for being a dumbass.

A door slammed outside, and I leapt back to the wall and collapsed. Jonathan and the paramedics burst through the door, my son's eyes finding mine.

"Mom!" He rushed to my side—his gaze barely gliding over Stan. His eyes scanned me as if I'd been the one hurt, but I could see the deep pain behind his concern. He touched my arm and when I didn't respond, prodded me harder. He rocked back on his heels and said, "You're in shock." Jumping up, he retrieved the blanket from my chair and wrapped it around me, kneeling in front of me. "Mom, it's going to be okay."

I sniffed and the tears started. It cut me to the core that I wasn't truly worthy of his care and concern, but I wasn't exactly sure what I was crying for. Relief, fear, regret? I was in trouble. They were going to find out. *He got what he deserved.* He hadn't been that bad. I should have just called. *I'm free.* My mind skidded and scrambled as it tried to find stable footing, as it tried to make sense of this scene. We had just been sitting here. I was letting him think I was fine. I asked to go see Roxanne. Maybe if I'd have asked years ago, he would have said yes and I wouldn't be here. My shoulders shook with sobs as the panic finally settled in.

I watched the paramedics work on my husband, both dreading and praying that there was no hope.

"We need to get you cleaned up," Jonathan said.

I frowned at him. His curly, black hair was flat on one side. He must have been asleep already.

He motioned to my chest. "Your nightie."

"Oh, yes." It suddenly struck me that the vomit was almost dried.

"Just give me a second." He stepped over to the paramedics and they conversed in low tones. Jonathan's eyebrows creased and he glanced at me before turning back to them nodding and whispering. *Oh shit, they know.* Was Stan too stiff? Colder than he should be for a recently deceased person? Ignoring my pounding heart, I forced my gaze away from them to the fireplace mantle and the family photos that lined it. Three children. Seven grandchildren. They would never see Stan again. They were so young, most of them would not remember the caring grandfather he'd been. My tears renewed themselves in earnest.

Jonathan returned and bent down to lift me by the armpits. He led me down the hallway and turned into our bedroom. "Do you need help washing up and changing?" His brown eyes were full of empathy and wet with tears, easing my earlier worries a fraction. Not only did Jon look like me, but he had always been the softest with me of my children. The girls were the hard, determined ones.

"No, I should be able to manage." *More than you could possibly imagine.*

As I turned away, he said, "What's that on your arm? Looks like finger marks."

I saw the chance to build my case and jumped on it. "Oh. Um." I looked at him and searched his face. "I didn't put mayo in the mashed potatoes," I whispered.

"What does that mean?"

I thought of all the times my father had dragged my mother around by her arm. She must have always been covered in such marks. "Your father didn't like it." Really, it wasn't a stretch. I was simply reordering the timeline of this evening's events. "He didn't like a lot of things I did." The hitch in my voice was real and the tears renewed themselves unbidden.

He blanched. "Mom… I… I never saw him touch you?" It came out like a question, as though asking whether he'd missed something that had been in front of him all along.

A tremor ran through me. I kept my mouth closed, not trusting myself to go too far. He gave me a once over, assessing me before giving me a sad smile. "Just go change. I'll deal with this out here, alright?"

I nodded and closed the door behind me. I stepped out of my nightie and let it fall around me, my cell hitting the floor with a thump. I had forgotten it was in my pocket, against my hip the whole time. Standing there only in my underthing's, the shaking worsened. I had only intended to change, but there were not enough clothes in the world that would warm me now, so I made my way to the shower. I needed a good scalding.

"MOM?" JONATHAN'S VOICE cut through the steam. "The paramedics just want to ask you a few things."

Shit. This was it. I took a deep breath and turned the tap off; certain I could still smell vomit.

I slipped into a pair of black jeggings and my heaviest sweater. I was still freezing, but didn't want to come out dressed in pyjamas and a housecoat like I was about to have a relaxing evening in.

I entered the hallway and Jonathan smiled at my getup. "Still cold?"

I smiled weakly and he stepped to the living room and returned with my slippers. Stan's body had been removed and I breathed a sigh of relief. Jon took my hand, and we settled on the couch as the female paramedic sat on the edge my chair. "I'm so sorry for your loss, Mrs. Copeland."

I nodded but stayed silent.

"Can you just give me a quick timeline of the events of the evening and then I'll be out of your hair?" Her gentle smile lit up her eyes, fringed by beautiful long lashes.

I cleared my throat. Should I say anything about the coughing and sweating before his heart attack? Because now I'd realized it was a warning sign. *Say as little as possible.* "We were watching *Jeopardy!*—"

"*Jeopardy!*?" Jonathan cut in, glancing at the clock on the mantel.

I immediately registered my mistake. *Jeopardy!* is on at eight. Shit. I blinked several times and before continuing. "And suddenly his arm swung out, knocking the lamp off the table." I nodded to the amber lamp still lying on the floor, its white shade crushed on one side. "And when I looked over, he was clutching his chest and gasping. I knew right away it was a heart attack."

"He's had two before," Jonathan added authoritatively.

I frowned at him before continuing. "It was bad, I knew it right away. The last two were not like this. I used to be a nurse," I added to bolster my observations.

"Most likely sudden cardiac arrest. They happen very quickly. And given his history, an event this immediate is not out of the ordinary." She took in the litter around his chair and stood, seeming to be satisfied already.

Jonathan rose and saw her to the door. "So, there was no stopping it?"

"Most likely not." She looked back at me. "Again, I'm very sorry for your loss. We'll be transporting your husband to the University of Alberta Hospital. They will contact you to determine your wishes for his body."

"Will they do an autopsy?" Jonathan asked.

I stiffened. Why would they do an autopsy if the cause of death is known? I searched my son's face for suspicion, but it was open and line-free. *He's in shock too*, I reminded myself. The word *autopsy* was stuck in my throat though, choking me. Would that determine the time of death and reveal the length of time that passed before I called? I glanced at the clock, confirming that I'd blanked out for two hours. I couldn't believe I had sat that long lost in thought. A question bubbled up in my mind. *Don't ask!* But I had to. I cleared my throat. "Is it standard to do an autopsy if the cause of death is known?" My voice was brittle and weak.

"No, but sometimes the attending doctor will order one, or the coroner. They'll let you know." She nodded and gently closed the door behind her, which was immediately thrust open again as Vivian and Tanya barrelled into the house, followed shortly by Jonathan's wife, Annette.

The stricken look on my daughters' faces renewed my tears.

IT WAS HARD to breathe with the five of us crammed into my small living room. I took a long, slow gulp of air to coax away the feeling of passing out. *No one in this room can ever know.* No one single person in the world could ever know, I realized, leaving me utterly alone. But wasn't that what I wanted—to be alone? A wave of sadness washed over me at what that really meant: in freeing myself I had created another prison. Like a puppy rescued from a mill only to live out her unadoptable days at an animal shelter.

I eyed the kids, who were busy hugging each other and settling in. Vivian and Tanya's husbands had stayed home with the kids, but Annette's friend Mags had come over so she could be here. My phone buzzed from the coffee table. A text from Roxanne: *I'll start planning it.* I frowned, not understanding what she was talking about, and opened our conversation to see that I had texted her with an all-caps *YES* at nine-thirty. I stared in horror at my phone. I had no recollection of sending this. The blank in my memory caused a wave a panic to roll through me. I slowly set my phone down, my face burning, wondering what else I had done in my stupor. I suddenly had a terrible feeling that I would not get away with this in the long run. The truth always found a way to come out. *My kids will never talk to me again.* After spending a large chunk of my life raising them, it was my worst fear. I should have called immediately.

"You okay?" Vivian's tear-streaked face loomed in front of me, her azure eyes still brilliant like Stan's had been in his younger years.

I yanked her into a tight hug. "I love you," I sobbed into her hair. *Please don't turn your back on me.*

Her chest heaved as she held me, rubbing the back of my head. It was a long minute before she gently pressed me back to look me in the eyes. The worry I saw made my heart ache and I forced a weak I'll-be-alright smile.

She nodded and wiped her cheeks. Jonathan lifted his head from his hands, his face red and puffy. He seemed to have powered through making sure I was alright and now was feeling the loss of his father.

"Oh, Jon." My voice broke. I hated seeing my kids in pain.

"I just saw him yesterday." His voice cracked and Annette tried taking his hand, but he pulled it away.

I choked back a sob. The kids loved their father deeply and didn't get a chance to say goodbye. His grandchildren didn't get to say goodbye. I would never be able to make it up to them. A small part of me wished I could go back in time and do things differently. A larger part of me didn't.

Jonathan's eyes roved the room, jumping over Stan's chair and landing on the empty pork rinds bag. *Please let them believe that this was Stan's own fault.* Because it was. Mostly.

Jonathan wiped his face with the sleeve of his plaid shirt. Finally, he asked, "You told the paramedics that you didn't notice anything wrong before?"

The sweating hairline. The coughing and choking. *Play dumb.* "You know how I am, Jon, I don't notice the little things sometimes." A bald-faced lie. I noticed everything.

"Was he on a daily Aspirin? You know, because of his last two?"

I shook my head. "He was supposed to be, but to be honest, I didn't check in with him every day."

He turned to me, narrowing his gaze. "Shouldn't you have been?"

There was a beat. A thundering silence as I held my breath, my defenses kicking in. Why did he think I was in charge of keeping his father alive? There was only so much one person could do for another.

Stan's lamp suddenly buzzed bright from the floor and then died with a pop, making me flinch. I had been so steady sitting alone here, but now that I was faced with the reality of what I'd done, my nerves were in tatters.

"No, she shouldn't." Annette sat up straight beside him, saving me. "She wasn't his mother."

That's right. I surveyed Annette's face—my third daughter and the woman who made my son walk the line. My head swam and I forced myself to start breathing again. Time seemed to be jumping around. Had Stan been gone nine hours or ten minutes? I could still feel him in every part of this room, in every old piece of furniture he wouldn't let me replace, the gross beige carpet that 'still had life in it,' the scuffed and chipped tan paint on the walls that had 'years to go.' Meanwhile I'd bit my tongue when he'd had his brand-new sixty-five-inch widescreen TV attached to the wall, taking up half of it and looking atrocious.

"You know how your father was, Jon. He never listened to anyone, especially when it came to doctors and stuff. I could never tell him what to do." I cast my eyes down to the old coffee stain on the carpet I hadn't been able to get out. Even after Stan had spilled the cup, he still insisted on taking his morning coffee in the living room, angering me to no end, because when a mess happened, who was expected to clean it up?

He pinched the skin between his eyebrows. "I know."

I relaxed a little. He was just upset. There was no reason for him to suspect anything nefarious went down here tonight.

He nodded, apparently satisfied. He glanced back at Annette and pulled a little further away from her. "Maybe I should stay with you tonight. I don't think it's a good idea for you to be alone."

I thought of the call I didn't make, the text I had no recollection of sending. Maybe I was slipping. "Sure, dear, whatever you think is best." As much as I wanted to be alone, a small part of me wondered if I did need watching.

"I really don't think that's necessary, Jonathan, she's not a baby," Tanya finally spoke. Her cheeks flushed, mottling her already ruddy complexion. Tanya had forever battled with her little brother *and* eczema. "Maybe she wants to be alone, to process," she added firmly.

It had a nice sound to it—alone. Nicer than I liked to admit.

Jonathan glared at his sister. He was all over the place with his facial expressions. I wondered if it was the emotional pain of losing his father or something else, because he seemed to be allergic to his wife the way he was leaning away from her. Maybe the heated vasectomy argument had been resolved and not to his liking.

Everyone settled into a quiet conversation about Stan's funeral and burial wishes. Tanya's face soured as Jonathan advocated for a church service to celebrate his father's seemingly monumental life even though we rarely attended church, and I noticed a delicate gold cross hung around her neck that I had not seen before—a red rash irritating the skin beneath it.

Vivian—who had orchestrated the most lavish sixtieth birthday bash for me—had the scene set within ten minutes, complete with how they'd use fishing line to string up pictures of Stan's life. I was torn over how she spoke of him. All of the good things were true, but already the bad was being glossed over. As it always was with deceased people, but it rubbed me the wrong way. Had no one else seen how Stan controlled everything? I pulled up the sleeve of my sweater to look at the bruises again, to remind myself of what he'd done, what he'd called me.

I glanced up to see Jonathan watching me with concern. I yanked my sleeve down. Telling Jonathan the fib about the bruises suddenly seemed like a terrible mistake. I should have portrayed a happy marriage, one with no animosity or reasons to not call for help when needed.

My relationship with their father was not their concern. It was no one's concern any longer. Vivian reminisced about the time Stan pulled all of the kids into the garage for a 'life lesson.' I forced a chuckle, adding that Stan's biggest concern was that his children knew how to change a flat tire.

The least I could do was let Stan go with high praise.

- 3 -

IT WAS THE thick of the night by the time I had the kids convinced I was fine to stay in the house alone. Jonathan had been the hardest to persuade. I sensed that he didn't want to go home, confirming my suspicions that things with Annette were seriously off.

I picked up my cell and read my message to Roxanne again, unable to comprehend the blank in my memory around sending the text. Was I getting dementia? I closed my eyes and yawned deeply. I should just go to bed. Instead, I found my fingers tapping the Call button under her name.

"Are you finally for real?" Roxanne's gravelly voice was bright and alive, even though it was past three in Tofino.

I rose from the old brown couch and paced the living room, still clutching myself against a chill. "Shouldn't you be sleeping?" I asked, though I'd known full-well when I'd called that she'd be around to answer.

A loud laugh erupted over the line. "I've been searching for flights since you texted. Why the sudden change of heart?"

I hesitated. Should I give her details or just embrace this? It would look so very bad if I was running away. "Because Stan's dead." The words slipped from me with no emotion. It felt better than it should have.

Silence. More silence. Finally, she let out a low whistle. "Shut the fuck up."

"Heart attack."

"Well, that's not surprising." A dog barked in the background. "I'm sorry, Willie."

Don't be. "Hmm."

"So here we are. Finally." Her voice was full of relief.

I stopped pacing to eye the couch, imagining it flying out the front door and a new, lovely floral one settling back in its place. *Too soon,* I scolded myself. I pushed my hand through my thick, curly hair. "Finally."

"You know what this means." Roxanne shot straight past the sympathy and into opportunity. My best friend of almost fifty years lived her life ready to pounce—a human-sized feline, always waiting for her golden moment. Stan hated her.

I nodded to myself, only partially listening to her epic plans for my trip out, taking in once again the family pictures cluttering the mantel. So many years put into raising a family. So many hours dedicated to making their lives happy and comfortable. An eon of minutes spent making Stan's life easier. Still… *I should have dialed sooner.* Then again, there were a lot of things he should have done over the years, too, but he happily rode the wave of comfort I'd provided. When we'd married, I'd thought I'd be able to hold my own, keep the nursing career I loved *and* raise a family like so many women I knew were doing. But as the years wore on, it became apparent that Stan had no interest in making it that easy for me. In fact, at every turn, he made it harder—sleeping through hours of babies wailing in the middle of the night, claiming incompetence when it came to changing diapers, refusing to take a day off work for a sick child, feigning stupidity when the kids needed help with homework. Always saying the kids only wanted me or that I did everything better than him as a way to defer the load of parenting.

After several years of trying to do it all—the first of three breast cancer scares behind me—I simply gave up. I didn't work again until Jonathan was in kindergarten and even then, it was in retail, something that gave me the flexibility needed for a run-down mother. Ringing up people's purchases at the dollar store didn't challenge the intellect in me, but it provided a dependable paycheck.

I looked down at my left hand and the metal noose on my third finger. Fifteen years ago—days after Jonathan moved out—I'd met with a lawyer to start the divorce process. With the kids all gone, there was no reason for me to endure Stan any longer. That very night I'd come home to new engagement ring to replace the simple band I'd worn for years, his 'I can't live without you' proclamation renewed. The diamonds glinted as I faked appreciation of his thoughtfulness, and he'd settled in his chair, satisfied he'd secured me for another eon.

He'd always had an uncanny ability to know when to work harder to keep me. For a month after the ring appeared, he actually tried to be more useful—one night even taking me out to a romantic dinner and making love to me in a way that was more tender than demanding. In the morning, I'd cancelled my next appointment with lawyer. But eventually, it went back to how it always was.

I ripped the ring from my finger and flung it across the room. It bounced off the wall and disappeared beneath the couch.

"You still there?"

"Yes." *Fortunately*. Roxanne and I had been thick as thieves in high school and then in the four years we lived together in college. Our friendship existed in that special place women reserved for kindred spirits, full of love, acceptance and shenanigans. Thirty-six years ago, I'd married Stan and she'd moved to Vancouver Island within the same week, and we vowed to each other that neither distance nor men could keep us apart—that I would come visit her as frequently as possible as she had no desire to return to dreary Edmonton, especially after her dad moved to Vernon. Eleven months later I was holding Tanya in my arms, the promise sailing out the hospital window. I had held resentment against her for years that she wouldn't make the trek back as it would be easier for her. I always thought if she loved me enough, she would come back, but she never did.

"I can't just up and run away," I told her, a tiny part of this resentment speaking now. "Why don't you come here?" There was a sharp note to my question.

"You know I hate that city. It's so ugly." Roxanne growled her displeasure, but then let out a long breath. "But, if you want me to, I will."

I didn't really want her to. What I wanted was to finally join her out there. "There's not much point of you coming here. Just... let things settle here. I'll come out eventually."

"You said that thirty-six years ago," she grumbled.

She had no idea what I had just done to get myself into a position to finally fulfill that promise. But still, it was too soon.

Once we'd said our goodbyes, I looked around the living room, frowning. I may not be able to escape right away, but I did finally have this place to myself. Even if it was still a prison, I could make it tasteful. Floral patterns and bold colours to replace the sad beige palette would be a great start.

As I made my way to bed, I swung past the kitchen and threw away every single bottle of condiments that Stan used to insult my cooking with. His excessive consumption of this crap had probably sped his passing along. Soon, the garbage can was full of steak sauces, sandwich spreads, and ketchup-mayonnaise concoctions. Lying curled up on the edge of the bed, I remembered there was no one to make space for anymore. I rolled over, my body a starfish, and passed out.

BY LATE AFTERNOON, the house was buzzing with people. I'd

slept solidly for two hours and then awoke with a start thinking I heard a banging in the living room. It had taken me a full five minutes to gather the courage to go check if there was an intruder. Unable to find the source of the noise, I concluded it was my conscience coming for me, torturing me into sleeplessness as retribution for my immoral decision. I'd slept in fits for the rest of the night. I hadn't known how reassuring it was having a man in the house all these years. It irritated me.

Food was piled on the kitchen table. There were enough meat trays to feed fifty people. I was in the process of dividing some of it up into plastic bags for everyone to take home. The grandkids lunches would be set for days.

Connor and Gabi occupied the other chairs, stuffing their little mouths full of crackers. Gabi reached out and plucked a cracker from Connor's hand. "Don't." He smacked his little sister's hand away. Annette was always on top of this behaviour, but I'd noticed Jonathan often let it slide. Not in my house.

My reprimand was swift. "Connor. Do not hit your sister."

"She was trying to steal my food!" he whined.

"She's only two. You're five and should know better." He eyed me as he slunk away. He was always the grandkid that challenged me.

Ainsley—Vivian and Bruce's six-year-old daughter—came and sat next to me and began helping me. "You're so good to Grandma." I smiled at her as I pushed a handful of sliced ham into a bag.

She lifted her big blue eyes to me. "Grandpa was supposed to take me on my first fishing trip next month."

Gutted, tears sprung to my eyes. *This* was the price of my freedom. I swallowed. "Yes. Yes, he was, sweetie." I reached over with my clean hand and tucked a strand of blonde hair behind her ear. She looked so much like her mother, and in turn, her grandfather. She was Stan's favourite grandchild. A tear slipped down my cheek as I held her gaze. *I shouldn't have done it.* All the bonding time they would have shared, gone.

Bruce popped his head into the kitchen, a smile lighting up his face at seeing his daughter helping me. "Willie, I noticed that there's a couple loose shingles on the roof. I went up and had a peek at them and they are pretty worn. I know this is a terrible time, but with spring coming, you might want to get that roof replaced. I can arrange it if you want?" The earnest look on his face touched me. He saw a problem and he looked into it and then offered to help find a solution. Vivian had hit the jackpot with this one.

"I noticed that a month ago and mentioned it to Stan, but we never got around to getting it quoted for repair. I think I can take care of it, but thank you, Bruce." Since this was my house now, I was in charge of its maintenance. Not that I wasn't in charge of it before, but I always had to go through Stan for every cent spent on this place. This morning, clutching a cup of coffee, I'd quickly gone over my financials before everyone arrived. The fact that the house had been paid for a long time ago helped immensely. I was going to be okay. This eased my mind a lot, but it made me wonder why I continued to work. Yes, Stan made it *seem* like we were always broke, but maybe it had more to do with getting out of the house than anything.

Mila and Oscar—Bruce and Vivian's three-year-old twins—tore through the kitchen. "Hey," Bruce said. "No running through Grandma's house when there's so many people here." They eyed him, slowing to a fast trot, only to take off the second their little feet touched the carpet of the living room. Ainsley rolled her eyes at me, grinning.

Tanya came into the kitchen, holding the phone out to me. "It's Grandma." I hadn't even heard it ring. I quickly washed my hands, dried them and took the receiver. Tanya was still wearing the cross necklace, her skin redder today than it was last night. I wondered why she wouldn't take it off.

I stepped quickly to my room to talk, closing the door behind me. "Hey."

Mom cleared her throat dramatically. "Tanya told me the good bad news."

I made a noise in my throat. "Mom. Really."

Fran chuckled. "Ask me who the happiest people in the nursing home are?'

I sighed and sat on the edge of the bed, rolling the knot between my shoulder blades. "Is this a trick question?"

"Nope."

"Alright. Who are the happiest people in the nursing home?"

"Women who have outlived their husbands. Bada-bump." I could practically see the jazz hands my eighty-eight-year-old mother was likely displaying right now.

I picked a lint ball off my slacks and dropped it on the carpet. "Mom. I watched my husband die of a heart attack last night. It was horrid. I think it's a little too soon to start celebrating."

"Shoot. I'll cancel the lawn flamingoes, then."

Mom had changed dramatically after Dad died twelve years earlier, morphing from a submissive housewife to a rowdy granny. Within a month of his death, she had the house sold, most of their belongings dropped at Goodwill, and she'd moved into a retirement home where, "Someone can look after *me* for a change." Her mind was clear, and the cross-armed declaration made it plain she would no longer accept *any* challenge to her wishes. My four older brothers sat mute while she told them.

"Probably a good idea," I finally said.

I knew my mother would be the safest person to joke about surviving long enough to see the good days, but anyone could overhear my words through the thin walls of this old bungalow. It would just be best if I steered away. "How are you feeling?" I asked. Last week she'd been hospitalized for several days for a severe bladder infection. Who knew that basic function would cause so much grief in old age? I was not looking forward to it.

"Pretty damn good. I don't think I'll make it out for a visit, though, if that's fine with you. I'm still a little wobbly on my feet."

"Yeah, that's fine, Mom. Honestly, the less people I have to entertain the better."

"That's the idea! You're fighting for yourself now. Put your foot down when you need to. No one's going to stop you now."

I sat a little taller. "You're right." I couldn't change what I'd done, but if I played my cards right, no one would ever know. It was time to embrace the chance I'd given myself.

"The kids are all there. Let them do the heavy lifting."

"Okay."

"And count your lucky stars you made it to the other side. The view here is *magnificent*." The wonderment in her voice lit me up from inside.

- 4 -

MY LIFE BECAME a revolving door for several days. For guests and my emotions. Everyone took my sudden outbursts of tears to be grief, but the truth was much more complicated.

After the funeral—which we did at the church, as Jonathan wanted—I dragged myself around the reception at the house. Who knew Stan had so many fans? The house was packed to the gills with people. I moved between rooms, collecting dishes to ease my restlessness.

I came up behind a particularly obnoxious neighbour wondering about how long I would be able to keep the place up by myself. I bit my tongue so hard I tasted metal. I tried to urge my legs to move on—to get myself out of an escalating situation—but as her simpering voice talked about him, my façade crumbled. I'd barely talked to this woman over the years, but as she listed all of the things she'd seen him doing around the yard while I apparently loafed around inside, the demon inside me grew uncontrollably.

I gripped the crumb-covered plate in my hands. I had picked out this house. I had decided this neighbourhood would be a good place to raise a family. I had furnished the rooms. I had kept everyone alive and fed. And *I* was the one who now took care of the yard.

I marched straight up to her wrinkly face and snapped, "I find it funny that you've replaced me with Stan in your lovely reminiscing. I was the one mowing the lawn every week and pushing the snow around after every storm. I was the one raking leaves and trimming hedges. How *dare* you tell her"—I jerked my head to the other wide-eyed neighbour—"that it was all him."

"Well..." she blubbered, eyes darting from me to her friend. "Stan had those bad knees! He couldn't have done it all himself."

I had a bad knee too, but heaven forbid I used it as an excuse. "Bad knees?" My laugh was acidic. "Bad attitude is all he had." I spun and strode away, but the sight of Wendy Walleye—Stan's stuffed prized trophy fish—enraged me further. I slammed the plates on the coffee table, plucked her lacquered body off the wall and stomped to Stan's fishing room. I opened the door, flung the fish inside and slammed it shut, breathing heavily.

"It's hard to keep running into his stuff, hey?" Curtis's voice behind me made me jump a mile into the air.

"Oh!" I closed my eyes and steeled myself. "Yes, it's just… It's such an awful reminder that he's gone." I turned my mouth way down, clutched my hands to my chest, and turned to face my second-favourite son-in-law. He'd never usurp Bruce as number one.

"Aw, Willie." Towering over me, a red scape bright on his bald head. He was such a klutz—one of his endearing qualities—and probably stood up under a shelf. He reached out and touched my arm. "It'll be alright. He'll always be here in spirit."

I hope not, I railed internally. I lifted my eyes, trying to look morose. "I hope so."

He nodded and gave my arm another squeeze, then returned to the living room. I shuffled behind him, but Jonathan was standing in the entrance to the kitchen, watching me, his hands shoved in his pockets, and his features screwed up with worry.

Shit. My entire body tingled. Had he seen the whole exchange? His eyes bore into mine and my stomach gave a great lurch, moving the ham sandwich I'd just eaten back into my throat. Why was he looking at me like that? He knew I despised that fish, surely it didn't look that bad. My words to the neighbour came back to me. *Bad attitude is all he had.* Did Jon hear that part? Did it make him think of the fingerprints? The sandwich rose higher, but I swallowed it back down and gave him a weak smile. I turned back to the living room and continued to collect dishes.

I PACED THE living room, unable to decide if and when I should act on my impulse to redecorate. Did I really want to take down all reminders of Stan? In the days since the funeral, my mind had painted his actions toward me in a softer light. Surely, he had seen in my eyes that I was thinking of letting him go. If that didn't deserve an arm grab and being called a cunt, I didn't know what would.

My phone buzzed from the coffee table. A text from Tanya saying the coolers for the flower shop were arriving in an hour and if I wanted out of the house, she'd love the company. I dropped everything I was (not) doing and sped over to her house.

Between myself, Tanya, and her girls Claire and Abby, we managed to wiggle the largest of the coolers into the corner of the garage. I stood back, puffing, and wiped my brow. "Where's Curtis?" I chuckled. "We could use your dad's muscles right now, girls."

Claire smiled weakly, but Abby blurted, "He said to Mom this morning that he would have no part in this." She lowered her voice and put her hands on her hips to mock him. At eleven years old, I could already see that she was going to be the sassy pants her mother had been.

I raised an eyebrow to Tanya, and she shrugged with a sheepish smile. "What do you do about these little independent women, hey?" A loud bang came from inside the house. Tanya flinched and watched the garage door intently. Was she scared Curtis would come in?

We worked silently for the better part of an hour, assembling racks. Tanya was normally quiet, but there was something discomforting about her silence today. When Claire and Abby ran out of patience for work, they asked to be excused. Tanya just nodded, but I was happy to have a moment alone with my daughter. It rarely happened anymore.

"What's the matter, love?" I asked once it was just us.

She wouldn't look up from the nut she was tightening, her red hair falling out of her messy ponytail. "Nothing."

Maybe it's still her dad. I had to keep reminding myself that even though I was relieved to be alone, he'd only been gone from my kids' lives for six days. Also, becoming an entrepreneur must be stressful. I loved her idea of running a floral business out of her garage, but there had been dissenting voices over the idea at Easter dinner. One of which was her own husband. "Are you worried about the shop not doing well?" I cut the tape on a cardboard box so it could be broken down.

"Not you, too!" The anger in her voice startled me.

"What?"

"Mom, you're the one person I can always trust to have my back, I can't handle you doubting me on this."

She finally looked up and I was saddened to see tears in her eyes. "Oh, sweetie. I've always thought this was a fantastic idea! In fact, I've had dreams about it doing so well that I could quit my job at the dollar store and come work for you." If I never had to face my asshole boss Ivan again, I would be a happy woman.

She sniffed, relief washing over her face. "Thanks, Mom."

"Is Curtis having a hard time with having to park his car outside in the winter now?" I smirked.

She barked a laugh. "Yeah, something like that." Her hand drifted to the cross necklace that was still around her neck. I wanted to rip it off but had to trust that there was a reason she was keeping something that obviously bothered her. I just hoped it was a damn good reason.

AFTER FIGHTING MY way through rush hour traffic for thirty minutes on Whitemud Drive, I pulled up to my mother's nursing home. As I located her window on the third floor, I wondered what she would have done with a little more freedom. I should be happy I had years to explore that notion before I ended up here.

I nodded and smiled to several residents before spotting my mother waiting for me in the lobby. I smiled and held up the McDonald's bag. She clapped her hands together and shuffled over to meet me, arms outstretched. She was wearing her 'uniform' as she liked to call it—black elastic-waisted slacks and a light blue button-down blouse. She hated making decisions, claiming that raising five children overworked her decision maker.

She pulled me into her signature fierce hug, smelling of coffee. I didn't know how she slept at night with the amount of caffeine that coursed through her veins, but at eighty-eight, she was not going to take being told it was bad for her. I really wanted to be like her when I grew up.

"My little free bird." She sang and rocked me back and forth.

"Mom. You're not supposed to say that kind of stuff."

"He's dead, who cares?"

I breathed heavily out my nose. "Here's your fries."

She moaned as she released me, taking the greasy bag from me, we walked to the lounge.

Settled in the comfy chairs by the fireplace, she started eating her fries one by one, savouring each.

"Has Tanya been in lately?" I asked.

She shook her head, the loose skin below her neck wobbling. "Not for a few weeks, actually."

"That's weird."

"Yes, she's normally here at least once a week."

"I'm worried about her."

"She did say something strange to me last time she visited." Fran licked her fingers and crumpled up the bag. "She asked if I wanted to have five kids or if it was Henry's idea."

"Really." I tipped my head. "More kids isn't an option for them. Curtis had a vasectomy years ago." Tanya had been a part of the vasectomy argument between Jon and Annette, I remembered. Annette had tried to tell Jonathan that Curtis and Bruce had been responsible, selfless husbands who did what was best for the family, but that had only made Jon dig his heels in further.

Fran shrugged. "I love you and your brothers, but it's not like I ever had much say in the matter."

Neither had I. Not really.

An evil grin spread across Fran's face. "You going to visit Roxanne now that he's finally dead?" My mother had always loved Roxanne, even when we got into all that trouble in Grade 12. And she had known about the vacation plan since its inception thirty-six years ago. She'd always blamed Stan for holding me back from that promise. I looked around to see how many old people were watching us, but everyone was either used to my mother's antics or involved in their own affairs. "Mom."

"Oh, it would be so fun though." Her smile grew, deepening the lines on her face. "I always wanted to skinny dip in the ocean. Promise you'll do that one day soon?" Her watery grey eyes lit up and she grasped my hands. *They're so soft.* I rubbed my thumb over the top of her hand, realizing Jon did this to me often.

I chuckled. "In the Pacific Ocean? Freezing my wrinkly, jiggly bits off?"

"Fuck 'em," she snarled. "You earned those wrinkly, jiggly bits. And find some young, hot guy to screw while you're out there."

"Mom," I gasped, pulling my hand away. "My husband literally just died. I spent a big chunk of thirty-six years dreading doing the deed."

"Why? Orgasms are *fun.*"

I put my head in my hands, unable to believe this was the contrite, controlled woman I had known most of my life.

"What?" she barked.

I looked up at her. "Orgasms and sex don't go hand in hand for me." How had I just uttered those words to the woman who gave birth to me?

She nodded deeply. "Ah, the selfish sexer. You know, wise men figure out before it's too late that making a woman come is the greatest thing they can do for us."

Just when I thought this conversation couldn't get any worse. My face burned with the heat of a thousand suns.

"Don't be embarrassed. Hamil over there"—she nodded to a grey-haired man in the corner of the lounge playing cards with a young woman—"taught me that. It's not like your father ever gave a shit about my satisfaction. As long as he got what he needed, all was good."

I sat up a little straighter. She was right. Why should I be ashamed of this conversation? I had been quite aggressive in my own pleasure back in the old days. Where had that woman gone? I deserved orgasms just as much as any dickhead man did.

Mom looked pointedly at me. "I'm proud of you."

"For what?"

"Getting yourself here. You're not the only one." She leaned back and folded her hands in her lap, eyed the small crowd, and winked at me. "Now fly."

- 5 -

I WAS CARRYING a stack of outdoor life magazines to Stan's fishing room when a light knock on the door startled me. I scowled at the clock, wondering who bothered people at ten at night?

I quickly threw the magazines on the floor of the room and closed the door before returning to the living room. I peered warily through the clouded peephole. "Jonathan?" I pulled the door open, my heart sinking when I saw he was carrying a duffle bag. It had been a week since we last spoke. Normally, I'd be suspicious of not hearing from him in so long, but given the circumstances, it had been purely a relief and I had been relishing the solitude, picking away at making the house my own.

"I'm sorry to bother you this late, Mom." His eyes were red and puffy.

I automatically reached for him. "It's alright. Everything okay?"

He shook his head slowly. "No, actually."

"What is it?" My heart galloped as I pulled him in.

He took off his shoes and moved to the living room, squinting around at the space, clearly realizing most of his father's stuff was gone. Twisting my hands, I sat in the chair across from him. "What is it?" I repeated, my voice tight. *Has he figured it out?*

"Annette asked for a divorce." His words sat stonily between us, his face red. He was mad. Really mad.

"Oh." And here I had been so sure this was about me. "Oh," I repeated, realizing how serious this was.

"Mom?" Jonathan's voice broke.

"Yes?"

"Can I stay here for a bit?" He blurted the words and then winced. "I know that sounds so lame. I'm a thirty-year-old man for God's sake! But maybe if I give Annette some space, she'll come around."

"Of course." My gut answered before I could check it. *Always a mother.* I looked around the room. Did I really want Jon to move in after I had just gotten my freedom? I hesitated before asking, "How long do you think?"

He shrugged and I saw a hint of the old Jon in the lifelessness of his face. It worried me. He'd only had one serious relationship before Annette and when it ended, he sank into our couch for a month and didn't move. And this time it wasn't just a break-up, but a potential divorce. There were children involved. Maybe I should push him now to find a long-term solution. "I am more than happy to have you, but I'm wondering if you won't be more comfortable with an apartment or something?"

He tipped his head at me. "This kind of works out, though, doesn't it? Like, who's going to look after you and the house now that Dad's gone?"

"I can look after myself," I bit back, purposely ignoring the fact that I'd barely slept since Stan had died. Every night, I'd startled awake to strange noises and had a hard time falling back asleep.

"You sound like Annette." His voice was laced with bitterness.

I figured that was a good thing. Since the first time I'd met Annette, I'd loved her. Confident and caring, she'd always known her own mind. And with her own parents far away in Ontario, she had vocally adopted me as her mother the second her and Jon were married. The thought of losing her to divorce frightened me. *Maybe I should disown you and keep her.* I recoiled at my acidic thought. I needn't take out my frustration over my relationship with Stan on my son.

He chewed a nail and turned slightly away from me. "The truth is, we can't afford me getting my own place. They've cut my hours at work because the company's not doing well, and the last year's been hard. Honestly, a divorce is the last thing we can afford right now. If we could just have some time apart, remember why we love each other..." He turned back to me, head hanging. "You know I wouldn't ask if this wasn't my last option." He smiled at the carpet before looking at me again. "It can be like old times, when I came back after that Lisa mess."

That's what I'm afraid of. I prayed it would be short-lived. It won't kill me to give my son a month of comfort. And if it helped keep him and Annette together, then it was something I needed to do. "Yeah. Yeah, it can."

He stood and motioned for me to do the same, pulling me into a tight hug. "Thank you so much, Mom."

I swallowed hard and hugged my son back.

WE MANAGED TO co-exist for several weeks. Even though I had to find more and more excuses to get out of the house because Jonathan always seemed to be *there.* Sitting where I wanted to sit, occupying space I wanted to myself, eating snacks I'd bought with the intention of enjoying myself at the end of a hard day, leaving a mess wherever he went. I came home from work one day to find him sitting in his father's chair a beer in hand and a hockey game on. I froze on the threshold of the living room. *No, no, no.* This was too much like how it used to be. It was creepy actually. If he asked me to do his laundry, I would scream.

"Hi, sweetie." I sat on the couch across from him. That was when

I saw several more cans of beer on the table beside him. And a box of Hot Rods. My heart stopped for a second.

"These are really expired," he said flatly.

"Oh?"

"You said Dad was still eating them after the doctor told him not to, but I found this box stuffed in the back of the pantry. They are three years expired. That means he *wasn't* eating them."

"Oh?" My voice was barely a whisper. I thought of the wrappers I found tucked in Stan's chair.

"And that *Jeopardy!* timing still bothers me."

I didn't trust myself to answer, not even to defend myself. He was trying to get somewhere, and I didn't like it at all. I stood and faked a yawn. "I'll think I'll go to bed."

"Mom. Something's been bugging me, and I didn't want to say anything about it, but it's become too obvious."

I froze. *Here it comes.* My gorge rose.

"I think you blanked out for at least an hour after he died."

"Um." That was not quite what I was expecting.

"And there's been other things that have been off." He held up his hand and flicked his fingers up as he listed things. "You keep moving his stuff around. What you said to the neighbour at the funeral. The quote for getting the house reshingled, which is dumb because I work in the trades and can find you a way better deal than those shitheads. Plus, Onyx Black is a terrible colour. This house will be boiling in the summer. The condiments I found in the garbage only a day after Dad died. I'm starting to worry about your, um…mental state. It's starting to feel like I should stay longer, that maybe you need help taking care of this place and you don't want to ask."

My relief was replaced by anger at the realization that he'd been compiling a list of evidence against me behind my back and snooping through my personal things to do so. And seemed to already conclude that I was incapable of looking after this place. I dug my toes into the carpet to steady my fury. "I'm perfectly fine." The only good thing about him being here was that I was finally able to sleep decently.

"Dad had mentioned to me that you didn't seem like yourself over the past couple of years, and I'm starting to see what he was talking about."

So, Stan *had* known I was living with one foot out the door. "You *don't* have to worry about me," I said pointedly. "What about you and Annette?" I needed to divert this conversation before I lashed out.

"Until Annette gets her head screwed on straight, that's a lost cause. She wants to put her career before her children and have me be some pussy stay-at-home dad. I'll be dammed if I stand back and just let her do that."

I winced at his insult to mothers who chose to stay home, but it was clear why he was making this so difficult on her. It was simply a power move. I suddenly didn't recognize my own son. It seemed everyone was hiding some kind of latent rage that just needed a trigger to be released. I had my own mixed mind to contend with, I didn't need to worry about anyone else's. "I'm really tired, Jon."

His eyes bored into mine. He still wanted to fight. It was the beers. He opened his mouth, but then closed it and focused silently back on the TV.

I put myself to bed in tears. I did not like how this was going. I needed to get him out. And the sooner the better. Because I sensed permanent damage was coming to our relationship if I didn't.

I MET VIVIAN for an early Sunday breakfast and risked telling her everything about Jonathan. It had been several days since our confrontation, and we had existed in a tense silence ever since. She told me point blank that I needed to get him out—confirming what I knew to be true. She admitted that Jonathan had raged to Bruce at the funeral about how Annette wanted to go back to being a realtor because she knew she could make more money than Jonathan's carpentry contracting was pulling in. Apparently, when Bruce told Jonathan he was being ridiculous in not supporting the breadwinner of the family, especially in this economy, Jonathan had hissed at him, "You're a real saint, hey?" Just when I thought I couldn't love Bruce more.

But that still didn't clear up what was going on with Jonathan. And Vivian jumped on the obvious answer. "It was Dad," Vivian said as she grabbed for the bill. "Seeing how he got away with what he did set him up for this."

My jaw dropped open at the insight. All through the funeral and following days, Vivian had never hinted that she knew how it had been with Stan and I. But of course she had seen. Why else had she chosen the husband she did? To change the narrative. I was happy for her, but in a way, furious at myself for letting it go down like this. Another thing that would have turned out better if only I'd stood up for myself from the beginning.

Knowing that Annette was capable of financially supporting their family if Jonathan would only help her out angered me more. Feeling empowered, I went home prepared to do battle. I found him sitting in the living room.

I sucked in a breath, my eyes darting around the room. Wendy had been restored to her place by the mantel. Stan's outdoor adventure magazines were back under the table. In fact, everything I had moved into the fishing room appeared to have been returned to its original spot, right down to the stack of stained Coors coasters on Stan's side table. My face burned. "What is going on here?" I demanded, my head swimming with deja vu.

"Why are you erasing him from this house?"

I came here to kick him out and with a single question, he flipped this on me. It reminded me so much of Stan. I took a deep breath, trying to gain control of myself. "It's... I don't want to see reminders of him everywhere." It wasn't really a lie, depending on how you interpreted it.

He stood. "Mom, I love you, but I don't think you're being fully honest with me."

"I am!" I clenched my fists. The demon I thought I'd sent along with Stan was back and it was even more pissed.

He looked at me for a long time, the tiny muscles in his face working. Before I lost my courage, I blurted, "I think you should move home."

He looked as if I'd slapped him. "I can't go home."

"You are *choosing* to not go home."

Anger worked over his face. "You're really kicking me out? I can't afford to live on my own and you have all this space now." He levelled a look at me. "This isn't like you. What are you trying to hide?"

I blanched. Whether he knew it or not, he'd struck a nerve, a deep worry inside of me. If he found out that I didn't call 911, he would hate me. Or worse.

We stared at each other in a frozen faceoff. It appeared he wasn't going anywhere soon.

But that didn't mean *I* couldn't leave.

I turned on my heel and walked to my room, hating myself for being the one that backed down. I may have freed myself, but it was beginning to seem it was only halfway.

I DOWNED A glass of water that was sitting beside my bed and called Roxanne.

"What's up sweet cheeks?" Roxanne's bright voice brought on tears.

"Get me the hell out of here," I sobbed, choking. "Everything's falling apart." How had it all gone so wrong?

She sniffed. "Just get on a flight and I'll take care of putting everything back together."

The tears intensified. I couldn't remember the last time someone had taken my needs seriously—and so easily, without question or hesitation. The relief I felt in not having to explain myself or what I wanted overwhelmed me.

Finally, when I caught my breath, Roxanne said gently, "I can't wait to see your ugly mug again."

I laughed—hard and long—as fear rolled off of me, anticipation of this long-overdue journey taking its place.

WITHIN HALF AN hour I was packed and on my way to the airport in a cab, having uttered only enough to Jon to ensure he'd look after the house while I was gone. I'd decided I would just wait in the terminal for the next flight to Comox, even if I had to sleep there overnight. There was no way I was confronting my son again because I couldn't trust myself to not blurt something irretractable.

I knew how stupid it was that *I* was the one leaving *my own* house. But the fracture in our relationship would have become a fault if someone didn't distance themselves from it.

As the cab moved down the highway, I couldn't fathom how I'd gotten here, running from the life I created for myself. I tried to focus on finally seeing Roxanne again. After all these years, would we be able to pick up where we left off? Was I handing Jon the opportunity to happily settle into his new place—*my* place. Where had my sweet Momma's boy gone? All I could see now was a bitter, wife-hating dictator. I cleared the sob from my throat.

I suddenly had no idea where my life was headed, but as we drove south out of Edmonton, I sat a little straighter, knowing one thing for certain: I was going to make this trip away the best time of my life. It was all I had right now.

- 6 -

FOR A HEFTY fee, I got onto the 4:55 pm flight. The last time I'd been on a plane had been to visit Tanya at university in Saskatchewan probably fifteen years ago. I was still surprised that Stan hadn't insisted on escorting me, but Tanya was having 'girl' problems and the second I uttered that to him, he claimed he was very busy at work. She had only been homesick, but the fib had gotten me some quality time with my oldest.

The sun was still high and as I passed over the foothills and mountains, toward the ocean. I was stunned by the brilliant majesty of the peaks. They were still covered in snow and impossibly white. Able to see them above, I felt big, bigger than I had in a long time.

I craned my neck, trying to catch a glimpse of the ocean, but the cloud cover was thickening. I let out a long breath and leaned my head back on the seat, letting contentment settle over me. After the fallout with Jonathan, I wasn't sure where I was going or what I was doing, but alone in the clouds I began to realize that this was the real adventure I'd wanted from the second the word *cunt* had passed Stan's cruel lips. I should thank Jonathan for making it happen.

It was a short flight, but by the time we started our descent, a pair of old ladies several rows ahead of me had gotten wound right up on the many little bottles of booze they'd devoured. One clear bottle of vodka had even rolled down the aisle, stopping at my feet. When the woman had jumped up to retrieve it, she winked at me before swaying back to her seat. I wondered if this was what Roxanne had in mind for me—a grannies-gone-wild calamity. If I was only going to return home to Jonathan's suspicious gaze, maybe this was my first and last hurrah of freedom and the best way to approach it would be guns ablazin'.

I pulled an imaginary pistol from my hip and blew on the curl of smoke rising from its tip, smirking. My fantasy was interrupted by the guy across the aisle muttering, "Crazy old bat."

You have no idea. I pointed my fake gun at him, and a deranged giggle bubbled up my throat. I pulled the trigger and whispered, "Bang." His eyes flared with shock before a look of deep disgust took over. Fran would be so proud of me.

As I put my gun away, the air vents whooshed on, and a deep chill ran through me. I was acting all tough, but I knew I wasn't totally off the hook just yet. Maybe I was mentally slipping. Maybe Jon's accusation held more truth than I'd like to admit.

The plane touched down and I gripped the armrest. Whatever was going on back at home, I would let go of for a week. I would not let anything ruin this trip.

AS WE TAXIED to the gate, I powered my phone up. I had sent a group message as I boarded the plane alerting Vivian, Tanya, and Annette to my plans, and now the screen exploded with messages. I scrolled through them quickly as the passengers around me started to stand. Vivian told me to have fun. Annette asked me to call her when I had a moment. And Tanya asked if I would be gone more than a week, which angered me. What if I was? What if I decided I wanted to stay longer than seven days? Surely to Christ my kids could survive without me for a few weeks?

There was also a message from Jonathan giving me a quote from his preferred roofing company. I was irritated that he went ahead and looked into it the second I was gone, but after seeing the lower price, I figured I should thank him for being proactive in saving me money.

I sent a quick note to Ivan that I was taking a week off, not caring if he fired me for the lack of notice I was giving, and immediately shut the phone back off and collected my things, my stomach turning at the thought of seeing Roxanne again after thirty-six years.

I was delighted to realize we would be deplaning outside. The crisp, coastal breeze was refreshing after the stifling, fart-filled air of the plane. I breathed in deeply as the warm air hit my face, pushing out of my mind the leery look on Jonathan's face when he asked me what I was trying to hide. I was here to enjoy myself and that was it.

On the ground, I fluffed my curls and smoothed the wrinkles on the front of my black slacks, moving along with the other passengers in a slow line to collect my suitcase. I spotted Roxanne, my guts giving one massive leap—my youth rushing back to me. The dancing, the drinking, the laughing our asses off. We'd texted random, low-quality photos to each other over the years, but to finally see my friend in person brought back how stunning she was.

She towered over most of the small crowd. In Grade 9, she had shot past me, leaving me six inches permanently behind. "Willie!" Roxanne squealed from behind a row of people waiting for their loved ones, a bright red scarf around her neck, her white hair woven into a side braid that trailed over her shoulder. "Over here!" Her arm swung back and forth over her head in wild arcs, attracting looks from the people surrounding her. The air hummed with her energy. A smile crept across my face. What a boob.

I moved forward to the front of the line and was handed my blue suitcase. I pulled it along, dodging people as I rushed toward her. Every step I took shaved five years off my life. By the time I reached her I was twenty-one again, full of piss and vinegar.

Roxanne's fingers scratched at the air as she reached for me—a land-dwelling octopus—finally pulling me into a deep embrace. "I. Am. So. Glad. You. Are. Here!" Roxanne said over my head as my face was smushed into her neck. Respecting my personal space had never been her strong suit. I'd missed it.

I relaxed into her—the smell of her musky, sun-kissed skin a sudden comfort—a sob jumping into my throat. "Oh, dear. I've got you," she murmured into my hair. "Did I say I'm so glad you're finally here?"

I nodded. I was so glad I was finally here too.

ROXANNE GRIPPED MY hand tightly and pulled me through the crowd. People seemed to part the way for her. I'd lost that type of visibility over the years. There was something about her stride that made people automatically step back, and I gratefully slipped through in her wake. I squeezed Roxanne's hand tighter. She glanced back at me, her cornflower blue eyes flashing.

In her car—an old grey Honda Civic—I settled into the front seat and pulled my phone out again. "I need to call my daughter-in-law."

"Wait until we get home to call. Everything is easier to handle with a glass of wine and the smell of ocean salt in the air." She winked, a motion embellished by her still-abundant lashes, making me—and my nearly bald lids—jealous.

She's right. I nodded and slid the phone back into my purse. "Tofino, right?"

She started the car and zipped out of the parking lot. "Yup. The most beautiful place on earth."

"You were always such an exaggerator." I rolled my eyes, a weight gently pulling me down, anchoring me to the earth and this moment in time. This was where I was supposed to be. Jonathan scaring me out of my house was exactly the push I'd needed to leap into this adventure.

She wheeled onto the roadway, and I clutched the door handle. "Wait until you see. Then you can tell me if I'm exaggerating."

I QUICKLY LEARNED that the beauty of Vancouver Island cannot, in fact, be exaggerated. I stared out the window, only partially paying attention to Roxanne's incessant chatter as the forest grew in thickness—the pockets of light streaming between the trees slowly vanishing. There were plenty of trees in Edmonton, but these were somehow more vibrant, as if the ocean air had zapped them with an electrical current. I tried to take in the lusciousness, attempting to name the various shades of green as they passed my window: emerald, moss, crocodile, seaweed, olive, sage, pickle, basil, avocado. Even Roxanne fell silent as we drove deeper into the grove, a natural archway over the highway bowing in welcome as we passed.

My lungs released another long-held, stagnant breath—similar to the one that had escaped me after I let Stan go. How many of these life-altering sighs were still inside me?

Part way to Tofino, I caught a glimpse of a large lake through the thicket, a flash of dark teal quickly buried again behind a wall of conifers. As we drove, I compiled a bucket list a mile long, knowing the first thing I would do was go to the beach.

Only two hours in and this trip was already better than the past ten years of my life. "He's been dead thirty-two days." I'd meant to sound more sombre, but a hint of awe had leaked out with my words. My eyes slid to Roxanne but she either didn't catch it or didn't care.

"But who's counting, right?"

Me. I gazed out the window at the trees, letting the silence become comfortable. It had been a long many years since I'd been able to. Silence with Stan was always born from resentment and irritation. Finally, I looked back at her, lifting an eyebrow. "I shot a guy on the plane."

Roxanne snorted. "What did he do to deserve it?"

"Called me a crazy old bat."

"Ohhh." Her head wobbled. "Not the classic dismissal of women of a certain age! I swear, they get more and more pathetic in their attempts to erase us as the years go by." The car growled and lurched as Roxanne pressed on the gas, and I remined myself not to provoke her while she had my life in her hands.

As I gripped the door handle tighter, I wondered if men would just be happier if women disappeared. Because some of them took every opportunity they could find to belittle us. But for the first time in many years, I was looking forward to staying and fighting for my place in this world. I lifted my head higher. "Let them try."

- 7 -

WE PULLED UP to an older condo building in the middle of Tofino. It was covered in blue vertical wood slats. Stan would have had a heart attack over the fact that someone had painted cedar siding. *I'll never have to endure one of his lectures again.* I smirked and got out of the car, catching a flash of red under a tarp from the storage area beneath the building. "Do you still have your bike?" I called out as I followed Roxanne up a couple flights of stairs. That thing must be fifty years old.

"Nope. Ol' Frankie was beyond uncomfortable. I upgraded to a Shadow about twenty years ago. Haven't rode it for a while. Maybe we'll fire it up while you're here."

"Uh…" The last time I rode on Roxanne's motorcycle I almost died. Seventeen and clutching her midsection, I could barely open my eyes as we flew down Whitemud Drive going dangerously fast, narrowly avoiding several vehicles as we zipped around them. "Maybe not," I finally finished.

As her keys rattled in the apartment door's lock, a commotion broke out behind the door. "Calm down," she shouted as the door swung open and we were hit by a wave of animals.

Two dogs, three cats and, "A ferret?" I didn't know Roxanne

housed a zoo.

"Oh, he's the sweetest, don't you worry." She scooped up the slinky taupe animal and thrust him onto my chest.

"Oh!" I eyed the animal as he circled over my boobs. "Aren't they vicious?"

"No more than any other animal."

I pulled my neck back from my body in case it decided to bite my nose. "But remember in college, Derek and Shawn had that one and you had to run from the front door to the couch or it would bite your heels?"

She blew a breath out. "That animal was abused. They thought it was funny to feed it beer and give it 'swimming lessons' in the toilet." She used air quotes.

"Oh, the poor thing." The ferret had curled up and I put up a hand to keep it safe from falling. "What's your name?" I murmured to the animal.

"Mr. Bo Jangles."

"Ha! Does he dance?"

"He does. I'll show you later."

We entered a tiny foyer—the kind where you had to step around and behind the door before closing it. The kitchen and living room were more open, a good size for an apartment. It was a bit dark and totally outdated, but homey, reminding me of Vivian's first place. I lifted my nose, sniffing as we made our way through the herd and into the kitchen, certain I could smell cherries. "Is that?" My eyes widened as they landed on the kitchen bar countertop.

"Black forest cake. Your favourite." She wiggled her butt happily, eyebrows lifted.

I hadn't brought anything for her. I was already a terrible guest. "It's just perfect," I whispered to the floor.

"A reunion this epic needs cake."

I nodded. "Yes, it does." I had never been more thankful that Stan wouldn't be able to follow every bite I took with accusing eyes.

If I remembered correctly, Roxanne made the best cakes in the world. My mouth was already watering.

She led me past the living room, the dogs trailing and the cats back to minding their own business. The couch had a lovely multi-coloured quilt draped across it and two blue armchairs were squeezed into the corner next to a small easel with a canvas that had a half finished oceanscape painting on it, tubes of paint and spray cans littered around its base. Roxanne's abstract realism scenes always stunned me. "Real life on acid," was always how she described her work.

A small flat screen TV was on a stand across from the couch and beautiful framed photographs adorned the walls. One directly across from me in the living room—a close-up of a light brown slug on a lime-coloured leaf surrounded by perfect water droplets—was oddly captivating, reminding me of the little silver tracks that lined the sidewalks on fall mornings. It was weird but lovely. With the slight mess and explosions of colour, Roxanne's place felt so *her*. My house felt like Stan, with its faded neutral tones and its forever tidy appearance. And I had just started to let myself dream of a newer, brighter palette when Jon showed up. I shook my head. *I need to stop thinking about Stan.*

Roxanne caught me staring at the photo. "My neighbour Dana took that. She's a naturalist. And a photographer."

"It's oddly beautiful."

"Like me!" Roxanne cackled and took my bag down a narrow hallway. She pointed to a door on the left. "This is my room." We walked to the end, where Roxanne again pointed to her left. "Bathroom." Then she turned to the right. "And this is your room. It's pretty small, but it's all yours." I poked my head in. It wasn't much bigger than a closet, with only a small dresser and a narrow bunk bed. One of her surreal oceanscape-at-sunset paintings hung on a tiny patch of free wall next to the closet door—blues and oranges of all shades jumping off the canvas—it was stunning. "You put my favorite painting up."

"Just for you."

The walls were a deep blue, and the white bedspread and curtains really made it pop. I turned to Roxanne and beamed. "It's perfect. Thank you."

"The bed is small, but it has a really good mattress—great support for our old backs. Why don't you get freshened up and I'll meet you on the deck with that cake and a bottle of wine."

I pressed my hand to Bo's body, holding back another wave of tears. "That's the best offer anyone's made me in years."

THE SUN WAS starting its slow descent. I stood on the small balcony, straining upward to get a better look at the water, but more trees blocked my view. A bird called far overhead—a sharp screech—but couldn't find it when I looked up. I turned to see Roxanne pouring me a glass of white wine, filling it to almost overflowing. "That's good!" I threw a hand up to stop her. It was already six o'clock—my stomach was rumbling non-stop, and I was ready for food. One huge glass of wine right now and I'd be yelly-talking in Roxanne's face.

"I never understood why they only fill the glass a third full in restaurants. Seems stupid." Roxanne put the glass to her lips and drank the whole thing in several loud gulps—just like how my kids drank when they were little, as if they hadn't seen water in two days. Roxanne set the glass down with a loud "Ah," leaned back in the red cedar Adirondack chair, and closed her eyes. Her manners were still perfectly atrocious.

I sat and took a sip of the wine, the fruity sweetness fizzing on my tongue. I avoided alcohol partly because of the blood pressure pills I was on, but mostly because I never wanted to encourage Stan to drink to excess by doing it myself. With every beer, he became more intolerable than the last, eventually getting handsy and harder to fend off.

"Wilhelmina Copeland," Roxanne murmured, interrupting my thoughts.

I winced. My mother had the best intentions when she chose that name for me, but I had not taken after the obscure Scottish feminist like she had wanted. "God that sounds horrid."

"So, change it."

I turned to her. "Well, I can't very well change my first name."

She laughed. "No, I mean the last name. Change it back to Bennet."

"That would look really bad, wouldn't it?"

"Who gives a fuck?"

I desperately wanted to not give a fuck. "My kids," I finally said flatly. That would really send Jonathan into detective mode.

She eyed me and I could tell she wanted to argue. I needed to change the subject. "How's your dad?" Roxanne loved talking about her dad who lived in Vernon.

"Great." She launched into a spiel about how Barry was now living the dream life being an artist in the culturally rich interior of BC. Roxanne had been raised by her dad after her mother passed away when she was two. He had always been so inviting when I spent half of my high school years at their house.

"How often do you see him?"

"Every couple of months. We facetime a lot, though."

I nodded and took another sip of wine. Sometimes I hated technology because I didn't understand it. I was a paperback person in a world of Kindles. But it was amazing that you could see people's faces halfway around the globe. It made being far away a little less painful. It also made me wonder about the places I could visit in the world, or even move to, with a little less guilt, knowing I could stay in touch. But I would never. My stomach gave a loud rumble and I laughed. "So, about that cake."

Roxanne coughed and reached for it, cutting large slices for each of us. "I don't want my precious friend withering away from starvation on her first night here. We have a lot of trouble to get into."

"Do we?" I lifted a forkful of chocolate, cherry, and whipped cream goodness to my mouth.

"You bet your tits we do. But tonight, we'll chill. My neighbors, Dana and Monique, invited us for supper at seven."

I closed my eyes and savoured the cake. After swallowing, I said, "I'm all yours."

"It's about goddamn time." Roxanne refilled her glass and tipped it toward mine and tapped it, the clink sharp and high.

ROXANNE QUICKLY WALKED the dogs and fed the other animals while I called Annette before going next door for supper—Bo curled on my bed.

"Hey, Willie."

"Hi, Hun. What's up?"

She let out a long breath. "First, I want you to know that I love you like my own mother."

"And I love you too, Annette. You're my third daughter, I've always said that."

She chuckled. "You've been so good to let Jon move in and I'm sorry I haven't called earlier, it's just that I didn't want to put you in a hard situation. It's already been bad enough with losing your husband."

My earlier thought came to me, that I should adopt Annette and ditch Jon. But the last thing I wanted to have to do was choose a side, because I knew at the end of the day it would be my son I'd have to align with. "Well, I'll do whatever I can to make this as smooth as possible. It's too bad it's come to divorce."

"He forced it." Her tone was cool.

"What do you mean?"

She let out a long breath. "I know you love Jon. He's your son. But I just wanted to tell you to watch out for him. He's not quite who you think he is. He can be controlling and manipulative."

I lifted an eyebrow. Sounded a little like Stan. "Was it the vasectomy thing?"

"Ha! That was just the icing on the cake. Did you know he's been trying to get me to have another baby for, like, a year?"

I stood and peeked out the little window in my bedroom. Roxanne was pulling the basset hound down the alley, and I smiled. "Why? You've always said two and done."

"So I have to stay home instead of going back to work."

"Ah." I thought we were well past keeping women barefoot and pregnant as a means of control.

"I was one of the top realtors in Edmonton before Connor was born. If I'm working full time, I can make really good money. More than him. So doesn't it make sense for him to help make that happen? We're barely getting by on his income."

He was telling the truth about not being able to afford to live on his own, just not the real reason. "Could you put the kids in daycare so you could work?"

She made an exasperated noise. "And rack up almost two grand a month just so he can continue to sit on his throne? Because that would be perfect for him—using the excuse that the added daycare costs make it not worth me going back. I'm so tired of having to defend myself." Her voice was drained, making me wish I hadn't suggested it. "Willie. I wasn't calling to complain, I was calling to tell you I think he's trying to take over your house so he has a free place to live."

I sucked in a breath. It was a bold suggestion, but the power play over the roof reinforced her claim. "I'll keep an eye on him." It wasn't so much an affirmation of what she'd said, but it couldn't hurt to keep my senses about me.

"I'll do my best from this end, Willie. Now go enjoy your

vacation. You've earned it."

MY CONVERSATION WITH Annette left me feeling dedicated to keeping a handle on my house even from out here. Maybe I'd even get Annette's friend Mags to swing by and quote the house for a total interior repaint.

Roxanne and I walked up to the third floor and knocked on a door that had a rainbow butterfly painted beneath the number three. Edna from The Incredibles answered. "Rox." She leaned in and kissed Roxanne on the cheek before taking my hand and holding me at arm's length. Her black bob and dark glasses made me smile. *How many times have I watched that show with the kids?* "I'm Dana, and you must be the astonishing Willie."

My cheeks warmed. "Well, that's a bit much, but I'll take it."

A radiant, tall, blonde woman called from the kitchen, beaming. "Welcome! I'm Monique. Dinner's ready. Dish up."

As I moved to the counter, she touched my shoulder. "Pleased to finally meet you, Willie. We've heard so much about you from Roxanne." She smelled like roasted garlic. I breathed in deeply.

I chuckled. "Please remember she's prone to exaggeration." My mouth watered as I heaped my plate with a salmon steak, new red potatoes—butter, rosemary, and chunks of said garlic covering them—and roasted asparagus. We settled ourselves at a small table on the balcony.

Roxanne popped a potato into her mouth, closing her eyes. "You're a wonder, Monique."

I nodded quickly. "This is absolutely delicious. The salmon in particular." I let another flake melt on my tongue.

Dana held a hand to her mouth and asked, "So, Willie, what are your plans while you're here? Or is having no plan the plan?" She winked at me knowingly.

Roxanne piped up. "Let's see. First, we're going to get shitfaced, then we'll get naked, then we'll splash around like lunatics in the ocean, freezing our asses off."

Monique snorted. "Why does all your fun involve nudity?"

"Free the tits, *baby*." Roxanne lifted her hands to give peace signs and jiggled her modest chest.

Roxanne had never gotten over her bra-burning phase in high school. It was easier for her though. Stan's favourite part of me had been my boulders. Now, they'd be at my knees if I didn't keep them strapped in. I should have cut them off when I was twenty and then Stan would have never looked twice at me.

"Sounds like you ladies have a lot to accomplish," Dana said.

"Oh, that's only the first day!" Roxanne chuckled.

Everyone laughed along with her, and I suggested the first item on my bucket list, "How about we hit the beach first and go from there?"

"Sounds like a plan," Dana said.

Monique sat back and patted her ample stomach. "I overdid it. Again." She looked down at herself and winced.

Dana's black eyebrows puckered together in a frown. "Food makes you happy."

Monique smiled sadly at Dana, and I knew instantly that Monique lived with me in the detesting-one's-own-physicality space. Seeing it on someone with such a bright light bothered me deeply.

"Your food makes *me* very happy, too." The smile my comment brought to Monique's face delighted me.

We chatted for the next hour, and I immensely enjoyed getting to know this group of women. Monique told me excitedly about being an English professor at the University of Victoria, and Dana rambled on about a seemingly never-ending list of occupations she had. I couldn't exactly tell if she was a scientist, a photographer, a cat-rescuer, a naturalist, an insurance representative, or an EMT. As she delved into the intricacies of each one, it slowly occurred to me that she was quite possibly the smartest person I'd ever met.

My mind wandered as Roxanne told a story about how, in Grade 12, we had removed the screen from my bedroom window so we could sneak out and go to the biggest party of the year. I didn't want to ruin Roxanne's memory by telling her that Fran had found out and—instead of grounding me for it—had shoved a box of condoms and a pack of birth control pills into my hands. Everything in my mother's eyes that day had told me to not make the same mistakes she had. And I thought I had done so much better.

And here I was trying to use Annette's children to keep her where Jon wanted her. I was ashamed of myself. Her warning rang through my mind again, so I excused myself to use the washroom. Protecting myself was my top priority now. I quickly texted Jon: *Thank you for taking care of the roof, go ahead and hire your company.*

The bubbles appeared: *OK.*

Do they require a deposit?

Yes. $500.

Why don't you give me their number and I'll call them tomorrow with my credit card?

ABC Roofing, 780-457-7777.

Perfect. I checked myself in the mirror, noticing the half an inch of grey at my roots. Guess I'd have to go get a touch up kit at the store while I was here. Not only would I pay for my own house repairs, I would make sure it was what I wanted, just in case Annette was right.

ALL FOUR OF us stood with our feet in the coarse sand watching the sun fully disappear behind the ocean. I absorbed the marvel of standing in the ocean for the first time in my life, trying not to think about the mess we'd left in the kitchen of Dana and Monique's place. Stan would have flipped. I curled my toes and then released them, hoping he could see me from above.

I quickly snapped a picture of the sunset and texted it to

everyone. It was more stunning than I could have ever imagined. A living Bob Ross oil painting. The bright orange sphere reflected in the water, rippling and distorting as the waves moved forward, a bouquet of blues surrounding it all. The horizon seemed impossibly far away, at the edge of the world. Was Japan beyond here? No, Russia?

The waves rustled up the beach and gulls screeched and swooped overhead. Every wave that came and went sunk my feet into the sand a little deeper. Roxanne reached out and took my hand. "Life's weird, Willie-Fillie."

"Yes, it is."

Monique and Dana joined hands and walked away from us. Roxanne continued in a low, deliberate tone. "We've come so far to get back to where we need to be."

"What do you mean?"

"You and I. We've officially survived a massive interruption in our plans of world domination."

I glanced over to see her eyes crinkled as she tried to contain a giggle, and I busted out in laughter. I remembered our high school graduation pinky promise clearly. Women were making strides in the late seventies, and we embraced it with vigor. We had both attended the University of Alberta—me in nursing and Roxanne following in her father's footsteps with fine arts. "Well, you seemed to have kept conquering the world. I was the one who bailed."

"Oh, don't worry. I got tripped up plenty. Two failed engagements under my belt. And we don't talk about the granola-crunching, free-love commune fiasco." Roxanne fake shivered.

I chuckled. "Yeah, but you stayed pretty true to yourself. Your artwork has been in galleries all over Canada! That's something to be really proud of. What do I have to be proud of? Diddly squat." Even making employee of the year at Dollarama six times in my nineteen-year career there meant very little to me. In fact, all it meant was that I was excellent at following my boss's orders to a T.

"Well. What do you want now? You have a fresh start. Make some new goals."

I gazed at the deepening dark. "I want..." The house to myself. To not be pushed around. To be seen as capable. To be heard. To be respected. To be selfish. I thought of the flicker of fear that had filled Stan's eyes as he realized my intentions as he died. Maybe I wanted a little more of that, too. The *Jeopardy!* category came back to me. *What Women Want.* Maybe some women only needed a pair of Levi's and a cup of Sleepytime Tea. But I needed more. Much more. It was such a relief to finally admit that to myself. "I want everything men have."

Roxanne rubbed her chin and pursed her lips. "That's broad, but we can work with it."

A bird screeched nearby again, but this time I looked up to see a large raptor circling overhead. "Oh!" Roxanne hummed in a long, drawn-out whisper. "An osprey." The large brown-and-white bird circled around on an updraft, swirling up, up like spring releasing in slow motion.

"Magnificent," I murmured.

"Like you."

I stopped myself mid-eye roll. I deserved better, even from myself.

- 8 -

FIRST THING IN the morning, I called the roofing company in Edmonton. The man was pleasant as I rolled off my credit card number, stating that they would get to work in a couple days. "I just want to make sure my son chose the colour of shingles I wanted," I said. This company carried the same line of shingles as the other company I'd contacted which was handy so I didn't have to pick a new colour.

Papers rustled in the background. "Yes, he ordered Russet Fleck."

Potato brown? That little shit. "Oh, I'm sorry! He must have misspoken. I wanted Onyx Black."

"Oh. Let me see..." The man hummed as computer keys clicked. "That was a fourteen hundred square foot bungalow, right? No peaks?"

"Yes."

"Alright, looks like we have enough Onyx in stock to make the change."

"Thank you kindly." I ended the call, reassuring myself that changing the shingle colour was not Jonathan's attempt to take over my house. I threw on a robe and made my way to the balcony.

Roxanne and I sat in the morning sun, enjoying our coffee. The sky was cloudless save for a single, white puff high in the sky, the air completely still. I couldn't remember the last time I'd felt so relaxed—my shoulders were not up around my ears, my jaw wasn't clenched, my stomach wasn't pulled in. I took in a deep breath and let it out slowly. I should be working all day, but the sudden change in events had brought me here instead. I was that cloud, floating, having nowhere to go, nothing to do, no wind to push me—the great big blue surrounding me. "I could get used to this," I whispered as I took a sip of coffee.

"Trust me, it's not hard." Roxanne turned a palm up in question. "What's on the docket for today?"

"Well, I need to do something with this." I pointed to the part in my hair.

"Okay, we can run to the drug store and get a touch up kit."

I looked over at Roxanne's wild nest of hair. "You never did dye your hair, did you? When did you start going grey?"

"Hmmm, about twenty years ago?"

I pinched my lips into a thin line. In the beginning, I'd ignored the greys that were creeping into my black hair, kind of liking the salt and pepper look. But once, when I was forty-six, a cashier at a store asked me if I qualified for the senior's discount and Stan had erupted in laughter, stating gleefully that he'd tried to tell me how old the grey made me look. Face burning, I'd strode down an aisle and plucked a boxed dye from the shelf. Later that night, Stan had told me the new look was beautiful, and that's when my high-maintenance hair upkeep began. "I don't want to dye it anymore." I looked over, expecting an appalled reaction, but she barely moved.

"So, let's bleach it and then dye it as close to your natural colour as we can."

"That sounds good."

"Can we watch Magic Mike while we sit?"

"Sure?" I had no idea what she was talking about.

"Trust me, you won't regret it. And then, tonight, the drunken shenanigans begin!" She whooped, causing a couple walking in the alley below to look up at us frowning.

I pressed my hands to my ears. "You're so loud."

"I know!"

I MUNCHED ON Skor bits while the bleach got to work, my eyes never leaving the screen as the half-naked men gyrated around.

"Hot, right?" Roxanne said from the couch where she lay. "Like, I swear I got pregnant just *watching* this the first time."

I nodded slowly, slipping another Skor piece into my mouth and then sucking all the chocolate off. Mike's loose penis bounced around in his sweatpants. *There are other things I could suck.* I shook my head violently. No. No more of that bullshit. After my conversation with Fran, I'd made an internal vow to come first, if I ever found myself involved with another man.

The timer went off. Roxanne paused the movie in mid-thrust and my groin stirred. It seemed losing my husband had resuscitated my libido.

"Let's rinse you off."

I tipped my head in the sink as Roxanne rinsed the bleach out, my eyes watering from the stench, but the mini scalp massage she gave while doing it was nice.

"Umm," Roxanne murmured nervously.

"What?"

"Well... it's just.... a weird colour, but I'm sure it will go away." She dug her fingertips more aggressively into my hair, trying to scrub it out.

"What do you mean?" I yelped from upside down, twisting my neck to peak at the colour of the curls that hung past my eyes. "Orange?" I squeaked.

"Close your eyes, you nut, you'll burn them." Roxanne grabbed a towel and wrapped it around my head. "Maybe we needed to leave the bleach in longer. Should we put more in?"

"I don't know! I'm not a hairdresser." I ran to the washroom and pulled the towel off. *Oh no.* I reached up slowly and touched my Halloween hair. "What have we done," I asked Roxanne who was behind me trying to suppress a giggle.

I wheeled on her. "This isn't funny!" But I felt something light rise up in me. It *was* a little comical. I turned back to the mirror and leaned closer. It wasn't pumpkin orange, more of a copper orange. Maybe it wasn't too bad.

"Let's do another twenty minutes and see what happens."

"See what happens," I muttered. "*See what happens?* I'm not an experiment."

"I beg to differ, actually."

Half an hour later, Roxanne stood back with her hands on her hips, inspecting me. "It didn't change much more. Want to just go ahead and put the grey dye in?"

"Sure," I said with a shrug. "I've got nothing to lose now."

"That's the spirit." She looked at her watch. "And we should have just enough time to make our reservation at Shelter for seven."

"Oh, God, you might not want to be seen out with me after this is all over and done."

"You wear that red dress of mine and I'd be seen with you anywhere." She winked.

She'd made me try on a couple of her sundresses this morning since all I'd brought with me was "grandma attire" as Roxanne had put it—blouses, cardigans, clamdiggers, and slacks. "My girls were busting out of that skimpy thing."

She lifted a single eyebrow and replied deviously, "I know."

I laughed. Stan was right. Roxanne was trouble. And I loved it.

SHELTER WAS A gorgeous timber-clad building that shouted West Coast—high wood ceilings, river rock fireplace, and earth-toned decor. We decided against the outside patio, even though it had a view of the bay, and seated ourselves inside in the back corner on comfortable black padded chairs. The waiter was prompt and had taken our orders and arrived back with a bottle of wine quickly.

"So, when are you coming back?" Roxanne asked, settling back in her seat, swirling the red wine around her glass. The bright blue dress she had chosen made her eyes look like jewels.

I laughed. "I haven't left yet, and you want to know when I'll be back?"

"Yes." She looked at me like I was crazy for not suggesting it first. "I'm thinking in a month or two."

"I don't know..." Laughter erupted across the bar, and I looked over. "Drunk plane ladies!"

Roxanne laughed. "What?"

I tilted my head toward the pair of women. "They were on the same plane as me." The one with short, white hair actually slipped off her chair as Roxanne turned their way.

"Well, they look like they're having the times of their lives."

I watched them wistfully. *They sure do.* "In a few months it'll be summer, and that's when the kids need me the most." Roxanne's features crinkled in anger as I talked. "And I'm never allowed to take August off because Ivan goes to his lake house."

Roxanne pressed her hands on the table. "Okay, I understand you have responsibilities, but are you really going to let your kids and boss dictate your life now that you're finally free of that dickhead? Summer out here is gorgeous! We could go to Victoria, visit the butterfly sanctuary, go to Butchart Gardens, walk along the sea wall, go to Craigdarroch castle, visit my paintings at the art gallery, go to the Victoria bug zoo—"

"A bug zoo?" I exclaimed. I mean, I didn't mind insects, but the thought of watching a herd of beetles rolling a giant poop ball along didn't sound like my idea of a great time.

Roxanne chuckled, a deep, rumbly sound. "Well, if that doesn't strike your fancy, there's always *other* famous artists to visit besides me. Emily Carr, Robert Bateman..."

"Oh, yes! He has those lovely wildlife paintings."

The food arrived, but Roxanne seemed to have lost interest in eating and only picked at her truffle fries. She must really want me to come back. I couldn't stand seeing her upset. "Look, I'll try my best alright?" I emptied my glass of wine. "Anyway, we have lots of time, Rox." I tried to gently reassure her. "Years, really." I wanted to enjoy my calamari, which was delicious, but her sulking had taken away some of my appetite.

I poured the last of the bottle into my glass and drained it, looking everywhere but at her. *I need to turn this around.* I refused to sit here like this all night. I hiccupped and covered my mouth. I felt lightheaded and wondered how much of the bottle I had downed. "I'm going to get tipsy soon, if we don't stop." *Too late.* I pushed my plate away suspecting I was halfway there already.

That brought her back to life. "Do it! Then we can go dancing after! Just like the King Eddy!" Having not seen her in person for so many years made me forget how undulating Roxanne's moods could be. Her eyes sparkled at the thought of us getting up to our old hijinks.

"Are there even any dance clubs here?"

"Nope." Roxanne grinned. "We'll just have to start our own dance party. I'm sure your friends over there are up for it." A deep grin spread over Roxanne's face, and she raised her hand to catch the attention of the waiter. It may have been years, but I still knew *that* look. "That's it—I've decided."

"What?"

"We'll dance here."

"Ladies." The grey-haired waiter approached the table, smoothing the front of his black dress shirt, eyes lingering on Roxanne. "What can I get you?" He'd been paying her an undue amount of attention since we'd arrived.

"Another bottle of this, handsome." Roxanne tapped the empty one.

"Certainly." He smiled at her and winked. He was attractive for an old fart, with his sweep of thick, white hair and his bedroom eyes.

I watched the exchange, realizing there was a familiarity between them. Or insane chemistry. Once he was out of earshot, I leaned toward her. "Have you, you know?" I flared my eyes in an attempt to convey what I was thinking.

"Fucked him?"

I choked. "Well, yes."

"I may have slipped and landed on Etienne's dick when it was icy outside the grocery store last January."

"You did not," I breathed, ashamed that the scene flitted through my mind. Magic Mike really did a number on me.

She sipped her wine innocently. "He'd be down with you too, if you wanted me to hook you up."

I touched my hair—which was now an *interesting* shade of yellowish grey—my eyes sliding to the waiter as he watched us.

"He's a slut, doesn't mind being passed around one bit." She lifted her hand to him. "Let's get this shit show on the road."

My heart leapt. Was she going to say something to him?

He sidled up to the table and Roxanne said, her eyes bright, "Bring this magnificent young lady a Rocky Mountain Bear Fucker, please."

As he nodded and turned away, relief washed though me. But as I caught him look back at me and wink, a little bit of disappointment did too.

FOUR SHOOTERS AND another half a bottle of wine later, I stood on a chair, Mavis's arms wrapped around my legs, wiggling my butt back and forth and not giving one iota as to who was staring. Etienne had clocked out, disappointing me a little, but Leon the bartender had been having so much fun watching the four of us go downhill he put on The Guess Who at our insistence. "No sugar tonight!" I sang loudly to Roxanne as her arm rammed in circles playing her air guitar, an intense focus on her face. Pork chop Mondays had been replaced with drunken chair dancing Monday.

Dee drummed on a tabletop, laughing as a group of young men cheered her on. "Nah, nah, nah, nah..." I wailed, jiggling back and forth, Roxanne's red sundress brushing over my knees. Roxanne and I had pranced on many a table back at Suki's in Edmonton, thriving in that late-teenage space where no one's opinion of me mattered. What a joy that had been.

I stepped a little too close to the edge of the chair and, before I could react, found myself lying face down on the floor, Mavis's body breaking most of the fall. I rolled off her, hoping I hadn't hurt her, but both of us laughing so hard I thought I would surely puke.

"Can I give you a hand," a gruff voice said. I glanced up to see a guy that looked exactly like the Brawny man smirking at me, holding out an arm to the both of us. I reached for it, and he easily pulled us up together. "Thank you!" I twirled away, Diana Ross coming over the speakers. I gave Roxanne goo-goo eyes, and she began serenading me, no mountain could keep us apart. She kneeled in front of me and took my hand, throwing her head back. "To keep me from gettin' to yooooou!" After the song was over, the four of us sidled up to the bar. "One more fucker, please!" Roxanne slapped the bar.

"I can only do that if you drink a glass of water first." Leon winked and pulled four glasses from under the counter.

Dee gave him fish lips, her red lipstick reduced to a faint line around her mouth. "Oh, poo."

"You'll thank me tomorrow," he said.

It turned out that Dee and Mavis were also on a girl's trip. They were from Saskatchewan, and this was their third annual retreat to the island. Murmuring over her glass of water, her eyes alive with mischief, Mavis said, "Robert Redford's watching you."

I glanced to the guy who'd helped us out, his red flannel shirt, strawberry blond hair and stubble giving off a rugged look that could be straight off a romance novel cover.

"Yum," Mavis said, draining her cup, ready for the shooter. I peered over her shoulder, realizing that he was watching me with a captivated smirk. *Yum, indeed.* That would be a real kick in Stan's barely cold pants if I hooked up with this hot, young thing tonight. He wasn't schoolboy young but couldn't be a day over fifty.

"Make Fran proud." Roxanne appeared in front of me, two more shooters in hand—each full to the brim—but somehow she held steady, not spilling a drop of the clear liquid.

Holding the shot glass to my lips, I lifted my eyes to the attractive stranger. He was leaning over to say something to his friend, but his gaze never left me. I imagined myself strutting right over to him, twining my fingers through his hair, and planting a kiss on his full lips. My pulse accelerated. I tipped the shot back and winced as it burned its way down my throat. *No.* I had just gotten rid of a man, the last thing I needed was another. I faced Roxanne. "Nah. I'm too busy having fun with my friends." My phone vibrated and I pulled it out of my purse. "Ivan?" I burped. "What right does my boss have texting me at ten at night, while I'm on holidays?" I yelled, reading the text. "To ask me to email him"—I squinted—"*Lyssa's contract*?" I was a salesclerk, not his personal assistant.

"Gimmee that!" Roxanne swiped the phone from my hand and started typing. "Nogoodfuckinguselessprick." She handed it back to me. "There. FIXED IT!"

I blinked at the screen, the words screaming at me from the blue bubble: *Suck it.* I moaned. How would I be able to live if I lost my job now? "Oh, Rox, what did you do?"

"Only what you've wanted to for years." She leaned over and kissed me loudly on the cheek.

She was right. I stared at my phone, blinking, as the laughter built in me. If I was ever going to do something irrational and fueled by emotion, now was the time. I couldn't imagine I would miss aching feet and dealing with customers' shitty attitudes—taking their frustrations out on lowly saleswomen was some people's favourite thing to do. I reminded myself that the house was paid for, and I had a decent little sum of money in the bank. And in a couple of years, I will be collecting my old age pension along with Stan's. Roxanne had started it, now all I had to do was end it. And if it became a struggle, I would simply find a new job. Maybe Tanya's flower business would do so well she could afford to pay me a small wage.

With determination, I texted again. *I quit.* I closed my eyes, relief coursing through me, but the swaying that resulted forced them back open. Maybe I would regret this in the morning, but a deep part of me knew I wouldn't. "Looks like I'll be able to come back this summer after all," I shouted to Roxanne, but she didn't hear me because she had just shimmied off as the iconic piano gliss of *Dancing Queen* came on.

I raised my arms high, immediately letting go of the whole ordeal. Dee pulled everyone to the centre of the restaurant for a dance off. I lifted my head and closed my eyes. This song would be my new theme—having the time of my life, indeed.

IT TURNED OUT sambuca and tequila, the two components of a Rocky Mountain Bear Fucker shooter, did not agree with me. But that hadn't stopped me from downing five. Or six. My head slammed forward again into the toilet.

I heaved, urging my body to get it all out this time. Long strings of spittle, bile, and squid chunks hung from my mouth in a searing reminder at to why I hadn't done this since I was twenty-one.

"Good grief," I moaned, and swiped toilet paper across my lips before laying down on the floor, half curled around the toilet. Leon had finally kicked us out of the restaurant at midnight, and we'd tumbled into the street singing ABBA songs and parting ways with Dee and Mavis in the parking lot as Roxanne and I piled into a cab.

"Knock, knock," Roxanne said, pushing the door open and scraping my heels. "How's my widdle muffin?"

I whimpered but remained limp on the tile.

"Great. So you won't mind while I piss beside your head." Roxanne stepped over me, bending down to move my head a few more inches away from the base of the toilet. She lifted her dress and sat, so that when I opened my eyes, the side of Roxanne's naked, white bum was barely ten inches from my face.

"Roxaaaaane…" I reached up and pushed on her leg. But there was nowhere to go. The wall was right up against my back, giving me little space to work with. I gave up and dropped my arm over my face.

"Just pretend we're in high school." Roxanne farted loudly into the bowl.

"Gah!" I flinched backward and hit my head on the wall. "You disgusting sow."

"You're welcome!" Roxanne cackled before wiping her butt and dropping her dress down. She flushed, closed the lid, and sat back down, ready for a chat.

"Why aren't you drunk?" I muttered.

"My booze tolerance is apparently way higher than yours. Seriously! You only had a bottle of wine and half a dozen shooters."

"That's A LOT!" I yelped into the side of the toilet and Roxanne's legs. "Are you an alcoholic or what?"

"Possibly." Roxanne reached over and moved my hand off my face. "You were really working it, girl!"

My stomach started rolling again as Roxanne continued to babble. "You still got the moves, Willie-Billie! That shoulder roll thing you do? Phew! Had that young stud practically drooling. I saw him *lick his lips* while watching you!" Roxanne hooted and clapped loudly, and I winced. "I bet he had a giant hard-on too!"

My brain let that image in, causing my groin to stir again and my stomach to heave simultaneously. A small moan escaped me, and Roxanne leaped off the toilet and flipped the lid open.

"I know that noise." She heaved me up by my armpits. "Come on, pukey panties."

"I did *naw*"—I hiccupped—"puke my panties." My body clenched as it once again heaved my innards—complete with my dignity and self-respect.

"There, there." Roxanne patted my back. "You'll be okay."

As I vomited again, I did not believe her, because at this rate there would be nothing left of me by morning.

- 9 -

I COULD LIVE the rest of my life never being hungover again. "This reclaiming my youth is a shit idea." *Free bird, my ass, Mom.* This was what happened to free birds—they went wild, ate too many fermented Mountain Ash berries, and crashed into windows. Roxanne laughed as I lay flat on the couch while she watched a movie. It was almost supper and all I'd managed to keep down were a handful of soda crackers and a cup of peppermint tea. I couldn't even handle Bo laying on my stomach and after the last time I pushed him off, he finally went to one of the blue chairs, curled up and pouted. What a giant waste of a beautiful day.

My phone lit up with another text from the coffee table. I'd been waiting all day for Ivan to respond and here it was. His one simple word made me happy: *good.* We'd never seen eye to eye anyway. Any time I made a suggestion about improving the look of the store, he shot it down. He only seemed to listen to the forever rotating crew of college girls that worked there. Now here I was—free of him and that shitty job. It had taken a lot of liquid courage, but I had finally spoken up for what I wanted. And it felt fan-fucking-tastic.

Another message came in, this time from Tanya: *Mom, I hope you're having a blast, just checking again if you will be home by April 29. Love you.* I clenched my jaw. What could possibly be so important? Tanya never needed me, so this sudden interest in my itinerary seemed strange. Most of the favours I did her were at my own offering. My face relaxed. If she was asking, it must be important. I texted back a yes. Since I was no longer employed, I would book my flight home for April 28 and not a day sooner. That gave me two weeks to enjoy out here. I lay back down and closed my eyes, willing the evening to hurry up so I could go back to bed.

I WAS UP early and feeling like my normal self the next day. *I will never drink that much again.* I quietly prepared coffee while Roxanne slept and settled myself on the deck as the sun rose, zipping up my sweater all the way to my neck. Closing my eyes, I lifted the mug to my face and inhaled the organic aroma deeply. It was so quiet out here. I smiled to myself. This was what I wanted.

It was a full hour before Roxanne appeared, blinking at the sun, and almost dropping her coffee as she stumbled onto the deck.

"You know what feels good?" I asked slyly.

"A dic—"

"Stop," I cut her off. "We're not going there."

She growled. "You're no fun."

"I am, in fact, tons of fun."

"Ok, what feels good?"

"The thought of not only having a place of my own, but now, not having to ever work for an asshole again." I leaned back in the chair.

"See! And if I hadn't texted your boss, that wouldn't have happened."

I nodded and watched a man below taking his garbage out. Sitting up straight, I lifted my finger gun, sighted him over my thumbnail, and pulled the trigger. "Pew. Another one down. I could just sit here for a week picking men off."

Roxanne snorted lightly. We sat silently for a long time. It occurred to me that I could tell Roxanne the truth about Stan's death, and she would not judge me. I opened my mouth to form the words, unsure how to start. In the beginning, I'd been smitten with Stan, but Roxanne had always disliked him. Stan commented that Roxanne's hatred of him was unhealthy for me, even saying once that he thought Roxanne was a lesbian and probably in love with me. It occurred to me suddenly that this might have been the real reason he never wanted me to visit her all these years. *Stupid ass.* Everything had to be sexual with men. Two unrelated people could not be close without it boiling down to animal urges. It was no wonder he didn't have any real friends.

But what would I gain by dragging her into this? I may alleviate some tension or need to unload within me, but it almost seemed unfair to put that on her. Plus, that would open me up to repercussions should Jonathan ever talk to her. Right now, the 'blanked out' alibi worked. I closed my lips and held it in. Maybe one day.

"I'm sorry that we lost so much time because of him," I said instead. For almost ten years after the wedding, Roxanne and I had barely spoken, but as the years passed, we overcame the hard feelings and settled into a long-distance friendship. "I know you never liked him, and I was forced to choose."

She shrugged. "What do you do."

"It was the wet t-shirt contest, wasn't it?" My nose tingled at the memory. I had never been so humiliated. But Stan had thought it was the best thing ever.

"That definitely sealed it for me." She turned to look at me. "It broke my heart to see that done to you. By a man."

I wiped a tear away, cringing at the memory of a drunken University pub crawl. One of Stan's friends suggested the women have a wet t-shirt contest since half of us already weren't wearing bras. Roxanne and I declined, but then Stan smiled wickedly and spilled his vodka and seven across the front of my white shirt. There was no getting out of it. Mortified, I knew the only way to win against Stan at that point was to own it, so I pushed my pride down and pretended I was in charge, swinging my saturated tits around for all to see. After that I became the favourite girlfriend and Stan's friends never looked me in the face again.

A man jogged down the alley, and I lifted my gun again, my face burning as the tears tracked down. "Bang," I roared. Crows took off from the spruce tree next to the apartment and the guy's head whipped around, searching for the sound of the noise. As he hunched over and picked up his pace, I grinned back at Roxanne, who hadn't taken her eyes off me the entire time.

FOR AN ENTIRE, blissful afternoon—dipping homemade chocolate chip cookies into iced coffees—we lost ourselves in the past. By supper, we'd brought ourselves up to discussing the future. Our friendship felt healed, as if Stan and the decades-long interruption, had never existed. I insisted on another beach walk to end a perfect day, and we invited Dana to join us.

A light mist hung in the air as waves crashed on the rocks at each end of the long stretch of taupe sand. I smiled, thinking that the beach was almost the same colour as Bo and simultaneously realizing that I'd grown quite fond of the little ferret. The constant movement of water rolling onto the beach filled the air with a gentle rumble. I breathed in as deeply as I could—the scent of fish and seaweed sharp in my nose. The sand and my feet were both perfectly warmed by the setting sun, and I couldn't tell where my skin ended and the beach began. I was rooted deeply in place, connecting to the earth in a way I never had before. How had I lived my whole life in the prairies when there was *this* to enjoy? I wiggled my toes and felt the grains gently grind beneath them.

"Willie. Come here," Dana called from a nearby rock formation.

I walked over to her. "Look here." Dana leaned over and pointed out a tide pool full of trapped critters, an amazed *oh!* escaping me.

"So, they just live here for twelve hours until the tide comes back?" I bent over to inspect a particularly beautiful red starfish. If I stared hard enough, I could see the infinitesimally small movements of its limbs.

"Yup. The tide's on its way out now and in a couple hours will be at its lowest." Dana crouched to point at a green tube-like blob thick with little feelers. I shivered, almost able to feel this strange creature crawl on me, tickling. "This is a green surf sea anemone. Anthopleura xanthogrammica."

"Antho whata?"

Dana patiently sounded it out for me. "Antho. Pleura. Xantho. Grammica." She used a stick to point at one. "These are their tentacles. They use them to catch prey—little fish, crabs, mussels."

"They eat meat?" The soft, delicate-looking thing didn't appear a carnivorous monster. I reached out, fighting the urge to pet it.

She laughed. "Yes, they do. They use their tentacles to sting and paralyze prey."

And poisonous. I pulled my hand back.

"And over here's some crabs." Dana continued with her sea-life education class while I listened in awe.

The longer I stared into the shallow pool cradled in the rocks, the more movement I detected. The tiniest things eventually twitched or slugged along if I stared hard enough. A bowl of life.

"Dana loves a rapt audience." Roxanne materialized beside me. "Converting regular people to nerds since 1983."

"I like it, it's interesting," I said, defending Dana.

"Oh, I agree! In fact, if everyone loved the earth as much as Dana did, we wouldn't be in the shitastic predicament we now find ourselves." Roxanne rolled up her leggings and stepped toward the water, a small, round bruise on her calf revealed. I touched my forearm where the fingertip bruises had finally faded. I could almost feel Stan's crushing grip. In this moment, I didn't ever want to return to the house where it had all happened. Maybe I'd sell it and get a nice little condo. *Screw the kids and their constant neediness.*

Dana had moved down the shore, and I stepped toward Roxanne. "Are you going to stay out here forever? Will you ever go back to Vernon to be with your dad?"

Roxanne clasped her hands behind her back. "I'll go back soon. But not yet. I feel like I need to be here, you know?"

"Maybe you stayed because you were waiting for me?"

"That's a pretty astute observation."

I wiggled my eyebrows at her. "*Maybe* I'm your reason for being."

She grinned at me and walked away.

We found a big piece of driftwood to sit on and watched people meander along the beach while Dana inspected the tide pools.

A tiny crab—a tan colour that was almost translucent—dashed past, just in front of my toes, slipping into a hole in the sand. I smiled as she cleaned house—little bits of sand shooting out the front door. I lifted my head, letting the water mesmerize me again, shielding my eyes, the glare almost blinding. A couple decked out in Tilly hats and sunglasses drifted past. I closed my eyes and let the sun warm my eyelids. The delighted squeals of the kids I'd seen running in and out of the waves earlier made me smile. There was something I'd always wanted to ask Roxanne, not as a judgment of her choices, but more of a gauge of mine. "Do you regret not having kids?"

She let out a long breath. "If I'm being honest, sometimes. Like, when you talk about your kids with so much love, a part of me aches for not having that. And the grandkids, that's something I know I miss. I would have been the best grandma."

"Yeah, you would have been." I inspected a new age spot on the back of my hand.

"It's just, like I *knew* how it would go if I had kids," she continued.

"Even if I found the best guy in the world. Marriage is one thing, but as soon as you pop a kid out your vag, they've got you. You're no longer human. You know what I mean?"

"Yeah. It was almost impossible back then. Things have gotten better, though. Vivian made Bruce sign a contract before they got married." I lifted an eyebrow at her.

"Really?"

"Yup. She lived for her research and made him agree that when they had kids, all tasks would be divided equally. The detail of that document was astounding."

"So, things are changing."

Annette and Jonathan came to mind. I dropped my head. "But not fast enough."

My phone vibrated and I pulled it out see who it was. A text from Vivian: *Hope you're having fun, just passing along a request from Ainsley to get a selfie with an Orca!* I started laughing and couldn't stop. Tears streamed down my face as my mind imagined me luring the beast to shore with a limp mackerel.

In that moment, I missed the grandkids immensely. Hardly a day or two would go by at home that I wouldn't see at least one of the seven. I knew I could never actually stay out here, but maybe a vacation condo was a great idea, and I could bring a different grandkid with me each time.

I wiped my cheeks. "Have you ever been on a whale watching tour?"

"No, surprisingly that's one thing I haven't done."

"Well, that's the next item on my bucket list."

"Fantastic." Roxanne jumped up and began walking back toward the ocean, her red knitted shawl falling off her left shoulder. Roxanne's way of dressing was *eccentric*—like a mix between Ainsley's wild, colourful attire and a hippie. Roxanne halted, bent down, and dug in the sand. A loud crack caused me to jump up and look behind me. I frowned as a teenager threw another large rock against the previous one he'd tossed, making the same ear-splitting noise.

Something cold suddenly hit me squarely on the neck. "Ahhh!" I leaned sideways and swiped at it, realizing it was wet sand. I jumped up, turning, to see Roxanne laughing. I yelled, "What did you do that for, you silly cow?"

Roxanne threw her head back and laughed to the sky and then, adroitly bending at the waist, went to grab for another handful.

She moved so quickly and fluidly. As I stooped to collect sand for a counterattack, another glob skimmed the top of my head. I scooped and flung a handful back at her. It fell with a splat a full two feet from its target.

Roxanne cackled and ran toward the ocean. Surprising myself, I seized another handful and delivered it with as much aim as I could muster. It hit Roxanne square in the back. "Yes!" I pumped my fist.

"Oh! Nice shot, dingle balls! Betcha can't do it again," Roxanne called over her shoulder, nimbly veering left, while scooping up another sand blob and chucking it at me. It half-hit my thigh, leaving a wet, brown smear on my lovely tan clam diggers.

"That's it," I howled and took off running as fast as I could toward Roxanne, my knee screaming the whole way.

We yelled and hollered and flung sand blobs at each other all down the beach, people staring as we went. I was gaining ground on Roxanne and in a final effort, leapt forward, frantically asking the higher-ups to end this with no broken bones.

"Ooof!" Roxanne bellowed as I made contact near her butt, wrapping my arms around her, both of us toppling to the ground in an uncoordinated mess. *Timber!*

"Gotcha!" I squealed, sitting on Roxanne's back. I dug up a huge handful of sand, feeling the grains sharply beneath my short nails, and squished it into Roxanne's hair. She gasped and yelled, "Stop!" I flopped off Roxanne, hoping I hadn't taken it too far and hurt her.

Roxanne rolled over and swiftly lunged toward me. "Tricked ya! You fall for it every time." Roxanne straddled my waist and pinned my arms into the mud. We were over the edge of the water now and were soaking wet and sinking. "You've always been too nice, Silly-Willie." Roxanne used a hand to scoop up sand and shove it down the front of my shirt, filling my bra.

"You…bitch!" I stammered, squealing and laughing at the same time.

Roxanne was laughing so hard she wheezed, tears streaming down her face, her hair loose from its ponytail and stuck to the side of her face. I had a vague memory that we had done something similar to this at Lakeview beach on Gull Lake where I had gone camping with Roxanne and her dad several summers in a row. Roxanne's laughter grew higher pitched, like it was being squeezed out of her, reminding me of the asthma attacks Vivian used to get. Pressing her hand to her chest, she finally breathed in deeply, erupting in a coughing fit. Slowly, she rolled off me and slumped beside me in the sand.

"You alright?" I peered into her face.

"Yup. Just some good old emphysema. Smoking for forty years will do that to a person."

"You should have quit." We had gone at cigarettes pretty hard in our early twenties, but shortly after the wedding, Stan demanded that I quit. He said he didn't want to kiss an ashtray and that it would age my face prematurely. In hindsight, it was one thing I could thank him for.

"No shit. But I haven't had one in over a year."

"Good girl." I patted her arm.

We sat up to see an old man walking by, shaking his head. With as much maturity as the boys up the beach breaking rocks, Roxanne stuck her tongue out at him. His eyes bugged out and he shook his walking pole at her before moving along. I gasped at Roxanne's immaturity, but the outraged look he kept throwing back at her was hilarious. Soon I was laughing uncontrollably, until I was hiccupping and crying.

We cleaned ourselves off as best we could and eventually made our way back to the car with Dana, who had reappeared after her walk down the beach. She shook her head at the sight of us, but the smile on her face was undeniable. The old guy who shook his stick at us earlier was getting into the car next to us. He glared at me and muttered, "Stupid cunts."

Red clouded my vision. I stood, unblinking, my teeth pressed together. I didn't need to wait until I grew up to be like Roxanne. I swiftly lifted my hand and gave him the finger. His bottom jaw dropped before he clamped it closed—his hatred for me in that moment etched in every pinched line of his face. It reminded me a little of Stan when he hissed that word to me.

We sped away from the beach still howling. I didn't need to wait until some prescribed time to embrace being myself. I was here now, doing and being me, and nothing had ever felt better.

BACK AT THE condo, my phone rang. Vivian. "God, they just can't leave me alone," I muttered, jumping out of the car and walking away, nodding at Roxanne to go up without me.

I took a quick breath. "Hello?"

"Mom, I'm so sorry to bother you."

"That's alright. What's going on?"

"I just got off the phone with Annette."

I rolled my eyes. "What now?"

"Gabby and Connor have been exposed to Hand, Foot and Mouth disease."

"Oh. It's not that bad is it? I mean Ainsley had it a couple of years ago."

"No, it's a pretty common virus, but if they actually get it, it's just that they have to quarantine for two weeks."

"Ohhh." *And?* I wanted to prod Vivian into getting to the point. As I paced on the tiny lawn, I could feel sand working its way into areas best left sandless. I needed a shower. "Honey, what am I supposed to do about it?"

"Kick Jonathan out of the house."

That was my Vivian, direct to a fault. I should just agree with her, but my need to avoid confrontation won over. I let out a long breath. "I tried."

"You have to try harder. Annette needs him at home." Her voice rose. "He's using your place as a staycation away from his family and is claiming that he's on call and can't watch the kids, in case he has to leave suddenly. To, you know, build an emergency cabinet." She snorted. "Right now, Bruce has to go over tonight to watch the kids so Annette can go to a showing. *Bruce.*"

I pinched the skin between my eyes. Why was Jon being such a jerk?

"Mom?"

"I'll see what I can do." I said goodbye and hung up, immediately dialing Jonathan, holding my breath the entire time.

"Hello?"

"Jonathan, go home and help your wife," I blurted out in a rush before I lost my nerve.

He scoffed. "So, you want the roofing contractors coming tomorrow and working unsupervised?'

"I'll postpone them until I get home."

"If you do that, they won't come back. They had to juggle other jobs to get you in. They'll be pissed."

I spoke through gritted teeth. "Let them be pissed then, because Bruce shouldn't be the one watching your kids."

"Oh, so turn this around on me, then? Annette asked *me* for a divorce, Mom! Why would I help her out now?"

"They. Are. *Your.* Children." My face burned. I had never talked like this to my son but being stuck in the middle of this was exhausting.

There was a long pause. "That drip in the roof will get worse with the spring rain. And I noticed you have mice."

Mice? In the forty-so years we'd lived in that house, I had never seen a single one. I squeezed my eyes tight. Was he lying? My shoulders sagged. *I just want a holiday.*

"And I'm still not convinced you should be left alone," he added.

I froze. I'd hoped he'd let that go. Surely there was no way to incriminate me. My stomach twisted and I feared I might throw up on the grass. There had to be a way to make this work for everyone. "Can't you stay at the house but still help Annette with the kids? If you continue to make things difficult for her, there'll be no chance of reconciliation."

"What if I don't want reconciliation?"

I give up. There was no way to win this. "Do what you think is best, Jon," I snapped.

I could hear the smile in his voice all the way from here. "I *always* do what I think is best, Mom."

For yourself, I wanted to scream. What about everyone else? Annette's warning came to mind. My jaw flexed and I hung up without saying goodbye.

I pounded my way upstairs, hating myself more than him. Why was he doing this to me? And why was I letting him? In the shower, I scrubbed the skin so hard—grinding the sand in more than rinsing it off—I was red and raw by the time I emerged. I didn't bother to wipe the steam from the mirror to see myself, as I normally did. I didn't want to look at my own, shameful face.

I PACED AROUND the furniture that took up about eighty percent of the tiny balcony, wine glass in hand, resisting the urge to kick something. The small picnic table, cedar chairs and metal railing would all emerge victorious against my bare toes. I stopped in front of the red Adirondack chairs. They looked heavy, but maybe I could send one sailing over the railing; I was sure that would be satisfying.

I couldn't shake the feeling that somehow Jonathan had outmaneuvered me. I had called him to give him shit and he'd managed to turn the whole thing around on me.

Kind of like the time Stan had found me curled up in the washroom when the kids were little, almost passed out from the pain that was tearing through my lower abdomen. He'd tried to tell me I was exaggerating, but it took Tanya crying with worry over me to prompt Stan to actually take me to the hospital. When the doctor admonished me for not coming in sooner, racing me to surgery for a ruptured ovarian cyst, I heard Stan telling the doctor he had been trying to make me come in for hours, but that I'd refused. I had almost died because of his inability to listen to or believe me. And then I was the one to blame for it.

"What's all the pounding for, snookums?" Roxanne slid the glass door open, her wet hair wrapped up in a towel.

I jumped. "Oh. You scared me."

She poured herself a glass of wine and eyed me over the brim. "So, what's the problem? Or should I say, who?"

I rolled my eyes. I knew I should let it go before Roxanne jumped on the hating-my-son bandwagon. But I really needed to vent. "Jonathan's being difficult."

She regarded me for a long time before responding. "Remember when I found out about Bobby?"

I laughed. Bobby was the first of her two abandoned fiancés. "Yes. You dumped him faster than a hot potato."

"You have to teach them how to treat you. That's why I have a no cheaters or beaters rule. Zero tolerance. People say I'm hard to deal with, but I truly don't believe these are hard rules to live by."

"And what's your rule on run-of-the-mill, pressing-your-luck dumbasses?"

"Oh, yeah, I got rules for them too." She cleared her throat dramatically. "If you can't handle my ambitions, opinions, anger, or body hair, then sayonara. That took care of Lance, fiancé number two. He said I was ugly when I was mad." She pushed a chunk of hair off her forehead. "I'd rather live with myself honestly, than with a man compromised. That doesn't just apply to husbands, you know. Any man in your life can be held to these standards, sons included."

But this is so much more complicated. Turning my back on a child was the worst thing imaginable.

We settled into the chairs, watching the clouds darken in the twilight. A couple of seagulls fought noisily over a crust of bread in the parking lot next door. Finally, I said, "The world does seem to need us to be perfectly hairless, doesn't it?" All the times I'd had to live with a nasty crotch razor rash just so I could be 'decent' in a bathing suit. Men's swimwear didn't need grooming prior to donning. I thought of all the hairy balls living under those baggy shorts. *Must be nice.*

"Maintaining ridiculous beauty standards is just another distraction so we don't have the time or energy to notice these men are still running the show. All of them. Even the shitty sons."

I downed the glass of wine, poured another, and gulped half of it. Even though I said yesterday I was never drinking again. But instead of calming me, the warmth of the alcohol only fueled my simmering rage. "Let's do something crazy."

Roxanne lifted an eyebrow. "What did you have in mind?"

I glanced back to the living room, thinking of the art supplies in the corner, then eyed her with an intensity that I felt deep in my soul. "I'll meet you by the front door in five minutes. Wearing all black."

She saluted me. "Yes ma'am."

There she goes again, complying without question. I jogged to my room. I could get used to being treated like this.

- 10 -

I MET ROXANNE back at the front door dressed in everything black I owned, a reusable shopping bag gripped in one hand full of her spray cans. Roxanne's eyes grew wide at the realization of the mischief we were about to engage in.

We crept down the stairs and slipped into the darkness behind the apartment building. *Three days.* The thought would not leave me alone. I'd abandoned my own house to only get three measly days of peace and quiet before they'd all started in on me again? My grip on the bag grew tighter. Three days before they could not function without me. It was my own fault. I'd made myself too available all these years.

I stopped short. What if I made myself…unavailable? I pulled my cell from my pocket, set it on the ground and heel stomped it with my sturdy Columbia hiking boots. I kept pumping my foot until glass shards lay around the mangled piece of technology. My chest heaving, I muttered to Roxanne, "We're going old school." Back to the days when no one could bother you if you wanted to disappear from the world for a while. It always made me a little sad that my grandchildren would never know the joy of not being tracked everywhere they went, would never be able to ditch school without an alert being sent to their parents devices ten seconds after their lack of attendance was noticed, to not have every little thing they ever did filmed and digitally documented for life. I let out a long breath. There was no point mourning the loss of the old days. Those were also the days men could do whatever they wanted without fear of retribution, and I was more than happy to move on from that.

Roxanne stepped beside me as I strode away from my obliterated phone. "So, what kind of message do you want to send the world, exactly?" She pulled a spray can from the bag and shook it—the sharp pinging of the ball inside felt satisfying.

I scowled, not losing focus on my mission. "I'm thinking." As we arrived in the small downtown area, I looked up and found the perfect canvas.

A fence that divided a park from a parking lot that was wide and white and not in the direct light of the main street or its lights. I found a can of black spray paint, held it to the fence and set my finger on the nozzle. The look of fear on the jogger's face after I'd shot him in the alley came back to me, warming me from the inside. Wouldn't it be amazing if *men* lived their lives always looking over their shoulders? Wondering who was out there creeping around in the shadows waiting to hurt them? I pressed the nozzle, the hiss loud as I wrote in blocky letters the first thing that came to mind, feeling strangely calm.

FUCK MEN.

That's for you, Stan. I stood back and admired my work, Roxanne nodding and silently stepping in with a can of red paint. She embellished the black writing with what appeared to be a severed penis. The knife that sliced through it was dripping with blood, a true work of art.

I stood staring at the two words, mesmerized. *I did that.* Even as a teenager, I'd never gone so wild as to vandalize something. It was so juvenile, but at the same time, a fierce power surged from deep within me—I had finally put something out in the world that spoke to my true rage. Blood rushed in my ears and I growled, "Perfect." We crept onto the next suitable canvas, a sidewalk, and did the same thing. That one was for Jonathan. Near the grocery store, headlights swept over us. "Car!" We dove onto the pavement, heads turned sideways, trying to make ourselves as flat as possible. As the car moved past, we erupted into giggles.

Roxanne finally breathed, "Should we stop before we get caught?"

"Nope." I wanted the world to know how I was feeling right now. I pushed myself up and finished the *-en* on the concrete. One for Ivan.

As Roxanne finished the tip of the penis, she turned to me. "Should we think of something more eloquent or poetic for the next one?"

My brows furrowed. But then I remembered the thought I'd had when I first arrived in Tofino, that men might be happier if we just disappeared. "No. It's just the opposite of what men have been thinking for years."

"Fuck women?"

"Yup." It was the silent message they sent us in the way they treated us, looked at us, thought of us. *The way they turn things around on us.* They could have a little of that sentiment right back.

Every single message I painted, I internally dedicated to a man in my life—my father, that friend of Stan's who'd kissed me, Damian the stalker from college, the shithead who'd decided the set of breasts that won the wet t-shirt contest deserved a fondling, the boy in 11th grade who'd conned me into believing he loved me so he could get a blowjob and then informed the whole school I was a slut, the neighbour boy who used to tell my father every single bad thing I ever did because I refused to date him. By the time we were done, we'd lost count of how many public places we'd vandalized.

Something rustled from the bushes beside us, and in one swift move, Roxanne was crouched facing it, a knife in her hand. "What the?" My head whipped between the bush and Roxanne, heart pounding. How had she moved that fast? The light caught the blade and flashed. And where did *that* come from? The leaves rustled. a cat emerging from the shrub, and we both let out a long breath. The black-and-white feline gave us the side eye as it crouched and took off. Surely it had been up to no good as well.

Roxanne straightened and pushed the blade back, slipping it into the pocket of her jeans. She saw me watching her and offered, "I'm always prepared."

"I... I see that."

A light drizzle started, warm and soft. It was the kind of rain that begged to be danced in. I pulled Roxanne toward me and spun her away, twisting my hips, my face lifted to the sky. It was a silent tango, but when I finally dropped my eyes to hers again, I couldn't tell if the wetness on her face was more than what was coming from the sky.

We crept back home feeling spent, but at the same time energized. "That was highly illegal," Roxanne mused as she linked arms with me.

"Sure was." I had a stab of guilt over making clean-up work for the town maintenance staff, for potentially ruining perfectly good infrastructure.

But what about me? What about every catcall, every groping, every dismissal, every belittling that I had been subjected to? In a small way, all of that had slowly ruined my psyche, my sense of self, my bodily autonomy.

I lifted my head. I would not feel bad about this. Just like I hadn't felt bad about letting Stan go. Sometimes ugly things had to be done for the greater good. And no one understood that better than men themselves.

THE NEXT AFTERNOON, Roxanne and I joined the other tourists queued up for the whale watching tour. We'd slept in until late morning after deflating from the high of last night and had to hurry to be ready for the noon trip. Several people at the front of the line were already into their huge red safety suits and were boarding the boat—a tiny little thing with inflatable sides.

The Orca selfie. I slapped my forehead. "Oh shit."

"What?"

"How am I supposed to take a selfie with a whale if I don't have a phone?"

Roxanne barked a laugh. "You didn't think that was really going to happen, did you?"

"Well, I was going to at least try."

Roxanne inhaled sharply and grabbed my arm. "It's him," she hissed.

"It's who?" I looked around but couldn't figure out who she was referring to.

"The Brawny Guy! From the bar that night." She bounced on her feet, her eyes sparking as she lifted her sunglasses to get a better look. "This is fucking *destiny* in action."

"Oh." My gaze landed on the captain of the boat, who was greeting people and helping them suit up. "*Him.*" There was a desire in my voice that shocked me. Even in his red safety suit he still looked very handsome. His strawberry blond hair and stubble, well, sexy.

"He has a Prince Harry vibe going on." Roxanne stepped closer.

"Don't you dare say anything." This was going to be a nightmare. I absolutely could not trust Roxanne to keep her mouth closed. I gripped my stomach. "I don't feel good. Let's leave."

"Oh, no you don't." She yanked me fully forward causing me to stumble.

"Well, hello." He grinned. "You two look familiar."

Roxanne gave him a look that was bashful and brash at the same time. "Ah, yes. You're the chap that helped my friend Willie here up after an unfortunate tumble at Shelter the other night."

My face heated up and I dropped my head, tucking a strand of my copper-grey hair behind my ear. He probably thought we'd looked like old, drunken fools that night in the bar and felt bad for us disgracing ourselves so publicly.

"I always like to be of service." His voice was nice, not too deep, but deep enough to be soothing should he ever find himself whispering sweet nothings in my ear.

Now I was sure an egg could be cooked on my face it was so hot. Why should I care what he thought of me anyhow? Roxanne nudged me and I finally looked up to face the music. He was looking right at me, smiling, his bright green eyes roving all over me. *He's checking me out!* "We should...uh...get on...the, uh...boat, don't you think?" My ability to string together a cohesive sentence had abandoned me.

He turned away, as if he realized he'd been caught ogling me. "Yes, yup. Here are your suits, and I'll meet you on board." He handed us the safety suits and—shaking his head and grinning—turned back to the other customers.

Once we were dressed and aboard, he slipped on behind me, pressing his hand into the small of my back to guide me to a seat. "Why don't you two ladies sit right over there where I can keep an eye on you?"

"Aye, aye, captain." Roxanne saluted him, leaning into me and growling. "He'll keep more than an eye on you if he gets the chance. Fingers, tongue—"

"Stop!" I hissed, moaning internally. Partly in regret for getting myself into this situation in the first place and partly because even though I was supposed to be on a man-hating streak, this particular man was causing a stirring in my nether region that I hadn't felt in a long time.

ONCE SEATED, I leaned over and whispered in Roxanne's ear, "Please don't make me regret bringing you today."

"But it would be so empty without me!" she sang lightly. "Eminem said that, you know."

"What? The chocolates?"

"Oh man!" Roxanne slapped her forehead. "You really need to prioritize your life, Willie-Dillie. Em-i-nem? *The rapper?* You know, Eight Mile, white boy on the come up, slim shady, word smith fucking extraordinaire." Roxanne fisted her hand, brought it to her mouth and started making noises, "*Uh uh uh.*"

She leaned back, pushing me away. "Two old white broads go lookin' for whales, lookin' for whales, lookin' for whales. Uh, uh, uhhh. Uh, uh, uhhh. One horny, hot lass, lookin' for tail, lookin' for tail, lookin' for tail. Uh, uh, uhhh. Uh, uh, uhhh."

My eyes bulged. "*Stop it,*" I commanded. Was I looking for tail?

Roxanne started laughing uncontrollably, soon doubling over onto her knees. "I'm gonna piss my pants," she wheezed.

I didn't want to laugh. I was sure the hot guy was watching us. Then again, so what if he was? A giggle started somewhere deep within me, followed by a snort I couldn't contain. Watching Roxanne lose her mind with joy was incredibly contagious. Soon, a full-bellied, braying laugh erupted from my mouth, and we were both bent over, tears streaming down our faces.

A throat-clearing from behind made me turn around to see him watching us with a huge grin on his face. As my eyes slid away from him, I caught a wink.

Roxanne's laughing turned to hard coughing. She put her hand up and shook her head as I leaned in to check on her. She dug in her pocket and pulled out a cough drop, righting herself and staring purposely out onto the horizon as she sucked on it, her body jerking a couple times as she held in several more hacks.

I looked into the dark water as the small boat pulled away from the dock. *My first time on the ocean.* I stared into the little eddies and whorls. There was so much beneath the surface that I couldn't see.

The Brawny guy talked over the chugging of the engine as we

pulled out of the harbour. "I'm Mark, your captain. Cross your fingers we see Orcas today." Diesel smoke spewed out the back of the boat, the wind throwing it toward me.

"I love that smell," I murmured.

"Really? Because it's making me want to cough again."

"Reminds me of my dad. Remember he worked in heavy construction? Always came home smelling like exhaust." I breathed in deeply. Why I was having nostalgic feelings about the prick now was unknown to me. He and Stan had hit it off right from the start, and Stan had been more upset than I'd been when my father passed away.

Mark continued giving safety instructions over the drone of the engine. As we made our way out of the bay, drops of icy water splashed on my face, but the sun was out, making it tolerable.

Roxanne made a moaning noise from beside me. My heart jumped. "What's the matter *now*?"

"This is why I don't do boats. They make me want to puke." Roxanne leaned forward.

"Why didn't you tell me, you dolt? I wouldn't have made you come."

"Do you think I'm the kind of person who lets a little discomfort stand in the way of having fun?"

I shook my head. *Nope.*

"It'll go away, just give me a few minutes to adjust," she said. I left Roxanne to her misery and inspected the horizon. I could feel my body sloshing with the waves and was surprised to realize I liked the feeling after having been land-locked my whole life. It was soothing.

Tall, bluish-purple mountains—the caps still topped with snow—rose up inland as we sailed away. The boat finally slowed as some rocks appeared to the left. Mark explained that this was a better spot for seeing whales than the open ocean, and that we just had to be patient. I crawled over to the inflated rubber edge of the Zodiac and held the flimsy rope, swaying back and forth on my knees. Mark came up beside me, touched my arm and squatted beside me. "I'm Mark. Just wanted to formally introduce myself."

"Willie. Nice to meet you." A sly smile crept over my lips. Was *I* flirting?

He nodded toward Roxanne. "Is your friend seasick?"

"Yes."

"I have some Gravol in my bag. Do you think she'd take it? It doesn't totally help, but it takes the edge off."

"Why don't you ask?" I smiled, knowing Roxanne would love for Mark to baby her.

He nodded, leaving me to contemplate the ocean. The sky was light blue, almost the exact same shade as Stan's eyes had been, so opposite my muddy brown ones. They had been one of his most striking features. I shook my head, not knowing why I kept thinking about him at the strangest times. White, puffy clouds cauliflowered over the ocean along the horizon. Now that the boat had stopped moving, the warm April sun could be fully felt, warming my chilled hands. I gripped the rail and closed my eyes, feeling the ocean churn below me. The slow rocking sloshed all the water in my cells. Getting brave, I widened my knees and let go of the rail. My small movements mirrored the waters, and I could feel the muscles in my hips flex and release to keep my balance. I closed my eyes and imagined Mark's naked body below me. I knew I should push the image away, but instead, I let it deepen. I slid my hands up his hairless, toned stomach as the tip of his penis sparked against my folds, sending a thrill through me. As I lowered myself onto him, my fingers curled against his stomach, the sensation almost overwhelming. As I sunk lower, a moan escaped—

A puffing noise came from out on the water, my eyes flying open. "Whale! I saw it!" one lady shrieked, more people shouting that they saw it too.

I blinked hard to rid myself of the vision and bring myself back to the boat. I glanced back to Roxanne, who was holding on to Mark's arm to balance herself. Seasick? *What a load of horse shit.* She repressed a smirk as she clung tightly to his arm, hobbling her way to the edge of the boat. "Looks like you're getting lucky today!" he called to the group after placing Roxanne's hands firmly on the rail. "Juvenile humpback whale. They are a baleen whale, which means they filter their food by taking in huge gulps of water and pushing it out, leaving the krill and small fish behind." His face was wide open with excitement, his mouth slightly open.

It was incredibly hot.

"Humpbacks have a distinctive shape, with long pectoral fins and dorsal hump and knobby head."

The whale suddenly popped out of the water much closer to the boat than the first time, making the group gasp. "Looks like we may be *very* lucky, today! He's coming in for a closer peek." The tip of the whale's tail caught the sunlight as it followed the body back into the water.

"Humpbacks typically migrate 25,000 kilometers a year—the distance always blows my mind." Mark was talking more quietly now. "This particular group comes up here in the summer, when the feeding grounds are rich, after spending the winter around Hawaii. I would guess this one is a couple of years old, now away from its mother, but still young enough to be curious." He took a breath. "Did you know the humpback, along with all whales, almost went extinct before the 1966 moratorium on the whaling industry? Only humans could cause such destruction." Mark shook his head. "The largest animal on the face of the earth almost wiped out by our own selfishness. But all species are on the upswing, although fishing nets, boat traffic, and noise pollution continue to be a problem."

I gasped as the whale came up right beside the boat. It rolled slowly, showing off its snow-white belly, before disappearing again beneath us. Roxanne kneeled beside me as we stared over the side, waiting for it to reappear. "This is pretty rare, folks," Mark said.

"Maybe once, twice a year we get an interaction like this, so enjoy."

"You must be a good luck charm," Roxanne said, smiling at me.

"Feeling better, you wretched lech?"

"Yes, I am, thank you so much for asking. Your pool boy was a great help."

I pursed my lips and shook my head slowly. If Roxanne could act in such a way, what was stopping me from doing the same? The whale's head reappeared, breaking the surface gently. It had the most ridiculously small eye I had ever seen on such a beast, and I could have sworn it was trying to look at us as it leisurely glided along the boat, slowly turning only metres away. Everyone was chatting and snapping pictures and crowding the edge of the boat to get closer.

"Remember, people in the front are sitting," Mark reminded us, speaking directly to a man who was trying to stand in front of everyone else.

The head shot out of the water, moving skyward. Water slid down its skin, slipping back into the ocean as it came to its full height out of the water. I guessed at least ten feet was exposed before it pirouetted and twirled itself back into the inky ocean. "It's so graceful," I murmured. For such a huge animal, it was incredibly agile and gentle.

One last time, the whale came up, almost nudging the boat and rolling past, its dark grey body marred with wrinkles and small scars. "Got it," Mark said. I turned to him leaning over us with his phone out.

Ainsley. "Oh! Did you take a picture?"

"Yes."

"You must be a mind reader." I'd have to give him my phone number so he could text it to me. Or rather Roxanne's, since mine was no longer with us. How convenient was that? "Can you text it to me, please? My granddaughter wanted me to get a selfie with an Orca."

"I would *love* to get your number." A mischievous, calculating look illuminated his face.

Roxanne elbowed me, but I just smiled and turned back to stare into the water until I couldn't see the flash of white fins anymore. A few minutes later, the whale popped up far away from our boat, on his way to say hi to some other tourists.

"Well, you lucky ducks"—Mark started the boat back up—"that was a once-in-a-lifetime experience. Now let's go find us some seals, shall we?"

We took our seats. I looked over to find Roxanne watching the water. I slid my hand over and took hers. "The magical moments just don't seem to stop coming while I'm with you."

She blew air out her nose, dropping my hand. "Just remember you can have this without me, too."

I frowned. "Why would you say that?"

Roxanne shrugged. "You never know when a whale will breach your boat and smash you to smithereens."

I made a *psh* noise. "Like that would ever happen." I glanced out to the water.

"It did down in Mexico a couple of years ago. Canadian woman, too."

I gasped. "So that *thing* could have jumped on me?" I imagined a grey bulk over the boat, dripping sea water on my head before it flopped, and I was squished flatter than a pancake.

"You need legs to—"

"You know what I meant, you…you beast!"

"Beast? I know after what you did last night you can do better than that." I grumbled and looked back out to the water, trying not think about imminent death.

"Don't be upset that I didn't tell you about 'death by whale' before we came. You wouldn't have stepped foot on this boat if you knew, would you?"

I sighed. "You could have still prepared me or something."

Roxanne took me by both my shoulders and gave me a hard

shake. "Willie! You could die at any moment. Do not—I repeat, do not—go anywhere or do anything. It could be the end of you." Roxanne leaned into my face and hissed, "For-eh-vah!"

I tried to stop the grin creeping onto my lips. "You're ridiculous." I turned back to the water.

"Don't do it!" Roxanne yelled, causing the budging-for-the-best-spot man to throw a death glare at us. "Don't you dare smile, you hoe."

I burst out laughing. As I wiped tears from my cheeks, Roxanne turned abruptly and pointed at a small island of rocks. "Seals!"

My Roxanne, she really hadn't changed a bit. As I watched the water spray around the side of the boat, I realized, though, that I had. Sure, reverting back to our teenage years was fun, but there was something missing from it. The depth that came from living many years. The wisdom and compassion born of having children. I couldn't, nor did I want to, erase the kids and grandkids from my memory.

As much as I wanted to, I knew in my heart I couldn't stay out here forever. Roxanne was right. I had to learn how to have this without her. There had to be a way to make my real life work. If I'd learned to do this years ago, Stan may still be here.

BACK ON THE dock after marvelling over bald eagles, osprey, far-off killer whales, and playful seals, Roxanne and I walked arm-in-arm onto dry land. We turned and waited for Mark to bid farewell to the other guests so I could give him Roxanne's number, a plan forming in my mind. As he strode over, Roxanne leaned into me and whispered breathily into my ear. "He seems the take-control sort. It's hot."

"I have to use the washroom. I'll be a minute." I pushed Roxanne toward the car so I could talk to Mark alone.

"That was a happy coincidence that you arrived here today." He dipped his head and pushed a piece of gravel with his shoe. "I did follow you out of Shelter that night, intent on asking for your number, but you were, um, pretty loaded and I didn't want to seem like I was taking advantage of that."

A true gentleman. Most men would have seized on the opportunity to possibly get laid, regardless of sober consent or not. "Well…" I watched a couple milling near the dock, kissing. My thumb found the dent on my ring finger from the rings that were still hiding under the couch back home. Surely it was too soon. Man-haters didn't date. My mother's words came back to me: *Orgasms are fuuuun.* I could use him just like men use us. I looked up to find him watching me, and I gulped. *Do it.* "Would you be able to show me to the washroom?" I lifted my eyebrows, feigning innocence.

"Of course. Follow me." He turned and strode toward the small building.

I can do this, I can do this, I can do this. I chewed my bottom lip as he held the glass door to the building open for me. Once inside, I asked, "Is it just you that runs this operation?" I winced at the formal, shaky tone my words had.

He stood stiffly near the reception counter. "Yes." His voice was even gruffer. "But I do have another tour coming in soon."

I took a quick breath and stepped toward him. He smelled like wood and ocean and sunscreen. "Then we'll only have time for a small taste…" I leaned toward him and slipped my fingers into his hair, gripping the strands and pulling his face an inch from mine. His breath was hot on my lips, and I closed the gap.

My entire body thrummed with tension as he yanked me closer, and for several blissful minutes, we went at each other like teenagers. When I pulled back, his mouth was wet and swelling. I licked my lips. "I'm free tonight if you'd like to get a bite to eat and then finish this."

"Yes," he blurted.

I tipped my head at him. What could he possibly see in me, a 63-

year-old woman with orange hair and sagging boobs? It was beyond me, but I didn't want to question it, or myself, any longer.

"Seven? The Hose and Hydrant?" Even though his eyelids were lowered, a fierce desire burned in his green irises.

"Sounds good," I said casually, slipping out of his grasp and turning back to the door.

"Don't you... Didn't you need to use the washroom?"

"Nope." I stepped out of the building and lifted my head to the sunshine, feeling more alive than I'd felt in decades.

- 11 -

AFTER ROXANNE GUSHED in awe for five minutes about what a floozy I was, we drove home. We passed the white fence where someone was vigorously painting over our artwork. "Shit, they're already removing it," Roxanne moaned. "That was expensive paint, ya' know!"

"Let's check out the other ones, since it's daylight and all." Several had already been covered up and one was painted over with the words, *Suck my dick*. We turned down another street and Roxanne whooped. "Of course, Max would embrace it!"

"You know the owner of the salon?" I spluttered, mortified that we had ruined the small chunk of fence beside her business. But as I watched the woman posing beside it, a man holding a baby—a toddler at his leg—taking her picture, I realized she was overjoyed with it. Roxanne stopped and rolled the window down. "Hey, Max!"

"Rox!" Max waved and stepped over to the car. "Have you seen all these? Aren't they awesome?"

"We've seen them alright." Roxanne glanced at me, grinning.

"I'm posting it to all my socials." Max's loose breasts were obvious under her tank top. So was her armpit hair.

"So, you're going to keep it?" I asked.

"You bet your ass I am." *She loves it.* My shoulders relaxed. She stuck her hand through the window and across Roxanne. "I'm assuming you're Willie?"

"Yes."

"Roxanne talks about you so much I feel like I already know you."

"I'm turning out to be quite the urban legend around here." I winked at her, and she tipped her head back and cackled.

"Did you do this to your friend?" Max eyed Roxanne as she nodded at me.

"Her hair? Yes, I'm afraid I did." She dipped her head to appear ashamed, but she couldn't fully hide the smirk on her face.

Max tutted. "It's only hair, right? And I quite like the colour. It's brash."

A hairdresser that wasn't judging me for doing my own hair? Marvelous.

The baby cried from the man's arms and Max pushed away from the car. "Sounds like he needs saving. See you ladies later!" She waved and twirled away.

We pulled away from the shop and made our way back to the apartment. Roxanne got out and slammed the door, calling to me over the roof. "What are you going to wear tonight on your hot date?"

"Clothes."

She lifted an eyebrow. "For how long?"

I snorted and strode toward the stairs, freezing as I looked up to see a cop coming down. *Shit, we're busted.* I glanced back at Roxanne who was eyeing the cop.

"Good afternoon, ladies." He stopped two steps up from me.

The car that drove past last night must have seen us. I fought the urge to bolt. "Hi," I managed, swallowing hard.

"I'm looking for Willie Copeland."

I squeaked. "That's me."

He squinted. "The description your son gave me stated that you had black hair?"

My son? *Oh shit.* My gorge rose up. This wasn't about the graffiti; it was about the "time lapse". Frozen, I stared at him. I felt pressure on my back and realized that Roxanne had moved behind me and placed her hand there to steady me. "She dyed it," she said, her voice sounding far away even though it was right in my ear.

"Oh. Well, I've just stopped by for a wellness check."

"A wellness check?" It seemed Roxanne was going to be my voice because mine was stuck in my throat.

The cop stared at me, surely wondering why I wasn't speaking. "Your son, Jonathan, said no one has been able to get a hold of you since yesterday, and they were worried something had happened."

I almost collapsed to the ground. My phone. Of course. "Oh, no... Well, I lost my phone, you see."

"Well, that explains it. You seem of sound mind." He smiled and I realized that he probably had better things to be doing than checking on old ladies. Like catching graffiti artists. *If he only knew.*

"Yes, yes, I'm perfectly fine."

"He was also worried since your husband had recently passed and he mentioned you haven't been acting like yourself since."

I'd been acting more like myself than I had in years. I stood up straighter and found my voice. "I assure you that I'm fine."

"It appears so." The cop stepped toward me, and Roxanne and I moved to let him past. He called back over his shoulder. "Just maybe give your kids a call and let them know you lost your phone. He seemed pretty worried."

"Will do." Roxanne waved as he got in his car and drove away. She breathed in quickly. "I almost shit my pants, right there, thinking he was here to arrest us for the graffiti."

I thought it was for Stan. "Yeah, me too." I laughed nervously.

I started up the stairs, my legs wobbly from the encounter. I was overwhelmed with how aggressively Jonathan was trying to make me look bad. I could not recall a single time in my life that he had manipulated me. We'd always had the best relationship. Annette's words came back to me: *He's not who you think he is.*

I knew this problem would not go away without a face-to-face confrontation, but for now, I hoped and prayed Jon would come to his senses before I returned.

As Roxanne stuck the key into the apartment lock, she added, "That would be epic if we got arrested."

"Yeah, epic." I was racking up illegal acts all over the place, so the day may come sooner than I ever thought.

I ONLY HAD two phone numbers memorized—my land line and my mother's—but Jonathan was the last person I wanted to talk to right now.

"Hello, love," my mother murmured. "Have you got laid yet?"

I pinched the skin between my eyebrows. "Mom. Why do you always have to go straight there? Not everything is about sex."

"My clitoris begs to differ."

Apparently, mine did too, but I was not comfortable enough to have this conversation with her. I sat on my little bed and squeezed my eyes shut. "Can you please not do that?"

"You should be happy for me. After all these years I'm finding my groove," her voice trailed off wistfully.

"I am happy, but I really don't need to know the details." Bo nudged the door open and jumped on the bed for a snuggle.

"Mom, I lost my phone, and the kids are worried. Can you call them all and tell them I'm fine and let them know I'll get a pay-as-you-go one soon?"

"Sure thing. But you know, being unavailable to them for a bit might be a good thing."

I laughed. "Funny you should say that because I was thinking the same thing."

"You do too much for them. You never relied on me to figure your shit out."

I hesitated. I wanted to tell her why, but what would be the point now, after all these years. A sharp pain zinged through my chest. Maybe it would be good to finally talk about it. "I didn't come to you because I couldn't stand the thought of you having more to deal with than you already did."

There was a pause and Fran sniffed. "It breaks my heart to hear you say that."

"I'm sorry."

"You have nothing to apologize for."

I recalled the time when I was twenty and I'd driven to my parents' house and sat outside for an hour, fighting with myself to do the thing I wanted to most in the world. "I came back to rescue you once, you know that?"

"You did?"

"Yeah, but in the end, I was too scared. Of him. Of what he would do to me—and more importantly to you—if I failed." I hiccupped as tears formed. "How stupid is that?"

"Scared to try for fear of a worse outcome? I don't think it's stupid at all. In fact, I think it's what men rely on to keep us where they want us."

I rubbed a tear that had fallen onto Bo's back. He looked up at me and I smiled. "Makes you wonder."

"Wonder what, sweetie?"

"What the real repercussions would be if we actually did all the things we wanted to. Maybe there wouldn't be any. Maybe it's just the *fear* that keeps us in line."

"Hmmm. You might be onto something. And speaking of, I think you have a little problem you need to nip in the bud. Annette called me." Her pointed words annoyed me.

I let out a long breath. Why was Annette going behind my back to try and turn everyone against Jonathan? Didn't she have her own family to get on her side? "I know. She's being difficult about this whole thing."

Fran snorted. "*She's* being difficult? From what I heard he is. And you're letting him."

Anger flared in me. Bo flinched as my hand pressed on his back and I immediately lifted it and mouthed *sorry*. "I'm not letting him. They are getting a divorce, and he needed a place to stay until he gets his life sorted out. I'm his mother and I offered to help him. It's quite simple, actually." The ease with which the lies flowed out of me to one of the people I loved and trusted most in the world pained me. But the second that I admitted to the rage I was feeling toward my own offspring, I was done. The truth suddenly dawned on me; I had no choice but to defend my son, because if I turned on him, the whole family would, and he'd be alone. I was the peacekeeper. *So, he would be wise to treat me better,* I thought.

Fran's voice was soft. "Being stuck in the middle sucks, love, but sometimes doing the right thing is more important than anything else. For yourself. Self-sacrifice is not the noble act we've been led to believe it is."

I looked out the window. Turns out I preferred when our conversation stayed within the realm of sex.

- 12 -

"OKAY. YOU ARE *not* wearing that on this date." Roxanne held up one of her colourful bohemian dresses up to my small frame.

"Why not? I want to be comfortable." I pulled at the waistband of my favourite black slacks. My gut had been churning since the encounter with the cop and the conversation with my mother. Where had the confident Willie who had pounced on Mark earlier gone?

"You look like my grandma!"

"I am a grandma!"

Roxanne sighed exaggeratedly. "What about the sexy red dress?"

I did up the top button of the plain blue blouse. "I want to be comfortable. My breasts spilling over the top of a dress does not make me comfortable." I needed something familiar with me in a potentially terrifying moment. Plus, I didn't want him to think I was desperate for his attention or anything. I slumped into the chair squeezed into the corner of my bedroom. "I can't do this," I whispered. "I can't go on a date. I don't want to go on a date. I obviously hate men—I just got rid of one!" I wiped sweat from my upper lip with the back of my hand.

"You don't hate men. You just haven't hung around many decent ones lately."

"But a date?" I gulped. "What was I thinking? I'm sixty-three years old! I'm a freshly minted widow! I have grandchildren. I have saddlebags *between* my legs—you should see them! They look like Ziploc bags full of thick, unmixed pancake batter! *Between my legs!*"

"So, you're planning on letting him see you naked? Did you trim your bush?"

"Roxanne! No. And no." I sat silent for a second before blurting, "You're supposed to trim down there?" I had spent several minutes in front of the mirror naked before I got dressed. It was not a pretty sight. I had lifted both my breasts, tried standing different ways to shift sagging skin around, nothing helped. But not once had I inspected my private area, worrying about its *condition.*

"Well, you don't have to, but it makes it a little easier for them to find the little man in the boat." Roxanne picked up a teal sundress and held it up.

I snorted. "Well, it's kind of bald down there now, anyhow."

"Me too! I'm personally rocking a Friar Tuck. Hardly need to trim anymore. A strange perk of getting older."

I put my head in my hands. "Exactly. That's the point. I'm too old to date." Too old to start over. I suddenly felt more exhausted than before I'd left Edmonton. Maybe the spell of the island had worn off.

Roxanne kneeled in front of me and reached out to push my shoulders back. "Look at you. Gorgeous exterior aside, you are a catch. Compassionate, funny, smart." She reached up and smoothed my cheek. "Ageless skin. So why do you think you can't do this? You're not married anymore. You're allowed to have a good time." Roxanne pulled my hands away from my face. "You are allowed to take up space in this world, on your own terms, as you are. Got it?"

"It's been so long, though."

She grunted. "This is what talking to the folks back home does to you. You became an entirely different person in just a few short days, then you have one phone call and boom, you're back in that shitty, compressed space again."

I eyed her, wanting to defend myself, but knowing she was speaking the truth.

The corners of her eyes crinkled. "Remember that feeling you had when you assaulted Mark this afternoon."

"I did not assault him!" I squealed. "He was practically begging for it."

Roxanne smirked knowingly. "Exactly." She pulled my hands into hers. "You don't have to pretend you aren't worthy, that you don't deserve it. The shrunken-woman act doesn't look good on you. But the brave bitch sure does." She pulled me to standing and held me at arm's length, eyeing me up and down. "You're right. You don't need anyone, including me, to tell you how to dress. If he doesn't want you, granny pants and all, fuck him! Let's go."

THE HOUND AND Hydrant looked like a typical pub joint with dark wood and large stones on the outside. The sign had a white dog sitting next to a red fire hydrant. At least it wasn't lifting its leg to pee on it, something Stan would have certainly gotten a kick out of.

Mark stood by the front door with his hands in his pockets, leaning slightly forward on the balls of his feet. "Hello again." His closed-lip smile was sexy. So was the tight black t-shirt he had on.

Roxanne whistled in a low tone as I closed the car door, muttering something about how impossible it was that she hadn't run into him years ago. I looked up at Mark, hoping he hadn't heard it.

I looked him over, reminding myself I could do this. *Remember the brave bitch.* "Hello yourself." I channeled my inner audacity and winked as I walked through the door he held open for me.

Mark scooted ahead of me and pulled out a chair. "I know it doesn't look like much," he chuckled as he settled himself opposite me. "But I promise the food is spectacular."

I opened the menu. "Great, because I'm starving." He shifted and fidgeted while I decided what I wanted. I lifted the menu a little higher to hide my grin. The fact that I could make someone young and handsome so uncomfortable was intoxicating. *So this is what the other side of the power balance feels like.* Decided, I closed the menu.

He reached for a water the waitress had set down when she seated us and knocked the saltshaker over, laughing tensely. "Oh, geez I need a drink."

His nerves were disarming. For so many years, I'd lived with a man who had the over-confidence of a little boy in the school yard, trying to prove he was better at, well, everything.

Mark smiled, showing a slight gap in between his two front teeth. He moved his hands from his lap to the tabletop, folding them and then unfolding them. The waitress came by and took our orders. "So, do you date much?" His cheeks turned red. "Sorry. That's none of my business."

I opened my mouth to tell him that I was a new widow, but I closed it. He knows nothing about me. I get to write the narrative here. I was tired of my story revolving around Stan. First, it was as his wife. Now, it was as his widow. "Not too often. I'm pretty busy with my work." I smiled. Off-the-cuff lying was addictive.

"Oh, what do you do?"

I flipped my hand like what I was about to say was no big deal. I thought of Dana and our beach stroll where she pointed out the slimy green blobs. "Oh, just manage an international research team for sea anemones. That's why I'm out here."

"Really? What a coincidence! My ex-wife was a marine biologist at Bamfield. She's in Hawaii now."

Oh fuck. I shifted in my seat. I just had to pick the one thing he would know something about. What was I thinking, anyway? Of course, everyone out here knew something about sea life or knew someone who studied it. I should have said I was an oil and gas executive or a farmer, something more Albertan. A bead of sweat broke out along my hair line. "Interesting," I murmured, trying to sound distant yet smart.

"Maybe you've heard of her? Tabby Wakefield?"

I pretended to think deeply, tapping my finger on my bottom lip. "Hmm. No, I don't believe so. I work a lot on the east coast, actually." And the quicksand deepens. Do they even have sea anemones in The Maritimes?

"Oh, I'd love to go out there. See the ocean on the other side. Where's most of your work out there?"

I'd read Anne of Green Gables as a girl. "Cavendish?" The waitress set our drinks down.

"Huh. I thought most of the research would be around Halifax."

I took a long slug of wine before blurting, "I'm also an EMT. A paramedic actually." Was I trying to steal Dana's life?

"That's...that's quite a different field." His eyebrows were both raised. He was impressed at least.

"Yes, well, I get bored easily." I waved the notion of work away. I needed to redirect this conversation before I told him that I was also an insurance salesperson and a cat-rescuer. "How long have you been out here?"

He beamed. "Life-long islander."

He delved into how he started his own whale tour company at the age of twenty-one, hellbent on making a living at it. "And here I am, forty-eight and still going strong."

Fifteen years younger than me. It strangely didn't make me feel like too much of a cradle robber. Hell, lots of guys had women three, four decades younger than them. I listened intently as Mark went on about his love for the island.

The waitress set our food down and I dove into mine. As I bit into a prawn, I closed my eyes at how delicious it was. I was raised in a beef world, but I could get used to living in a seafood one. "You said you were married?" I asked after a few moments of silence.

"Yes. For ten years. She was working here for years but moved to Hawaii for her dream job about five years ago. I visited a couple of times, trying to see if I could acclimate to the tropics, but it just wasn't going to happen. Honestly, we were both being a bit stubborn and selfish. She didn't want to hurt her career for a man, and I didn't want to sabotage my business for someone else's goals. It sounds terrible, but after two years of long-distance, we decided it was best to move on."

My mouth was hanging open. "You didn't try and stop her from going?"

"Of course not. It was her dream. We were never going to have kids and neither of us was willing to lose our careers. Things happen and sometimes it just doesn't work out. We still stay in touch."

I wondered if I'd just held strong to my desire to continue nursing, maybe Stan would have just relented. But I recalled barely trying at all. If I'd done that, I'd actually have something to look back on now and be proud of. I bit my lip. I had nothing to be proud of besides the kids. And pride in mothering was frowned upon anyway. It was just expected to be done without remark.

"Did I say something?" Mark asked after we'd continued to eat quietly for a few moments.

"What? No, why?"

"You just got a look on your face. Like something I said pissed you off."

I leaned back and wiped my mouth with a napkin. "No. It just made me realize I've missed a lot in life." My eyebrows shot up at the realization of my slip.

Mark laughed. "If you think you've missed a lot, after everything you've done, then I am *fucked*."

Maybe I could actually be one of those things I'd said I was. Surely people went back to school at my age. Maybe there was a way to renew my nursing registration. I smiled and sat up straighter. In this narrative, I was everything I'd never been allowed to be. And damned if I wasn't going to embrace it. And what I wanted most right now was that delicious-looking mudpie that I'd spied on the menu. And without dipshit here to make a fuss about my ordering it, the story I wanted to embrace was that of a glutton. "What do you say to desert?"

He licked his bottom lip and my insides rolled in anticipation of what I could turn this night into. "I say yes. To all of it." His eyes held mine for a long time before the waitress returned to take our order.

I SLOWLY SIPPED on my third glass of wine as Mark told me about his asshole father. I nodded and murmured along, knowing exactly what he was talking about. The door burst open and three guys stumbled in. Mark shot them a look. "That might be our cue to leave."

I looked over and watched them saunter up to the bar. It wasn't even nine. And it was a weeknight. Didn't these guys have jobs to go to tomorrow? "We'll just ignore them."

Mark winced as one of the men cat-called a group of girls in the corner. "We can try our best, but this group prides themselves on being hard to ignore."

We tried to continue talking, but I couldn't help noticing the guy with the bushy black beard would not leave the table of four girls alone. He kept shouting to them and asking if they wanted shots sent over. Their dropped eyes and hunched shoulders were a clear *no,* but this dickhead did not seem to understand. Or he did and he simply didn't care.

"Jesus," Mark breathed. "They just want to be alone."

I looked back to him. *He gets it.* So, it couldn't really be that hard. I pushed back from the table, my heart hammering. "I'm going to go talk to them."

Mark grabbed my wrist. "No, don't. They're drifters."

"What does that mean?"

"They've only been coming in for a couple weeks, and they'll be gone soon. They're working for a friend's fishing outfit."

"So?"

"They don't have a stake in their own reputations. Know what I mean?"

My upper lip started burning. "So, they're allowed to come to town, be assholes, and leave without repercussions?"

Mark winced at my words. "Yeah. Basically."

While the women of the town were terrorized. "Well, I'm a drifter too." I stood and marched over to them. "Excuse me?" I shouted, stopping a couple feet away. I didn't want to get too close. As all their eyes turned to me, my stomach churned.

"Yeah?" the blonde one said.

"I think you're bothering those nice girls over there, and I'd like you to stop." I put my hands on my hips, an attempt to erase the quiver in my voice.

The entire group broke out in laughter. "We're just trying to be friendly, *Granny,*" Black Beard said.

Mark was suddenly behind me. Blondie nodded toward him. "You need to take your mom home. She's had too much to drink."

In a heartbeat, I closed the space between us, my nails digging into my fists. "Leave. Them. Alone," I hissed.

Black Beard rose and towered over me, a flash of anger sweeping his face. A wicked smile crept over his lips. "Maybe you're the one I should be sending shots to." He licked his lips and inched closer. "You looking for some tail? Why don't you send your son home, and we'll get to know each other better."

"I'm not her son." Mark was pressed up behind me, trying to steer me away by the waist. I pushed his hand away. For all my life, I'd let shit like this slide. And if now wasn't the time to throw my own safety out the window and stand up to these guys, there would never be a time. I flashed back to myself standing mutely frozen while that guy squeezed and caressed my wet breasts. No one had stepped in. Not even Stan. Because that was just how it went for women.

My eyes slid to the girls, who were throwing cash on the table and collecting their things. It was ominously silent in the bar. I looked back to Black Beard.

"Well?" he spit. "You wanna have a go? *Granny?*"

I tipped my head back and howled with laughter. "If you think that's an insult, you better up your game." I lowered my face and gritted my teeth. "Because I'd expect more coming from a fucking asshole like you."

Something dangerous flashed in his eyes. Mark pulled on my arm, but I jerked away from him.

Black Beard leaned into me. "Well, you stupid cunt, I suggest you turn and leave before *someone* gets hurt."

I threw my hands up, feeling the last strands of my self-preservation unravel. "Oh no!" I used my best damsel-in-distress voice. "You did not just call me a cunt. Is that the best way you can think to put me in my place?" I turned to look at Mark, eyes wide. "Whatever shall I do?"

The corners of Mark's mouth turned down as he tried to suppress a smile. I spun back to Black Beard and his crew. "Next time I see you bothering any woman, I will call the cops." I took a step back and came to stand next to Mark, reaching my hand into the pocket of my slacks. "Let's go. I'm feeling a little stabby." Black Beard's gaze lingered on my pocket. I so wished I actually had Roxanne's knife on me. But maybe it was best I didn't.

We turned away from the men, who were temporarily stunned, and returned to the table. Our waitress brought us the check and I paid. My heart was slowing down, but the men kept giving me dirty looks right until I left the pub.

Outside, Mark asked if he could give me a ride home or wait until Roxanne came back to get me. But when I turned to him and suggested we finish this date off properly, with a nightcap at his place, the hot and heavy *yes* that slipped from his lips only added to the intense desire I had to see this man naked.

WE PULLED UP to a small grey apartment complex where Mark led me up to the second floor. It was a compact one-bedroom place, tidy and sparse.

Mark took my cardigan and purse and placed them lightly on the kitchen table—a simple pine two-seater squeezed into the space between the galley kitchen and living room. He pulled two beers out of the fridge. "You want one?"

I shook my head. First, I hated beer. Second, I'd already had enough alcohol. If I was really going to do this, I wanted my wits about me.

"Okay then, neither do I." He put them on the counter and stepped over to me, stopping inches away. I was certain he would be able to hear my heart pounding. I swayed slightly on my feet, suddenly lightheaded. He reached out and placed both hands on my shoulders. "You okay?"

I swallowed. "Yes. Just a dizzy spell. They pass."

He slowly ran his hands down my arms, stopping at my wrists, where he squeezed gently. "May I kiss you?'

What lovely manners. I couldn't remember the last time a man had asked if he could touch me. Stan was a reach-and-grab-without-asking kind of guy.

"Yes," I whispered. I closed my eyes as his lips brushed mine. They felt rough and chapped, but as they pushed harder, all I could feel was hot pressure. A little bolt of electricity flashed through me as my hands found the back of his neck, acting on some old, long-lost impulse. His body inched forward and pressed fully onto me, and my hips to pressed back as if on autopilot. *Oh God.* Entombed in old memories, my body knew how to do this. All I had to do was make my logical self step back. Nothing was worse than laying there waiting for Stan to finish, faking my own enjoyment for his benefit, telling myself I was simply fulfilling a wifely duty. As Mark gently bit my lip, any fleeting thoughts of dead husbands zipped away.

A small moan escaped me, causing me to flinch in shame, but when he mimicked the sound, I knew we were officially all in.

Swiftly, he scooped me up—his body curving around me, protecting me as he carried me to his bedroom. He set me down on the bed, backed up and took his shirt off, showing off the body of a man who does manual labour for a living. Back at the restaurant, he'd told me how physically demanding manning a boat could be. Plus, he was an avid hiker, a fact that I now appreciated. He threw a leg over me as I lay back, coming to straddle my hips.

Should I explain to him how truly inexperienced I was, that whatever he was expecting, he would be disappointed?

No. Instead, I pulled him down toward me, running my tongue over his bottom lip, pure desire surging through me. His movements were urgent in return, hands sliding up and gently pressing on my breasts. I arched my hips to meet his.

"You're so beautiful," Mark whispered, his voice husky.

When I reached down and felt the front of his shorts, I was shocked at the fullness there. My body throbbed with want. "Please." I breathed hard, all thought leaving me. "Now."

If this was what widowhood was, I thanked Stan for leaving while I still had time to enjoy it.

- 13 -

FRESHENING UP IN Mark's washroom the next morning, I noticed a piece of hair that looked out of place. Not out of place in a way that hair looked after you've been rode hard, but almost floating over the top of my head. I went to smooth it down and several stands came away in my hand. "What the?" I whispered to myself.

I put the hair in the toilet and flushed it away. I emerged from the washroom to find Mark scrambling eggs for us. He grinned when he saw me, stirring at the contents of the pan. "Thought I'd just make you a bite to eat before I take you home."

"Thank you." I sat at the small table as he served the eggs and a cup of coffee.

"Can I see you again tonight?" Mark asked.

Something in me suddenly wanted to bolt. Two nights of my time away from Roxanne? No, thank you. "I'm busy tonight."

"Oh." His disappointment was palatable. "How about Saturday night?"

"Look, Mark. I had a really great time with you, but this was a one and done kind of thing. I'm not here for long, and I can't spend my holiday with you. I'm here to be with my best friend." My directness surprised me.

He frowned and for the first time since I'd met him, a flicker of the man-rage passed over his face.

Come on, I urged, setting my fork down. *Just try and control me.*

But it passed. Or maybe I'd imagined it. He nodded and smiled sadly. "I understand. Maybe we'll bump into each other again while you're still here."

"Yes, maybe we will." I stood and regretfully eyed my half-drunk coffee. I needed to get out of here. I suddenly realized that I just spent the night with a man and no cell phone. Roxanne must be worried sick. "Do you know where I can get a cheap phone? I lost mine."

He jumped up. "Oh, I have a couple old ones. You're more than welcome to take one. You'd just need to buy a SIM card and get a plan, but the drugstore has those." He jogged off to his bedroom and emerged with an old blue iPhone.

"Are you sure?" I turned it over in my hand.

"Absolutely. I've been meaning to get rid of them but haven't gotten around to it."

"Well, thank you very much." I slipped the phone into my purse and pulled on my sweater. "I have to get going."

He stepped toward me. "Let me drive you."

"No, that's alright." I levelled a sexy look at him. "After last night, I could use a walk."

He laughed and let me go, but not before I laid a long, hard kiss on his lips, whispering that it had been the best night of my life. And that was no lie. I couldn't even remember a time before or after Stan came along when I had orgasmed so hard. It had been almost seizure-like in its intensity as his tongue expertly worked my clitoris.

My groin warmed again, but I bolted from the apartment before I could change my mind.

I made my way straight to the drugstore—only a two-block walk—and selected a card and plan. As I stood in line to pay, a display of Mars chocolate bars tempted me. *Why not?* I thought. This trip was all about indulgence. I grabbed two and held them lightly in my hand, so they wouldn't melt. *Slip them in your pocket.* The intrusive thought caused my heart to speed up. I wasn't a thief, by any means, but I was certainly on a roll with the illegal stuff.

My eyes widened as my hand slipped into the pocket and then came back out, leaving the bars behind. A thin sweat had broken out between my breasts by the time I reached the cashier, and my inner angel screamed at me that it wasn't too late to pull out the Mars bars and put them on the conveyor belt. I could pull the forgetful old woman card, and all would be forgiven. But the tiny devil in me cheered on the brazen theft.

The cashier peered at me through thick glasses as she swiped my stuff over the scanner. "How are you today, ma'am?"

"Just fine, my dear," I replied, though she was not much younger. "And how about yourself?"

"Oh, just lovely. Who wouldn't be with this weather," Louanne, according to her name tag, said, sweeping her hand toward the large window framing the sun-dappled trees and parking lot beyond.

I paid for my purchases and waltzed right out of the shop with a spring in my step. I reached inside my pocket and touched the bars, as if to confirm I had really just broken the law again. I was getting good at this. I giggled to myself and kept walking.

WOMEN ONLY WANT TO FUCK MEN OVER.

I stopped dead at the sight of the grey fence along someone's yard where we'd sprayed our best mural, which was now defaced—the new words added in blue paint around our original slogan.

Was that what they really thought? That our primary goal in life was to screw them over? Because if it was, no wonder the world still despised women. "Something has to change," I whispered. How had we gotten to such an ugly place? How hard was it to just let everyone do and be what they wanted to? Why did they need so much power? It didn't make sense to me.

This revised slogan spoke to men's deepest fears. But I was an average woman, and I had no desire to fuck men over. I only wanted equality. And maybe more orgasms.

Tears burned in my eyes. Would I live to see a truly equal day? I wiped at my face. *The hate.* It was the hate that I didn't understand. Even after everything with Stan, even after the bliss I'd experienced these past few days in finally telling the men around me what I really felt, I still knew in my heart I didn't hate them. Yet it seemed they despised us more than I could fathom.

I continued to Roxanne's, furious that my perfect night with Mark had taken such an unpleasant turn. But I would not let them get me down. I couldn't. I refused to return to that space. I forced myself to look up. The sky was a beautiful, Mayan blue, the sun was warm, the birds were calling. I was in paradise. *So why did my problems seem to follow me here?* I knew, though, that these were the types of problems that would follow me across the globe and into my grave, and I felt the exhaustion of that in my bones.

I turned the corner of Roxanne's street and made my way to the apartment. As I stepped over the curb and toward the stairs, a cop pulled up behind me. *Shit.* Maybe that cashier wasn't as inattentive as I thought. I forced my hand to stay still at my leg and not creep suspiciously to my pocket.

"Willie."

Great. Now I was on a first name basis with the police. "Yes?"

The same cop from yesterday strode over to me and held out a busted phone. The iridescent unicorn stickers that Ainsley had plastered over the back, glaring in the sun. I clenched my fist to still the tremble. "Happen to recognize this?"

Could they somehow trace this phone back to me even though it was smashed? "No. No. Why would I?" Without Roxanne here to brace me, I knew I couldn't stand up to scrutiny alone.

"It was found near one of the graffiti paintings. Have you seen them around town?"

I would be stupid to lie about this. I took a deep breath and found my brave bitch. "Yes. Such a shame," I tutted, shaking my head slowly.

"Yes. So, you don't recognize this phone?"

I dug in my purse and pulled out Mark's old one. "Nope. Got mine right here, officer."

He made a noise in the back of his throat. "Please let us know if you see anything suspicious. Several of the business owners are very upset about the graffiti."

Except Max. "Oh, I would be too."

I turned and practically ran up the stairs, threw the door open and entered the apartment, slamming it behind me.

Roxanne looked up from her coffee at the island. "You're alive."

"Yes, but we need to get the fuck out of here."

She stood and brought me her mug of coffee, reminding me that I had only half-finished the one at Mark's house. I took it and drank. She watched me for a whole minute. "What do you suggest?"

The red flash of the bike down in storage came to me. "How about we go for a little ride?"

She nodded deeply. "I like where this is going. Tell me more."

I drained the rest of the coffee and told Roxanne that I didn't care where we went, that I just wanted to get away, that everything seemed to be coming at me faster than before.

She tapped her foot, a look of deep concentration on her face. "I know just the place."

BEFORE WE LEFT, I decided the right thing to do was give everyone my new number. I stood on the balcony, trying to absorb as much sunshine as possible. To hell with age spots, I needed Vitamin D. I texted Mom and asked her to send me the kid's numbers since I didn't have them memorized.

Fran responded immediately. I texted Vivian and Jonathan my number but decided to actually call Tanya. I missed hearing her voice. After leaving my nursing career and becoming a stay-at-home mom after Tanya was born, meant I got to spend the most time with her. I wanted to make sure the flower business was still on track. Selfishly, I knew I needed something to do once I got back and thought I'd be an excellent shipper and receiver for her.

"Hey, Mom. How's it going? I see you're not dead." The sarcasm in her voice made me smile.

"Nope."

"I told Jon to not freak out when we couldn't get a hold of you for, like, one day, but he kept going on and on about you not being yourself since Dad died and how he'd found lots of stuff moved around the house." She cleared her throat. "But seriously, that stuffed fish was hideous! Of course, it was the first thing you got rid of."

"Yeah, Wendy was pretty ugly." I almost added the lie I'd told to her husband at the funeral. That seeing all of Stan's stuff made me miss him more, but I knew I didn't have to do that with Tanya. What I desperately wanted to ask was if Jon had said anything about me blanking out or him asking that paramedic about an autopsy, but I could not figure out a way to bring it up without sounding suspicious. "I'm having a great time, though. It's so beautiful out here."

"Yes, Curtis and I went there for our honeymoon, remember?"

"Of course. So, are you going to tell me what you need me to come home for so desperately on the twenty-eighth?" I blurted. *Because I'm thinking I'd like to stay out here longer.* I was startled by my own thought. I hadn't consciously given any energy to the idea, but really, what was stopping me besides this mysterious appointment?

Tanya took in a quick breath. "Mom, I really don't want to tell you over the phone. It's not... It's just something best discussed face-to-face because I'm not sure how you'll react."

"How I'll react? It's your life sweetie and whatever you do with it, is completely up to you."

She sighed. "You might not feel the same way once you know."

I frowned. What could possibly be so bad? Were her and Curtis breaking up too? Something wrong with the girls? No, she would have told me that. I had a feeling this was strictly about her.

Tanya sniffed. "I just, I need your support, if you can give it. I'm on a bit of a raft alone here."

My throat constricted. Even though they were adults, hearing my kids in any kind of pain or stress still hurt me deeply. "Oh, sweetie. I'm here for absolutely anything you need, okay?" I'd just make my return trip sooner rather than later.

Tanya sniffed again. "Thanks, Mom. I have to go watch Gabi and Connor tonight so Annette can go to a showing. I'll swing by your house and make sure Jon hasn't burned it down."

That shit. He was still trying to make Annette's life impossible. Even though I didn't want to, I knew I needed to at least try and correct this situation. Maybe I should have never let him stay at the house so he would have had to figure out life on his own. "Thank you. See you next week."

I hung up and immediately called Jon. A part of me hoped he would answer so I could yell at him, but a bigger part hoped he wouldn't so I could avoid a confrontation. When his voice came over the voicemail, I breathed a sigh of relief. "Hi Jon, it's Mom. You really didn't have to send a cop out to check on me, I just lost my phone. But anyway, here's my new number." I rattled off the digits and then paused. There was more I wanted to say and holding it in until I barfed was not the look I wanted today, not after that encounter with Black Beard, not after the added words to the graffiti, and not after hearing that Tanya was watching his kids tonight. I took a quick breath. "And look, I love you, but you need to be out of the house by the time I get back on April twenty-seventh." I pressed End quickly before I could launch into an apology or an explanation of why I was asking him to leave. I didn't need to tell him why, and I didn't need to say sorry. He just needed to listen to me.

I shoved the phone in my pocket and left the apartment, scratching the basset hound's head as I passed. "Don't pee on the carpet again," I admonished him as I closed the door, his droopy eyes telling me that such things were sadly out of his control.

ROXANNE WAS WAITING in the parking lot, the bike already growling, its cherry red gas tank and fenders sparkling in the sun. I was happy to see the bitch seat looked more comfortable than the one on her old bike. She handed me a small backpack and a helmet, then I swung a leg over and climbed aboard as Roxanne gunned the throttle.

Dana suddenly appeared in front of us. She reached over and turned the key off, the throaty purr of the bike evaporating. She put her hands on her hips and tipped her head at us, her black bob swaying to the side.

"Aw, man! Don't do that," Roxanne whined.

"Now. I'm all for living life on the edge, but I need to know that you are in the right frame of mind to do this, because the last time you took your bike out on a rage-ride you know what happened." She pointed to a scuff mark on the side of the gas tank.

"Dana! That tree jumped out at me."

"Yes, trees tend to do that when you're stoned."

I leaned over and looked into Roxanne's visor. "You drove when you were stoned?"

"One time! I was having a really bad day."

My arms tingled with fear and anticipation. Dana stepped around the bike and flipped Roxanne's visor open. "I know you have a penchant for living like your dying"—her eyes slid to me—"but this time, you have a valuable passenger. One who has a life to return to."

She was looking pointedly at Roxanne, so I jumped in. "I think we're fine, Dana. It's really sweet of you to be concerned."

Roxanne took Dana's hand. "I'm okay this time."

I swore Dana's face crumpled for a second before righting itself, and I had the sudden feeling I'd missed some critical exchange. "Alright, just text when you get there. Will you be back in time for supper and a beach walk?"

Roxanne squeezed Dana's hand and dropped it. "For you, yes."

Dana moved closer to me as Roxanne restarted the bike. "What's your favourite meal, Willie?"

"Um." I had so many. "How about something that involves prawns." I couldn't seem to get enough of these delicious little crustaceans.

"Paella it is." She stepped back and let us past. As we turned onto the highway, Roxanne screamed back at me, "You ready for the road trip of your life, Thelma?"

I cackled. "More than you can imagine, Louise."

- 14 -

AS WE FLEW down the highway, I clung tightly to Roxanne's midsection, feeling lighter and happier than I had in years. The end of Roxanne's red bird scarf escaped my coat and flapped around, slapping my cheek. Roxanne had emerged from her room after my we-need-a-trip announcement wearing it and when I told her how gorgeous it was, she had it unwrapped and was re-settling it around my neck in a flash, shushing my resistance to accepting it. "A gift for a gift," she'd murmured, securing it so carefully, almost reverently. I carefully let go of Roxanne with one hand, reached up and tucked it back in.

We cruised through the forest toward Ucluelet, the roar of the engine the only thing I could hear. A few times I caught a glimpse of the ocean through the trees, but as we turned east, small mountains began to rise up with tree covered peaks and a lake popped out for a few minutes before we were swallowed up by forest again.

Two hours later we arrived at Cathedral Grove—a famed hike located between two small mountain ridges. I stiffly climbed off the back of the bike and pressed my hand to my lower back. I didn't want to complain, but the thought of having to make the return trip caused an ache deep in my hip bones to sing.

Roxanne motioned for me to turn around so she could pull a water bottle out of the backpack. We both took a long drink. "So," she said.

"So what?"

"Are you going to tell me, or do I have to torture you for details?" She threw her free hand up.

There was no point playing coy, I knew exactly what Roxanne was driving at. I lifted my shoulders casually. "I had sex."

Roxanne screeched and lunged for me, grabbing me by the shoulders to shake me. "Tell. Me. Everything."

I laughed. "I just did."

"No, like *details*," she moaned. A couple passing us gave us a strange look.

"After a lovely dinner we went back to his apartment, and he asked if he could kiss me."

"He asked? Well, isn't that the sickly sweetest thing I've ever heard."

"We kissed, and then you know…"

"No, I don't know. Pretend I'm a virgin and have no idea." Roxanne's eyes searched me.

I grabbed the water bottle and stepped back from her, taking a swig. "Really, Roxanne. You are hardly a virgin."

"Pretend!" she demanded.

"Okay, okay!"

"So, he kissed you. And then?"

"I grabbed his, you know, man parts."

"Seriously, Willie. It's a wonder you even know how babies are made." Her eyes widened. "You do know, don't you? You weren't one of those women who just woke up one morning with a sore Volkswagen and a strangely swollen belly?"

I laughed.

"So, you grabbed his dipstick. Was it big? Hard? I bet you had him turned on brighter than a Christmas tree!" Roxanne clapped and hooted.

I lifted an eyebrow. Images from our romp returned to me; me squirming and losing control beneath him, then me straddling him, his mouth wide and distorted with the pleasure *I* was giving him. "It was… nice."

"Nice? Jay-sus, Willie! Cookies are nice. Cocks are ah-ma-zing! Especially when they're inside me, doing their thing." Roxanne closed her eyes and sighed, to which I instantly put my hand up and said, "Is this my story or yours? And I'm not entirely sure I want to continue if it's going to turn you on. That's kind of creepy." Roxanne rolled her eyes and made the lip-zipping motion.

"And then we went to his room," I continued.

"And?"

"That's all I'm going to tell you." I crossed my arms over my chest.

"What? That's not fair!"

"Behind closed doors, Roxanne. Use your imagination."

"Ugh. You are the worst best friend ever!" Realizing she wasn't going to get any more out of me, she turned and stomped over to the sign at the trail head, releasing a long, exaggerated sigh. "Cathedral Trail." Her tone was formal. I wanted to pat her shoulder and say, *there, there.* "See cathedral grove on a short loop walk that takes you through a forest of giant trees. The largest are 800 years old. But most sprouted when a fire opened the forest about 300 years ago." She let out a low whistle, already over her disappointment. "Now that's old. You're a spring chicken next to these bad boys."

Waiting for a family to move ahead before stepping onto the path, I linked my arm through Roxanne's. "This is the best day ever."

"It's barely begun."

"Doesn't matter."

We walked softly through the forest, a deep feeling of peace coming over me—and everyone here, I suspected, due to the quiet care with which everyone was talking. Fallen leaves and pine needles covered the path, moist from the air, our steps silent. Rotting, moss-covered wooden rails guided our way as we went deeper into the forest.

"Can you feel the oxygen waking you up?" Roxanne whispered.

I inhaled deeply, imagining a million tiny, sleeping little me's rising, rubbing their eyes, and stretching their arms overhead.

"Dana told me once that lichen is sensitive to air pollution," Roxanne continued. "So, when you see old man's beard hanging everywhere, it indicates really clean air."

I ran a hand gently over the green carpet that flourished on the wooden rail. I knew I wasn't supposed to touch it, but I just had to feel it. It was spongy and dense at the same time.

Dead trees lay everywhere, simply left where they had fallen, only cut if they blocked the path. I spied a large tree to our right. "Oh, this is perfect for a picture for the grandkids." I went to stand in front of an ancient, towering fir, feeling incredibly small next to it. Roxanne took several pictures and I turned to inspect the bark. It was thick and grey and deeply cracked. I strained my eyes to follow a fissure upwards until I couldn't see it anymore, disappearing into the branches and leaves only present at the top of the towering wood. I imagined the roots travelling into the earth, in search of water, as far as the trunk above ground—a connection deep into the earth that sustained it as well as a lifelong appetite for sunshine and air above.

Eventually we came upon a small lake. Clear and dark in the middle—the circumference was populated with fallen trees floating and jamming up against the shore. People were balancing along the logs, picking their way through the buoyant, wooden maze. Roxanne pulled my arm. "Let's try!"

"We'll freeze if we fall in!" I squeaked.

She tugged on me like a little kid. "Come on."

Laughing, I threw a hand in the air. "Why not?"

She whooped and took off her hiking shoes, laying her socks inside them and rolling her pants up and balling her hair into a low bun at the back of her neck. I followed suit, leaving our sweaters draped across a log next to a stranger's. I touched a toe in the water, surprised it wasn't the sub-zero temperature I was expecting. Roxanne hopped up on a log and held out her hand to me. We inched along the dry wood, inspecting tufts of grass, lily pads and tiny fish in the water. The tree turned darker where it descended into the water, Roxanne already ankle deep in the water. I touched a toe on it, feeling how slippery it was, knowing that submerged things tended to accumulate slime. "Too slippery," I said just as Roxanne stepped onto an intersecting log.

"Let's go this way," she said, as if the trees formed a maze and we had to follow them for a way out. We picked our way over broken branches that spiked out of the water, pausing to admire the occasional frog, until we emerged on the shore twenty metres from where we'd entered.

"That was like a choose-your-own-adventure book. Remember them?"

"I sure do. I loved those." I tipped my head up to the sky. "Honestly, I think I'd mostly forgotten what it felt like to choose my own adventure until now. Stan and the kids have driven my choices for so long. Thank you for asking me to come out here." There could be dozens—hundreds—more adventures in store for me now. All the little me's jumped and cheered, but Roxanne just smiled knowingly, as though this revelation had been her intention from the start.

We made our way back the way we'd come, stepping off the log and sitting by our shoes. I looked up to see Roxanne watching me pat my feet dry with my sweater with a sad look on her face.

I tipped my head. "What's that look for?"

Her eyes got glassy, and she smiled. "I'm just glad I stuck around long enough to see you through this."

I frowned at her. "That's a morbid thing to say."

She shrugged, pulling on her socks. "You never know what's around the corner, Willie-Hillie. Remember the whale." She stood and heaved herself up, then dropped sideways onto me, making strange noises that I assumed were meant to sound like a whale.

I laughed and rolled off the log, holding her close.

OUR SOULS CALMED, we continued to the waterfall. By the time we arrived, it had begun to drizzle, a mist hanging in the air. Stepping gingerly down a rock stairway, I was at the bottom when I heard a shout behind me. Clamping the rail, I twisted to see Roxanne lying flat out on the stairs. "Oh!" I climbed back up and knelt beside her. "I knew it was too slippery." I touched a scrape on her ankle.

"Ow! That stings," she stated. A couple behind us passed, asking if we were okay. "I'm fine, I'm fine," Roxanne muttered.

I got her back up and down the stairs before sitting her down on a stump and finding the small first aid kit she had packed. I gently patted the abrasion and applied a Band-aid. "Now do you think we bit off more than we can chew?" I smiled up at her.

She scoffed. "Never." She rose and continued tentatively along the path.

We eased our way down more stairs to Little Qualicum Falls, gripping the handrail the whole way. The falls were small but beautiful, and the water pooling at its base was a clear, bright turquoise. With the sun cutting through the mist to warm us, the scene was almost heavenly. We found a bench to sit on and listened to the water roaring. My mom loved waterfalls. I snapped several pictures to send to her once we had cell service again. It was one of the few things that brought her joy and living in Edmonton all her life, she rarely got the chance to see one. On a trip we took to the mountains when I was a teenager, she stood beside me when we'd stopped to gaze at the falls and whispered so my father wouldn't hear, "Please don't settle for anything less in your life." In hindsight, that was exactly what I had done, not just with Stan, but with the world. I never fought back; I rarely expressed my opinion. All I ever did was smooth the way for others. Even in my job. *Former* job. How had I gotten it all so monumentally wrong? "Would you change what you've done?" I blurted.

"What?"

"I've just realized that I made a lot of choices in my life that weren't the best for me, but I can't go back and undo them. Would you change the way you lived your life if you could?"

Roxanne watched the water, the light catching the side of her face. I could see tiny hairs, more like a fuzz along her cheek, and I smiled. It made her face softer, gentler, the lines around her mouth more sloping than cutting.

"I don't think so," she finally said. "Because if even a moment of the past was different, I wouldn't be here with you. A tiny misstep could have sent us on a completely different course."

Tears formed in my eyes at the fact that this exact moment in her life was irreplaceable to her—that she would do everything all over again, just to be sitting here with me at this waterfall. I reached over and squeezed her hand.

I focused on the waterfall, wondering where that particular sweep of water had been before it reached this spot. Had those molecules been around the world? Had they seen China and Antarctica and were now tumbling over a Canadian cliff? Where were they off to next? "You're so wise. I wouldn't change anything either, then."

When I looked back at Roxanne, her eyes were bright with tears, but the small smile she gave warmed from deep inside. I could tell her I was sorry that it had taken me so long to get here, but then that would go against what we'd just concluded. I leaned my head on her shoulder and sighed, absorbing into my soul the joy of finally being here.

- 15 -

ROXANNE SCREECHED INTO the apartment parking lot and braked hard, the momentum careening me into her back, jolting me back to reality. I had just been mesmerized by the pink and orange sunset as we'd tore back through the forest. I had never seen a sky so beautifully intense. "Jeez, lady," I yelled as she cut the engine.

"What? I'm starving. I can't live on trail mix forever." We got off and she quickly put the bike back into its storage spot and trotted back to me, passing without a word to head upstairs.

I pulled my helmet off and gasped. "What?" Roxanne asked, pausing at the bottom of the stairs, her foot hovering on the next step.

I reached into the helmet and pulled out a chunk of hair, holding it up for Roxanne to see. The were at least a hundred coppery-grey strands waving in the breeze.

"Oh, shit." She returned to me and inspected my head, her hand coming away with another chunk. "Um, Willie..."

"What?" My voice quivered.

"I think your hair is falling out."

"No," I moaned.

"It's okay," Roxanne patted my head. "It'll be fine. It's just hair, right?" The rising pitch of her voice did nothing to soothe me.

"Do you think it's from the bleach? Like, did we overdo it?"

"Maybe. Let's go upstairs."

By the time we made it to her apartment, I'd pulled out several more clumps. I ran to the washroom mirror, a sob rising up in me as I surveyed myself. "I look like a cancer patient."

"Trust me, you don't." Roxanne's voice was steely. "You look like a perfectly healthy woman who did something spontaneous that backfired."

"What am I going to do?" I wailed. My hair was my pride and joy. It was the one nice, feminine thing I had besides my boobs. My face was nothing to write home about, but I'd always had a luscious, curly head of hair. My second-best trait according to Stan. If I lost it, what would I be?

"Shave it." The casual nature with which Roxanne suggested such drastic measures pissed me off.

I wheeled on her. "How would you like to lose all your gorgeous hair? I sure bet you'd feel less beautiful then." My chest heaved.

Something dark flickered over Roxanne's striking features. She pushed past me, leaned into the cupboard under the sink, and pulled out a pair of clippers. Holding my gaze with an inscrutable look on her face, she plugged them in, turned them on and ran them straight over the middle of her head. The long chunk of hair floated to the floor.

"Roxanne!" I gasped. "What the hell are you doing?"

She buzzed off strip after strip, tears running down her face. "My hair does not make me beautiful. Living life on my terms, enjoying the company of wonderful friends, doing what fulfills me, standing up for what's important—that's what makes me beautiful. You don't see men conned into believing they are what they look like on the outside. They don't spend hundreds of hours and thousands of dollars on stupid things like *hair!*" She was practically screeching, her face bright red as the long, curly, white locks were freed from her skull.

I watched with an open mouth as my best friend became bald. When she was done, she handed me the clippers, eyebrow raised. I took them, my hand shaking. Roxanne nodded slightly, urging me on. "*You* get to define what being a woman means from here on out, no one else."

She was right. Hair was such a bother. Not being able to run to the grocery store unless it looked half-decent lest you run into someone you knew. Hearing Stan's comments on how wild it was most mornings—*"That's an interesting look"*—because I hadn't yet showered and got it back to right. At the funeral, I had flipped through family photos albums with Vivian, and I was amazed by the ever-evolving woman I had been while Stan stood beside me looking damn near the same in every picture. I held Roxanne's gaze and pressed the clippers to my head, inhaled sharply, and let everything go.

Laughing and crying, snorting and snoting. Our minds didn't know which emotions to embrace. Hair everywhere, we turned and surveyed ourselves in the mirror. Two bald old ladies who looked happy beyond belief.

"We've gone full Brittany Spears," Roxanne stated reverently, nodding with approval.

My stomach rumbled. It seemed that liberating oneself was hunger-inducing. We bolted from the apartment, hand in hand, cackling like the witches we were.

ON THE THIRD floor, Roxanne knocked and then walked into Dana and Monique's place, me right behind her. "Dana, Dana, Dana, I'm dying of hunger!" she sang.

The smell of seafood, saffron, and aromatic rice hit me. I closed my eyes and breathed in deeply.

Dana clicked off the stove. "You are just in time." She turned to look at us, her mouth dropping open.

Monique set her book down and rose from the couch. “Now that’s a look I can get behind! You two are positively glowing. Island life appears to agree with you, Willie.”

“I feel… absolutely, unequivocally fantabulous.” I beamed as we lined up to heap our plates full and make our way to the balcony. As the warm breeze caressed my freshly shorn head, I realized I was going to have to invest in some toques for winters in Edmonton, though.

“Thank you so much, you two,” I said before starting, making deliberate eye contact with both women. It was only our second meal together, but I felt like I’d known them for ages.

“It’s cliché, but a friend of Roxanne’s is a friend of ours,” Dana smiled.

We ate in silence for several minutes, stopping to sip the delicious sangria. It was another beautiful evening. “It doesn’t rain here as much as I thought it did.” I half-laughed, knowing it must, but other than that little shower the night of our painting escapade, the skies had been dry.

“Oh, yeah,” Roxanne said. “The winter is the wettest, but the spring is a bit more unpredictable.”

Dana tipped her head. “Actually, now that you mention it, it has been unusually dry since you got here.”

“Climate change.” Monique nodded deeply.

“Or…” Roxanne lifted her wine glass for a toast. “The gods conspiring to make Willie’s trip the best ever.”

We cheered to that and finished eating. I leaned back and burped. “Sorry.” My hand flew to my mouth.

Roxanne forced an even louder one out. “You ain’t got nothing on me.”

Monique folded her napkin and sat back. “So, ladies. Have you seen the graffiti around town?” Her eyelid fluttered. Did she wink at us? I chewed a fingernail, my eyes sliding to Roxanne.

Roxanne shot me a look back before responding. "Of course. It's fucking awesome, right?"

"A friend of mine owns the gas station and said they saw a couple of older ladies dressed in black creep across the corner of the frame of their CCTV footage the night it happened."

Heat rose up in my cheeks. We were doomed. "We didn't paint the gas station," I blurted.

Roxanne slapped her forehead. "Oh, man!"

Monique smirked and grabbed her phone. "It appears," she started as she scrolled, "that the artwork has gained a following." She turned her phone toward us so we could see the Facebook page she was viewing. "Along with Tofino, Victoria has gotten on board, as many as thirty murals popping up in the past couple days."

Roxanne and I looked at each other with wide eyes. "No shit," Roxanne murmured.

"Ucluelet has a couple too," Dana added. "It seems that this has taken on a life of its own. It even has a hashtag."

I frowned. I was not great at this technology stuff. "A hashtag?"

"It's for social media, more like Instagram and Twitter, to kind of like, start a group of sorts. Or a following."

"Like, back in the day when we were burning our bras," Roxanne said. "*Free the tits* would have been a hashtag."

"Huh. So what's this one? Fuck men?" I asked.

"Well, swear words will get taken down, and it would be considered hate, so they came up with, *#whatwomenwant.* I personally think it's brilliant because it makes the movement—and the conversation—productive."

I choked, spitting my wine back into the glass as the *Jeopardy!* category and my answers coming back to me. *For men to stop telling us to smile, to let our hair go grey, a bed to ourselves, to eat chocolate ice cream without thinking about our waistlines, to be able to go out at night without fearing rape, male birth control.*

Roxanne trumpeted. "I think it's brilliant."

Monique nodded. "It really is."

"Now the perpetrators can sit back and watch it unfold, instead of raising more suspicion among the townspeople and police than there already is by doing it again." Dana's eyes danced as she looked between Roxanne and I over the top of her glasses.

I took a long drink. "Indeed."

AFTER A DOUBLE scoop of cookie dough ice cream, we walked along Chesterman beach as the sun sunk behind the ocean. I stopped to stare at the darkening sky. "I could do this every night of my life," I murmured to Dana, biting the cone.

"It's really why I've stayed so long myself," she admitted. "I've thought about moving so many times over the years, but this"—she lifted her hands to the horizon—"I just can't leave." Dana peered at me. "It was a big step for you, the graffiti."

It was. I dropped my eyes and took another bite. I wasn't very good at this claiming-my-power thing. Roxanne had embraced the truth on the short drive over, going into great detail about how amazing that night had been. She seemed to have no problem sharing, though I felt a bit anxious that Monique and Dana were now officially accomplices to our crime through guilt-by-association.

Stars were popping out over the dusky blue horizon. I ran my hand over my head. It was so soft. And now I could grow it out naturally. Or keep it clipped. It sure would make getting ready every day much easier. I bit the last of my ice cream cone and shivered, pulling my sweater tighter around me. Maybe ice cream wasn't a good idea.

"We had so much fun today. I think we're ready for the big hike, Dana," Roxanne said.

Monique looked Roxanne up and down. "You sure about that?"

"You bet! You ready for a bigger hike, Willie-Tillie?"

"Yes," I breathed. "I'm ready for all the hikes."

Dana nodded. "Alright. I'll get planning it." My phone buzzed. *Jonathan.* I did not want to spoil this amazing day with his bullshit, but something in me felt ready to deal with him. Finally. I lifted a finger to the women and walked away.

"Hello?"

"Hi, Mom."

"Hi Jon. How are things at the house?"

"Good. The roof is already done. It looks great."

"That was fast."

"Yeah, these smaller bungalows only take a day."

"That's good." I paused. I didn't want to fill this conversation with empty words. Let him do the heavy lifting. I walked closer to the water so I could feel the coolness on my feet, even though I was already chilled. It spread over my toes and then toward my ankles. I shivered again and smiled at the sky. Every inch of me felt something. It was magnificent.

"Mom?"

I swore I'd heard his voice break and my heart stuttered. "Yes?"

"About the message you left? About you wanting me out before you get back? I've decided you have a point. This is your place, and I'm just loafing here."

This was definitely not the reaction I'd expected, but I tried emitting confidence rather than shock. "Yes, well, and you do have a family to think about."

"Yeah. That's what I wanted to talk about. Look, Annette is not taking me back. Ever. That ship has sailed. And we can't afford two places right now."

"If you let Annette work properly, it sounds like she could make great money. That would help."

"Well, yes, if we were staying together. But I should be able to support myself, so I've asked my boss to put me on more new builds." I could hear him swallow. "I need a place of my own so I can take the kids half of the time, but until I can afford it, could I..."

Had he suddenly forgotten about his accusations? Maybe if he needed me, they would be a thing of the past?

He barrelled on. "I know that's not what you want, but this is me trying to make things better, and I can only do it a step at a time."

He did sound sincere. And it would help Annette.

Surely, I could stand up for myself *and* help my son out at the same time? "Only until you figure out your own place to live."

"Yes. Absolutely. Thank you."

We chatted for a few more minutes and I could see the old Jonathan was back. The one who loved me and doted on me and cared about his family. Maybe his father's death affected him more than I realized?

I hung up and closed my eyes, listening to the sound of gulls screeching overhead and the waves rustling up the shore. *This has been the best few days of my life.* Baldness and all.

- 16 -

I LAY BLINKING as the morning light infiltrated my room, rubbing my face vigorously and smiling as the feeling of yesterday came flooding back to me. I popped out of bed and sang my way to the kitchen to make coffee, scooping Bo off the couch and pressing him to my chest as I went. I crooned to him, swinging my hips back and forth as I poured the first fresh cup. I nuzzled his fur and set him down, ignoring the clattering of the dogs at my heels. I reminded myself to never get a dog. They were too needy.

"What in the reborn woman is going on in here?" Roxanne drifted into the kitchen and joined me, singing along to the familiar tune. She grabbed me from behind and pulled my hips to hers. Her movements were slow and surprisingly sensual.

The dogs jumped and yipped in excitement of the display going on in the kitchen. I twirled away from Roxanne. My voice wobbled with unintelligible words as I tried to hit the high note. I'd always been the worst singer, and Stan made sure I knew that every time I tried.

Roxanne laughed. "I don't think those are the exact words."

"They are *my* words." A light tap on the door was followed by Dana poking her head in, the dogs rushing to greet her.

"I heard singing." She entered the apartment, coffee cup in hand, dressed in cargo pants and a white t-shirt. "What are you two up to today?"

"What do you want us to be up to, Dana?" I asked.

"Well, in a bid to keep you out of trouble, what would you say to ziplining?"

"Fuuuuuck no," Roxanne said. "You know better than to ask me that, Dana."

I looked between the two women. I was terrified of heights. But Roxanne had helped me so much since I'd gotten here, and what had I done for her besides be a pain in the ass? "Yes," I blurted.

"Aw man, no." Roxanne's bright blue eyes pleaded with me. "Dana's been trying to get me to go for ten years." She crossed her arms over her chest awkwardly trying to not spill her coffee. "Plus, you're supposed to be on my side."

"I'm firmly on your side. That's why I said yes."

"Willie," she moaned, and I knew I had her.

"I'll keep you safe, I promise. We'll use *all* the safety gear." I took another sip of coffee and realized my hand was shaking. Was I trying to convince myself or her?

Dana clapped. "We'll leave in an hour. She wheeled around and practically skipped out the door.

Roxanne gave me an evil eye my daughters at sixteen would have been proud of and silently went out onto the balcony to finish her coffee.

DOWNSTAIRS, DANA WAS already waiting for us in her car. I settled myself into the passenger seat, Roxanne in the back, still grumbling. Dana handed me a little brown paper bag and another one to Roxanne. "What's this?" I opened it and peaked inside to see a sandwich wrapped in waxed paper, a little bag of carrot sticks, and a bottle of orange juice. A little kid's lunch. I grinned.

"I hope you like tuna."

I smiled wistfully at her and her excellent caretaking abilities. "Thank you so much," I murmured, staring out the window as we left Tofino.

The buildings thinned and the trees thickened as we sped along the highway. I eyed Dana sideways and saw the gentle smile still on her lips that conveyed pure trustworthiness. I was struck by the sudden regret at not having *cultivated better female friendships over the years.* I'd had friends here and there, but the demands of my life made them hard to keep. Except Roxanne—she was never going anywhere. In the few days I'd been here, these women made me realize how much I liked the camaraderie. I decided right there that when I got home, I was going to start that women-only book club I'd thought about for years. And Stan wouldn't be there to hold his nose at our "clucking." I exhaled deeply and dropped my shoulders.

As we passed through Ucluelet, Dana mentioned that she often took the seniors from the assisted living centre on adventures, including ziplining.

"Is this another job you have, or a volunteer position?" I asked, marvelling at yet another thing she did.

"A casual job."

I shook my head. "How do you manage so much?"

"I have a lot of irons in the fire." She grinned, revealing a double dimple on her right cheek. "That's what happens when you don't marry a man and have kids."

Touché. We turned and drove even deeper into the forest, enjoying the revere. I stared out the window at the huge cedar trees, the undergrowth dense with ferns and other greenery that sped past, a light mist hanging in the air.

"Ha'uukmin Park," Dana said quietly. "H, a, apostrophe, u, u, k, m, i, n. It is the home of the Tla-o-qui-aht people." She went on to tell us a story about the history of the park.

Finally, after what seemed like an hour, Dana said, "Here we are."

The car turned up the road to West Coast Wild Zipline.

In the parking lot, I jumped out and stretched, noticing two guides approaching us. "Hey, Dana!" a young man in a blue t-shirt called.

"Brett!" she answered and then waved to the woman. "Angie! So glad you both are seeing us around today."

Roxanne came to stand beside me. "I'm gonna barf."

I turned to her in alarm. She looked fine, maybe just worried. I grabbed her hand. "I'm scared shitless, too."

"Then why are we here?"

"Because it's a core memory I want to have with you, overcoming a fear."

Something moved across Roxanne's face before she stood up straighter. "I'm going to hate you for this."

I swung her hand and turned my attention back to the guides. Brett and Angie talked about the forest and the Native American peoples that took care of it, while the group made its way to the first platform. The passion these guides had about conservation oozed out of them. It made me steel myself. Had I ever had that kind of passion for anything? Yes. Nursing. I had been confident and capable in my career choice. I had worked steadily, and with Stan's encouragement, right up until Tanya had been born. And then he'd started saying things that surprised me, things that I'd heard from my own father. *Babies need their mothers,* and *you don't want someone else raising them* and *this is nice that you're here at the end of the day when I get home.* And the truth was, I couldn't really argue. I wanted to be there to see my kids grow, I wanted to be the one to comfort them when they fell down, the same as my mother had. But I had given it my all and it wasn't until the kids were half-grown that I realized it had been too much, that there was nothing of the old me left. And by then it was too late to reverse time, so I moved forward with what I had.

As we walked along the gravel path, rays of sun cut through the canopy and streamed to the ground, giving the flora at the end of each beam a little spotlight as if the heavens were saying, *it's your time to shine.* Ferns, moss, gigantic tree roots, lichen—everything got its moment. The group chatted lightly as we walked, but I remained silent while taking in the beauty of my surroundings.

At the first stop, I tried not to look down into the river canyon as it made me swoon, but on the grated platform it was impossible. I gripped the handrail tightly and kept eye contact with Angie as she went through the safety spiel, talking loudly to be heard over the rushing water. I could feel the coolness of the canyon on my hairless head.

Everyone took turns stepping into the safety rigging that Brett was in charge of. He clipped everything up and Dana attached to the first line, taking off without hesitation, Angie right behind her. "Do you want me to go first?" I asked Roxanne. When I looked at her, I was shocked to see her face had gone completely grey. "Rox? Are you alright?"

She opened her mouth and shook her head, but no words would come out. I wondered if I should have let her out of it. I didn't want to be the cause of my best friend dying from a heart attack. But I also knew I wouldn't have gone on the whale watching trip if she had made clear the dangers beforehand.

I waved a hand in front of her face, breaking her stare into the canyon below. "Rox. Remember what you told me?"

She swallowed. "What?"

"That we only have one life to live." I couldn't believe *I* had to be the brave one now. "And that… and that playing it safe is for weenies." I winced. This wasn't exactly the profound, inspirational speech I was going for.

Roxanne lifted an eyebrow. "Did you just call me a weenie?"

"Well, a wild, creative, and beautiful weenie." I smirked. This seemed to lighten her mood a little, but she was still gazing at the river with a far-away look.

Finally, she looked back at me, scrutinizing. "I'm not all that. You have so much more than you know."

I shrunk back a little. She'd seen into the backhandedness of my attempt to make her be grateful for everything she had that I did not.

She continued, "You had a mother. How about that? Sure, your dad was an ass, but you have no idea what it's like for a girl to grow up without a mom. I would trade all of this"—she waved a hand over herself—"a million times over to have that one thing. And yes, Stan was a useless prick, but now you've got kids and grandkids, and your life is full. I'm going to blink out one day and no one will even remember I was here."

Her lecture stunned me. She was telling the truth, that I did have a habit of overlooking the good things I had. But what hurt me was that she felt that her existence was so hollow. We stood facing each other, inches apart, searching the other's eyes. I wanted to tell her that her artwork would live forever, that her father still loved her to death.

I took a deep breath. "I will *always* remember you." My voice broke on the last word. I knew I wasn't the be all and end all, but even just one person keeping another alive in their hearts had to be enough.

"Um," Brett interrupted, breaking our face-off. "Are you guys going?"

"Yeah, I'm fucking going." Roxanne stepped up to the line to be clipped on.

Even though I felt terrible for creating friction between us, a grin started at the corner of my mouth. Nothing was more incredible than a pissed-off Roxanne. "You could take on the world right now, couldn't you?"

"You bet your taco I could."

I laughed. "Taco?"

"Yeah. Since when did having *balls* become the phrase for courage and bravery and toughness? Vaginas are the toughest things around." She looked to Brent. "Balls are delicate little things. Right, sweetie?"

Instead of being mortified by this conversation, he chuckled and nodded. "I guess you've got a point there."

Roxanne stepped off the platform and screamed the whole way down.

Now that I was alone, the fear started to creep in. I focused on the ravine below, the water rushing past, my head swimming with visions of me falling to rocks below when the cable gave out. The headlines about my death would read: *Tragic accident or just desserts? Widow quickly follows husband to the grave following ziplining accident.*

I forced myself to open my eyes. No way I was going to let Roxanne hold my failure over my head. I stepped off the platform and my stomach plummeted, falling for a split second until the cable tightened, causing me to gasp. I screeched as I sped down the line, closing my eyes tight before the vertigo forced me to open them again. Pine trees and grey rocks sped past, and I could hear Roxanne and Dana cheering off in the distance.

This was it. I was living.

I looked up at the sky, almost perfectly cloud-free and a brilliant blue, the same shade as the wild blue flax that used to grow around the side of our house. My house. *My house.* "Yes!" I squealed.

As my feet brushed the platform, tears were streaming across my cheeks. "We did it!" I cheered as Angie detached me from the line.

"Yes! And I only peed my pants a little bit." Roxanne cackled.

Dana and Angie took off on the next line, and as Roxanne clipped in, she threw me a smug look. "I was always going to do it, you know."

"You're such a lair!" But as I watched her zip away, I couldn't help but wonder if she had outmaneuvered me into seeing past the anger and into the grace that was still present in my life.

MAYBE IT WAS the adrenaline buzz, but the tuna sandwich Dana had made was the best thing I'd ever tasted. As we drove home, chatting animatedly about the day, I felt a warmth growing in my belly. The only thing that could make this day better was an orgasm. And since I had a keener on speed dial, there was no need to do it for myself. I slipped my phone out of my pocket and texted Mark, asking if he was available for a booty call tonight. He immediately replied with a yes.

I smirked and tried not to imagine what *that* was going to look like but failed. Mark's chest came to mind, the image of my fingernails digging into it as I rode him, coming to a climax swiftly as he worked my clitoris with his thumb. A real moan rose up in me but was cut short by my phone binging again. I shook my head, realizing I was in the car with my friends, and prayed to God the moan had not actually escaped my lips.

A picture of my house came through from Tanya. *Oh yeah, I'd asked her to take a picture of the shingles.* I tapped the picture to make it bigger. This wasn't right. I spread it bigger. Yes, it was my house, the green wooden siding and broken glass stucco. The ugly, utilitarian aluminum screen door with the cattails on it.

But the roof. "Potato brown?" My eyes roved over and over the picture, my blood boiling by the time I admitted to myself that these were not the Onyx shingles I'd ordered, but the Russet ones Jonathan had wanted.

"What's got your knickers in a twist?" Roxanne asked from the back seat.

"I'm gonna kill him."

Roxanne squeezed my shoulder. "I'll supply the knife."

- 17 -

I STOMPED AROUND the apartment for an hour. Even the animals knew to stay out of my way. "I can't believe it!" I lunged for the couch, grabbed an orange throw pillow, and launched it into the kitchen. It landed with an unsatisfying plop on the tile floor.

"You can't *fucking* believe it. Use your words, Willie." Roxanne said from the safety of a chair in the corner of the living room.

"What am I going to do? I am not living with a potato brown roof for the rest of my life. I'm not."

"Make Jonathan pay for the right one."

"He can't even afford an apartment!"

"So, then tell the roofing company. You paid for it, right? They can fucking fix it."

I stopped pacing. "You're right. But, God, it'll be such a waste. Of time and materials."

"Time? Who cares? Materials? Yes, I don't love that. But what will the cost be to your psyche if you don't correct this?"

Irrevocable. "And he was being sweet as fucking pie on the phone yesterday while knowing full well what he had done." I realized in one heartbreaking second that I didn't really know who my son was. Annette was right. A sob tried to push past the burning lump of rage in my throat, but I pushed it back down. I wasn't going to cry over this. I was going to act. I took a swift breath and dialed the roofing company.

Roxanne leaned forward, a look of pure delight on her face. She only needed a bucket of popcorn to make this the best experience of her life.

"Good afternoon, ABC Roofing."

"This is Willie Copeland. Let me talk to Dave," I barked.

The receptionist stumbled. "Oh, um, yes, one second." There was a click as she transferred me.

"Hello?" Dave's voice sounded slightly frantic.

"Dave. Can you explain to me why my house currently has shingles that I did not order?" I was proud of myself for not putting *please* or *kindly* at the beginning of my statement.

"Well, um, I know you wanted the Onyx, but then your son called, and we had a really great conversation. He's in construction too! And he made some really valid points about getting the lighter colour and, well, we changed it. *At his request.* Plus, he said it was going to be his house eventually, anyway."

I deflated a little knowing it was Jonathan's fault and I couldn't really take my anger out on Dave. I pinched the skin between my eyebrows. "Did you say *his house?*" What kind of plan was Jon concocting? To somehow get me out of my house? To take control of it? My head was spinning, and I felt faint. I rallied myself. Someone still had to fix this problem. "Who paid for the shingles?" I demanded.

"Well. You did."

"When will you be able to return to the house and put on the shingles *that I paid for?*"

"You can't expect us to change them," he blustered.

"I can. And I do." I looked to Roxanne who gave me two big thumbs up.

"But that will cost us thousands." I could hear the defeat in his voice, and I moved in for the kill.

"Then send the bill to one Jonathan Copeland. I think you know where's he's staying." I hung up the phone and fell into the couch. I breathed deeply for several minutes, pressing my fingertips into my temples. "That was awful," I finally said.

"Stepping out of your comfort zone rarely feels good in the moment. It's after, when you can look back and realize that you had your own back, that it becomes clear."

Had my own back. She was right. It was not something I was accustomed to. I was good at standing up for the kids and even Stan when someone would say something disparaging about him. But having my own back? I didn't even really know what that looked like.

"Women are really bad at it," Roxanne said, as if reading my mind. "We've been told for so long that we're inherently untrustworthy, we don't even know how to show up for ourselves, how to trust ourselves." A wry look crossed her face. "Didn't you get the memo? It was sent out about two thousand years ago by a man who was upset that a woman destroyed his virtue."

Eve. But I didn't want to talk about the bible. I had other problems. "What am I going to do about my son?" I knew I should call him and screech, but on the other hand, it would be pretty funny when the roofers showed up to replace the shingles, bill for him in hand. I was avoiding the confrontation I needed to have the most, but I didn't have the guts for it.

Roxanne stood and stretched. "How about we contemplate that over a bottle of wine?"

"It's only four in the afternoon."

"Who gives a shit? You?"

I grimaced. "No."

BY SIX, ROXANNE and I were having a dance party on the balcony as the sun was starting to descend behind the trees.

"Let's go to Shelter and see if our buddy Leon is working again," Roxanne said, dragging me back into the apartment.

"Yes!" I sang. "I could use something to eat." I wrapped the red scarf around my bald head and grabbed my purse and fell into the wall.

Roxanne laughed. "Let's walk."

I righted myself. "I don't think we have another choice." We made our way carefully downstairs and started for downtown.

That asshole. The thought had been randomly jumping into my head since I'd called the roofers. I could just not wrap my head around the fact that my son had done that to me. Who the hell did he think he was? I pulled my phone out of my purse and dialed Annette. If he was going to be sneaky, so was I.

"Who are you calling?" Roxanne asked, bumping into me as she stepped up onto a curb.

My antagonistic daughter-in-law? No. I had been looking at this whole situation wrong. "A friend." The phone rang in my ear twice before she picked up.

"Hi, Willie." I detected exhaustion in her voice.

"How are the diseased little children?"

She laughed. "Still disease-free. But let me tell you, Willie, if I ever have to homeschool, kill me."

"Got it." Roxanne and I waited for a car to pass before crossing the street to Shelter. "Annette, can I ask you something?"

"Yes."

"Has Jonathan ever talked about getting my house? Like inheriting it or something?"

Annette let out a long breath that whistled into the phone. "Yes. The night he left, he mentioned to me that you'd been acting weird since Stan died and possibly it being time for a nursing home."

I gritted my teeth. How deep did his claws go? And he was supposed to have a decent career—why did he seem so desperate lately? "How much does Jonathan actually work, Annette?"

She snorted. "Not nearly enough. It's the whole reason I've been pushing so hard to go back to work. Honestly, it's rare that he works more than twenty hours a week."

It was the exact same shit Stan had pulled years ago. Claiming he couldn't handle his asshole bosses; he'd gone contract so he could pick and choose what he did. But it had only been a way for him to put in the bare minimum effort to help keep the roof over our head. I'd had to slowly increase my hours to make up for his lack. That was the one difference here. Stan had been more than happy for me to work more, as long as the household chores didn't suffer. So why does Jonathan not want the same from Annette? "It doesn't make sense that he won't use you for more money."

"No, it doesn't. There's a power struggle there that he won't admit to."

"So, he doesn't want to work, but he doesn't want you to work. Does that mean he wants to keep the family broke for some reason?"

"He knows if I make money, I'll leave."

That was it. That was the one thing Stan never had to worry about. He knew I'd never leave.

"But what he doesn't understand or believe," Annette continued, "is that I love him and would be happy to switch roles until the kids are more independent. I don't mind being the breadwinner if he would stay home with the kids."

"He would never. It would be an insult to his manhood."

"And therein lies the rub. It's all about control, Willie. And now that he's lost me, he's moving in on you."

"Well, he's about to get a rude awakening." I told her quickly about the roofing situation. She couldn't stop laughing.

"Willie, just so you know, I am going to tell Jonathan about our conversation."

I didn't want Annette to fight my fight, but the thought had certain appeal. She was so much better at it than me. I'd never had to stand up to one of my children. But Annette had been standing up to Jonathon for their entire seven-year marriage "Really, I should be the one calling," I finally said.

"Let me get my hands dirty. There's nothing I love more than bickering." I was happy Annette was going to do this, but as I ended the call, I felt more drained than I ever had. Why was I so weak? What about Jonathan made me shrink back into the same space I'd occupied with Stan? It had been so easy to become a person I admired out here, but this wasn't the real fight and I knew it.

"Well, I for one would pay money to see the look on your son's face when those roofers show back up and start ripping that brown shit of the roof," Roxanne muttered as she pulled the door of the restaurant open for me.

I rubbed my forehead. "Can we not talk about it anymore?"

"Done."

"Willie! Roxanne!" Leon called to us as we walked in. We went straight to the bar. "I almost didn't recognize you two. Did you have an unfortunate run-in with a pair of clippers?"

"You could say"—I glanced at Roxanne with a smirk, nudging her with my elbow—"that it was a *fortunate* run-in."

He reached for two shooters glasses. "That sounds like something that needs a celebration. Rocky Mountain Bear Fuckers?"

"No!" we said in unison.

He laughed. "Okay, something a little tamer. Sex on The Beach, perhaps?"

Sex. Shit. "I was supposed to have a booty call tonight," I said to Roxanne. Leon lifted his eyebrows, but if he was shocked, he didn't say anything. I guessed being a bartender left him hearing and seeing it all.

Roxanne slapped my arm. "You didn't tell me that."

"Sorry."

"Well, you still can. Tell him to come for a drink."

"You don't mind?"

"Not at all. And if he has a cute friend..."

"Ah. There's the real reason you don't mind."

She grinned as Leon set down two shot glasses piled high with whipped cream. I gaped at them. "How are we supposed to—"

"You put your hands behind your back, open your mouth and do this." Roxanne bent forward and gripped the little glass with her lips and threw her head back, dropping it on bar on the bar empty.

"Oh my God, I'll gag."

"You'll be fine. Just pretend it's Mark's—"

"Stop," I cut her off. Without overthinking it, I did the shot and was left with liquor dribbling down my chin. But it was tasty.

"You two need some food?" Leon asked.

"Yes please," I said.

"What do you feel like?

"Surprise us."

He nodded and went to talk to the waitress, who entered something into the computer. The door slammed open and Black Beard and his crew entered the restaurant. "Oh fuck," I moaned. I leaned toward Roxanne. "That's the dickhead who wouldn't leave those girls alone from the night I had a date with Mark."

Roxanne patted her purse that hung on the back of the bar chair. "I got my little friend if we need her."

As the men sat at a table, I noticed the waitress eyed them and then whispered something in Leon's ear. He dried his hands on a towel and grabbed several menus and made his way over to them.

Black Bread sized Leon up. "We don't want you. We want the redhead beauty over there. Isn't she the waitress?"

Leon, who was taller but much slimmer than the man glaring at him, set the menus down. "Yes, but I've got her mixing you guys her special drink."

The waitress was indeed behind the bar making something. *An arsenic concoction perhaps.* She dropped a thick glass, and it skidded away without breaking. She looked up at me and I knew instantly how she felt. I wished these assholes would just disappear too.

Roxanne and I sat at the bar and tried to ignore the idiots and enjoy the steak bites and sweet potato fries Leon had ordered us, but nothing tasted quite as good as it should. Leon kept one eye on the bar and one on the men. I leaned toward him and whispered, "Can't you kick those guys out?"

"Not unless they threaten someone or break something." Leon sighed and I realized sometimes this line of work must be beyond exhausting. "They know how to just barely toe the line." He loaded another round of drinks onto a tray and went to them.

"Okay, this is bullshit," Black Beard shouted. "I just have a question for her." He turned to the waitress and yelled, "Do the curtains match the drapes?"

The restaurant went quiet. The waitress's face turned pink, and she looked as if she wanted to cry.

I saw red. How dare these fuckers get away with such disrespect. Before I knew it, my hand had slipped into Roxanne's purse and back out. I stood and closed the space between us in three strides.

"What do you want, Baldie?" Black Beard hissed.

"I want you to apologize to that nice young lady." I jerked my head back toward the waitress.

He cackled and looked to his friends. "You hear that, boys? Granny wants me to say, *sorry*." The word came out in a babyish tone. He stood quickly, knocking his chair over. "What are you going to do if I don't?"

In one swift movement, I pressed the release on the blade—enjoying the satisfying click of it snapping into place—and swung it up and pressed it to the side of his neck. Panic flashed across his face and his hands went up in defense. The air around us seemed to freeze, as if we were locked in our own personal atmosphere. His deep brown eyes were wide with alarm, and it made me feel bigger. Standing as straight as I could, I still only came to his chin, but the way his body was curved back from me was delicious.

I pressed the tip of the blade harder and revelled in his flinch.

The divot in his skin pushed dangerously inward, and I wondered how much force it would take to puncture it. I pressed the blade even harder and rejoiced in his little gasp. I blinked at the red dot that suddenly appeared on his neck, realizing my heart was keeping a calm, even beat. I held the blade perfectly still, and Jonathan's face emerged before me, his finer features replacing Black Beard's weather-worn ones. Jonathan's black curls and brown eyes looked pained and beseeching, as if asking whether I'd really kill my own son. Over a roof.

The knife clattered to the ground, and I ran from the building.

I WAS HALFWAY back to the apartment, retching into a bush, before Roxanne caught up with me. "Willie," she coughed, grabbing my arm.

I wiped my mouth with the back of my hand, looking around for the cops, who would surely be coming to arrest me.

"That was"—hands on knees, Roxanne took a couple deep breaths—"the best thing I've ever seen in my whole life."

"Roxanne," I wailed. "I'm going to jail for sure now. There were, like, ten witnesses." I brought my hands to my face as the tears renewed themselves.

"Yeah. And? Guys like that do illegal shit all the time and get away with it. Leon said he's a known harasser. Everyone cheered after you left."

But I saw my son's face. I couldn't even admit this to Roxanne. I couldn't tell anyone. "I don't care! Don't you understand? I'm not a hero, I'm a monster. I don't actually want to kill anyone." Stan would argue otherwise.

"Of course you don't. You just have some things you need to work out."

I rolled my shoulders around viciously, trying to rid myself of the feeling of insects crawling over me. I needed out of here. Like, *out*,

out. I turned and kept walking.

"Willie."

"I can't keep going like this. Something is broken in me." I'd been swinging wildly between having the time of my life and having my life fall apart, and the whiplash left me wrecked.

"Something is broken with the world," Roxanne argued. "There's nothing wrong with you."

You don't know. And how could she? I envisioned stabbing my own offspring. Someone who I love more than anything.

I rubbed at my arms roughly. This was a level of rage I didn't know what to do with.

But I knew one person who maybe would.

- 18 -

AT SEVEN THE next morning, the four of us were barreling down the highway, starting the camping and hiking adventure Dana had planned for us a few days early. She hadn't hesitated at my request last night, and I'd bawled embarrassingly into her arms with relief.

I rubbed the moisture off the window so I could look outside, but the mist that hung in the air didn't allow much more of a view. My chest felt heavy with the knowledge that I just kept running away from everything—and that "everything" seemed to mean the various men in my life.

My phone buzzed from my pocket—a message from Mark, who was very upset about me standing him up the night before. *Too bad,* I thought. I was about to put my phone away without replying when another message came in. Tanya sent a picture of a new "fuck men" mural that I hadn't seen before. I squinted at it and realized it was the side of a grain silo. Good for you, Alberta. *Have you seen this?* The text from Tanya read. *Awesome, hey? I'm about to go do one myself.*

I swallowed. There *was* trouble in their marriage. I quickly tapped back, *do you want me to call you?*

No, it's ok, Mom. I'll tell you about it when you're home.

I wrote back that I was disappearing into the forest for a few days and would have poor cell reception, and she wished me a good time. When I looked up, Roxanne was watching me. She mouthed, *Everything good?*

I nodded and went back to staring out the window, hating that I'd lied to her. Everything was not good, not even close. But I didn't know how to put my feelings into words. Instead, I pushed it down and tried to focus on having a great time with my friends, because who knew what shit was going to hit the fan when I emerged from the hiking trail on the other side.

WE PULLED UP to Sombrio Point at nine. I ran through a mental checklist of everything I had: comfortable hiking boots, bandages for blisters, track pants where the bottoms zipped off into shorts, gaiters to keep the mud out of the boots, hiking poles, ball cap, wind breaker, two shirts, water bottle and treatment tablets, snacks, sleeping supplies.

Dana was obviously the more experienced hiker and we happily let her lead the way. Our timing had worked out with Monique's school schedule, making us a rowdy foursome. Roxanne jostled her backpack and an orange pill bottle fell out a side pocket. I bent and scooped it up. *Hydromorphone.* I handed it back to her with a frown. She swiped it out of my hand and turned on her heel, marching away.

My chest constricted. Such a strong pain killer seemed a little excessive for emphysema. I'd seen her using her steroid puffer several times since I'd been here, something Lisa at work routinely did for her COPD, but as I watched Roxanne's hunched back disappear into the forest, an uneasy feeling settled in my mind. She had more than emphysema. I was suddenly certain of it, and the realization hit me hard. I choked back a sob and followed the group.

Tears blurred my vision, and I tripped over a tree root and landed on my knees. Monique stepped over and helped me back up. Her hazel eyes searched my face and the tears ran down it. "Let's just enjoy this trip, alright?" she said gently.

I wiped my face and nodded. I focused on Dana's nature talk. "See the difference between western hemlock and sitka spruce?" She pointed from one tree to another, her features wide with excitement. "The hemlock has soft, flat needles, while the spruce has sharp ones typical of coniferous trees. Plus, hemlock tend to be a little lighter green." She reached out and grabbed a clump of needles from the hemlock, pulling them gently through her hand. I did the same, surprised at how soft they were.

We started moving again when Roxanne stopped dead in front of me, a gasp escaping her as her left foot froze in the air. I crashed into her back.

"What?" I peered around her to see the biggest slug I'd ever laid eyes on, inching across the path. "It's a travelling banana," I said, as the dull yellow creature slimed its way back into the forest—its black spots striking against the skin. This place sure had a lot of slugs. Every time I'd ventured into the forest I'd seen at least one, but this was certainly the most impressive.

Dana crouched beside it. "This is the only slug that's native to BC. And you're right, it's called a banana slug. They can grow up to twenty centimeters and it looks like this one is almost there." She reached down and moved a small rock out of its path, which at the speed it was going, was going to take an hour to get to. "This guy is nature's recycler. Eating and breaking down detritus as it goes. A wonderful creature!"

"It's antennae are so cute!" Monique peered from behind. They were moving back and forth as if sweeping its course for danger.

"Technically, they're tentacles. There are two sets. The top ones you see are for detecting light and movement and the bottom ones—much smaller—are for detecting chemicals and smells."

"Nerd." Monique beamed at Dana. We moved on, taking a detour over the Loss Creek suspension bridge. Soon we could hear the waves crashing. The ocean was announcing its presence, and this shush and rumble quickly became music to my ears. Stepping around a corner, it came into view. "Now, we have to hike quite a while on the rocks, so please watch your step," Dana instructed. "Use your poles, watch for loose and wet rocks. We aren't in a hurry." She pulled her Tilly hat over her forehead to protect from the sudden glare of the sun, her black bob tucked neatly behind her ears.

I used my pole to support myself around a particularly large pile of rocks, wet with ocean mist. The last thing any of us needed was to be carted out of here by search and rescue.

Roxanne suppressed a cough, her shoulders moving greatly from the effort. "Don't make me turn this caravan around!" I called to her, frowning. I would not hesitate to abandon this trip immediately if it was best for her.

"Like hell, you will!" Roxanne said loudly, straightening up. "Frackin' salt spray does it every time." She made a deep noise in her chest and spit a booger out onto the rocks.

Such a Stan move. "Gross!" I yelped, gagging.

"Don't be a prissy pants," Roxanne said, head hung, and cheeks flushed. It wasn't too late to go back, and I was about to voice my concern when Roxanne called back to me, "Let's keep going." Monique fell in behind Roxanne, leaving me at the back.

We hiked mostly in silence for the next two hours, everyone lost in the beauty of the ocean, passing a couple of tents set up on the shore along the way. By the time we stopped for a light lunch, my worries seemed to have been washed out to sea. For the first time in a long time, I felt completely present in the moment. We sat on a large piece of driftwood. I picked at our trail mix and cheese and crackers, my appetite lacking. I did finish off my thermos of tea—even though I would probably need a toilet in an hour—but sipping on a hot drink in the sunshine and ocean mist, watching the long rollers come in was about as close to heaven as I imagined one could get.

After inspecting the tide pools for several minutes, we took off again, heading back into the forest. Dana took us past a wonderful little waterfall hidden behind an outhouse and we crossed another suspension bridge over a river that ran into the ocean. There wasn't much wildlife to see in the forest—a squirrel here, a bird there—but the trees were spectacular. Every tree that I thought was the biggest I'd ever seen had a photo shoot, only to be replaced by an even bigger one twenty steps away.

By the time we arrived at Chin beach, our camping spot for the night, it was almost dark. The tide was just low enough for us to sneak along and into a place suitable for tent setup without finding ourselves adrift in the Pacific in the middle of the night.

Now I was hungry, and I watched in amazement as Dana pulled out a tiny stove and propane bottle and all the supplies to cook a gourmet dinner right on the beach. My feet and calves were covered in mud, and I was grateful Dana made us wear gaiters to protect the tops of our boots. I knew for sure it was going to be ugly when I took them off, though. I had felt a blister growing on both heels for the past hour. Sitting down, I carefully pulled off each boot, sighing at the sight of once-white socks now red around the whole back.

"Willie. That's terrible." Monique crouched down beside me; her curly blonde hair gone completely frizzy. "Why didn't you say anything earlier? We could have wrapped them up."

"I thought it wasn't that bad—you know how it is." I peeled the socks off, wincing. I inspected the small round, raw spots. "See, they're not that bad. Just bled a lot."

"Okay, let's patch you up." Monique pulled a first-aid kit out of her backpack and got to work. Roxanne walked down the beach collecting driftwood for a fire. I tried ignoring the stinging as Monique gently swabbed at me.

"Dinner in five!" Dana called out.

"Bald Eagle!" Roxanne shouted, pointing at the sky behind them, over the trees. Everyone turned to see not one but two huge, brown birds soaring, their white heads and legs unmistakable. Onc glided behind the other before they both slowly turned and disappeared behind the trees. I wondered if they symbolized the same thing as the Osprey I'd seen when I first arrived. Roxanne had said they were a sign of having power over one's fate. I had power over my own fate, just *not* over my son, I reminded myself.

"I could see them every day and never tire of it," Roxanne said, dumping a pile of wood near us. "What did you do to yourself, dingle-ball?" Roxanne stared at the bloody socks lying on the rocks.

I shrugged and carefully pulled my boots back on. "Just a little blister."

We feasted on a delicious meal that consisted of tuna, pasta, and spices. As I took my last bite, Roxanne said, "Hope you saved room for dessert."

"Oh, I'm pretty full."

"You'll fit it in." Roxanne winked and turned back to the ocean to watch the bright orange sun disappearing behind the dark waters.

BY THE TIME everyone finished, the dishes cleaned with ocean water, and tent set-up, it was fully dark. Monique had a roaring fire going with pieces of driftwood pulled up near it as seating. "Here it is!" Roxanne announced, holding up a plastic container. Across the cackling fire, Dana rolled her eyes.

"What is it?" I asked.

"Pot brownies."

"Ohhhh." It had been over forty years since I'd had marijuana. I stared at the small chocolatey squares. Did I need to be more of an old-woman-behaving-badly cliché than I already was?

Roxanne waved the dish back and forth in front of me. "Well? And trust me—I cut them to the appropriate size. I don't need anyone barfing into the ocean or tripping out and thinking beach pebbles are coming to kill them."

I reached out and took the smallest one and popped it into my mouth before I could change my mind. Stan would have shouted and raged at me if he knew I was doing this. *Good.* I pushed him out of my mind, wondering how many weeks needed to pass before I would stop thinking about Stan's reaction to everything I was doing.

"Yes, bitch!" Roxanne moved onto Dana and Monique, who each took one.

Roxanne licked her fingers and circled the fire. "Now we wait. They take a while to kick in."

The slight taste of trees lingered in my mouth, even after I tried swishing with several gulps of water. I watched the tops of the waves glisten in the starlight. It was so velvety black out there. So much emptiness, stillness, and beauty. Living my entire life in a city, connections to nature were hard to come by. Such a shame. It made me wonder if humans were going about it all wrong—always working and striving and pushing. In the end, you took nothing with you anyway. A tiny light streaked across the sky. A shooting star! I wanted to tell Roxanne, but I didn't dare let my eyes leave the spot. And then it was gone. If I had been looking anywhere else in that second, I would have missed it.

I realized, then, that if Stan hadn't died when he did, I would have missed *this*. I glanced at Roxanne. Our reunion was predestined by the stars above.

Dana and Monique engaged in a heated debate over which Schitt's Creek character was better. Dana argued for David and Monique for Moira. I'd heard about the show, but since Stan was in charge of the remote, I rarely got a chance to watch what I wanted. I added it to the list of things to do once I got back home.

A branch popped in the fire, sending a spray of embers into the air. The red and orange sparks lifted like a Phoenix, up into the endless sky. "I don't think this is working. Should we have more?" I asked, my voice lifting with the firebird.

"No!" Roxanne stretched her hands toward me from across the fire, slowly. "That's when you get into trouble. It can take up to an hour to kick in, and people get impatient and eat more before the original stuff has had time to start working. Just give a few more minutes."

I watched the waves glisten in the starlight. The top of a wave crested, bright white and glossy, then gone. Something suddenly moved on the rocks to my left. I leaned toward Monique for safety, just in case it was a snake.

"What are you looking at?" Monique asked, grinning.

"That." I lifted my hand to point but found it moving incredibly slow. *So heavy.*

"A stick?"

"It's a snake," I whispered.

"It's a stick."

"It… moved. Sticks… can't… move. It's a… snake." I feared I had developed a speech impediment. Roxanne burst out laughing on the other side of me and Dana leaned into her, giggling.

"Willie. You're stoned, and it's just a stick," Monique said.

"How…?" I frowned, pulling my head and chin back, trying to turn my head. Why did Monique sound so far away? She was right beside me. Monique snorted and found my hand again, giving it a squeeze. "I'm right here."

I smiled. *I'm okay.* My body swayed as the sounds of the ocean got louder and louder. "It's like a… an ocean orchestra. Do you hear it?" I leaned forward, tilting my head, cupping my ear dramatically to the water. The waves crashed and pounded in my ears. "I don't like snakes." I shook my head back and forth—slowly and seriously. When I was little, a boy that "liked me" threw a little garter snake in my face. I hadn't been scared of nature, but having that cool, slippery reptile wiggle around my nose and then slip down my neck had traumatized me.

Something hit me in the chest. *The snake!* I jumped up, brushing frantically at the front of my coat while everyone laughed and laughed. I scanned the ground, the light from the fire flickering over the rocks, to see… a stick. I growled at Roxanne, who was still laughing. "Meanie!" I lunged, making her squeal.

We collided and rolled off the log onto the rocks, a mess of arms and legs. I grabbed both sides of Roxanne's face, leaned forward, and licked her from chin to forehead.

"Ewww!" Roxanne squealed. "I've been slimed!" I started laughing, which quickly turned into a braying. Eventually catching out breath, we laid back and stared at the stars. "I love you," I whispered into the air.

"I love you, too, babycakes."

"I don't know why life worked out like this." I tried to lift my cement hand into the air.

"What's there to know?"

My exaggerated shrug made my shoulder blades dig into the rocks. Finally, I said, "I never let myself think before. I just *did*. Go, go, go. Make everyone happy. Now, look!" I waved clumsily to the sky, happy my limb finally complied. "Poof. I make *me* happy! Maaaagic!"

"It's called creating your own life, babe. Welcome aboard."

I squeezed Roxanne's hand. "I wanna do it with you."

Roxanne turned to look at me. The firelight dancing off her face made her look spooky and haunted. "Umm… I love you and all, but not like that."

I slapped her arm. "Not that *do it*." I giggled. "I wanna have more *life* with you." I felt myself sinking into the rocks, a heaviness pressing me down.

Roxanne puffed air out her nose. It sounded sad and I opened my mouth to say so when she yanked me to my feet.

"Enough of this melancholy. We're going swimming!" Roxanne started pulling off her coat. I rolled away, instantly slipping my boots and socks off. I'd beat her to it.

"Um, Roxanne? It's pretty chilly out." Dana had moved from the log to standing next to her.

"Then I'll have porn star nipples!" she screeched, fighting with the laces of her boots. "If you motherfuckers can believe it, I've never gone skinny dipping. What do you say, Willie-Millie?"

I already had my shirt over my head, the warm air twirling around my exposed stomach, my elbow caught in the sleeve. I pulled ferociously on the end of it like a little kid. Roxanne cackled. "Yes, bitch!"

"Beat you to it!" I sang, managing to finally free myself from the straightjacket.

"You guys are going to get hypothermia!" Monique yelled, standing from the log she had been occupying. Another large *pop* came from the fire, Monique screeching and jumping back with laughter.

"It was like, thirty degrees today, it'll be fine," Roxanne said.

"I brought one towel," Dana weighed in. "As long as they dry off well, they should be fine. It will be a good memory for Willie." Dana found her backpack and pulled a thick grey towel from it.

How much stuff could that bag fit?

I stood naked for a second, nonplussed, my embarrassment likely having melted away with the drugs. The warm breeze from the water caressed me, the firelight dancing off Roxanne's backside, highlighting the wrinkles and dips of old age. What a beautiful accomplishment to get this far in life.

Roxanne pulled my arm, and we ran for the ocean, rocks stabbing the bottoms of my feet. Our screams echoed across the beach as we hit the water. Monique followed us with the towel, laughing as she heard Roxanne cry out, "Ah! My sweet potato!"

I shrieked as a cold wave hit my naked bottom. We splashed and jumped, hollered and cackled as waves broke on our bodies sending droplets up to our necks. My hands wandered to my chest, and I lifted my boobs—two giant bags of pudding that had weighed me down most of my life. "Look at my juicy melons!"

Roxanne stepped toward me and started playing drums on them, a beat I was sure I'd heard before. We swayed together for what seemed like ages, lost in music only we could hear. An ocean melody to the rhythm of a tit bongo. *Jingle Bells.* That was what Roxanne was playing. I closed my eyes and tipped my head back, singing the Christmas carol to the stars.

One Christmas, my father had been particularly nasty—having got into the whiskey early in the day—and Fran had dressed me up in my winter gear and told me to go to Roxanne's for a sleepover. At sixteen, I was more than happy to spend all my time with my best friend, but I was terrified to leave my mother alone with him. I'd held her hands, begging her to come with me. I'd always had a fantasy about Fran and Roxanne's dad getting together. He was the kind of father I would have loved to have—he was everything his young children needed him to be, all on his own. "Dad will never notice you're gone," I had pleaded, my eyes darting to the living room, where I saw him lurch to the TV to turn the channel, and then back to her. I saw in her face that she desperately wanted to join me. But now I understood that if she'd left that night, she would never have come back. She would have dropped me off at Roxanne's and just kept driving. "I can't do that to you," she'd finally answered, and I knew she was talking about more than leaving for the night. By sacrificing herself, she was protecting me. I owed her everything for that. I made a (foggy) mental note to buy her something special from the island before I left.

Dropping my bosom, I cupped some water and splashed it on Roxanne, causing her to cough. I leaned toward her, holding out a hand. "Sorry!" The spell had been broken.

"Time to come in, kids," Monique called out. At once chilled, we trudged out, and Monique wiped down Roxanne, then me, and wrapped the towel around both of us. "Go get dressed, you lunatics." As Roxanne coughed again, I prayed our little stunt hadn't been a terrible idea.

Warmed up and full of dill pickle potato chips—which had never tasted so good—I fell into my sleeping bag before midnight. I was hoping what Dana had said was true, that pot made you sleep better, because the rocks beneath my thin sleeping mat were uncomfortable.

I rolled over so my face was inches from Roxanne's, my stomach dropping lower with every constricted wheeze that came from her mouth. I tried to keep my eyes open and focused on her, but the blinks became longer and longer until I eventually gave in. Right as I was drifting off, Roxanne whispered, "This has been the best night of my life, stink face."

I knew that must be quite a compliment because Roxanne had always existed in a way I could only dream of. It warmed me from the inside—taking away the chill I'd had from swimming as I drifted to the land of nod.

- 19 -

I BLINKED, MY eyes crusty, as the morning sun coming through the tent cast a blueish hue over everything, giving the skin of my hand an oxygen-deprived appearance. I'd been having a crazy dream about Tanya drowning in the ocean—twisted up in the tent, cut tulips floating around her—and felt the need to try calling before we disappeared into the forest for the day. Obviously, my efforts to not worry about my daughter had not reached my unconscious brain. The necklace rash, the delay in the floral business, the mysterious appointment, the husband-hating. I rolled off my mat quietly and slipped out of the tent.

I walked a way down the beach while my phone powered up. I saw one bar, then the second one. I stopped moving and dialed, hoping to not lose signal.

"Hi sweetie. Is it too early?"

She chuckled. "I've been up for two hours."

"Um," I started, not knowing how to tell her I'd had a dream she drowned. "I had a bad dream about you last night, and I just wanted to make sure everything was okay."

A lone woman appeared at the north end of the beach, geared up for a hike. She stopped and turned toward the calm ocean and paused. I looked away from her, feeling that she wanted to be alone in her reverie.

The line went quiet. Then there was a sniffle. Tanya was crying. My stomach dropped. "What's wrong?"

More silence followed and my heart tumbled around my chest with fear. "Please tell me what's wrong," I begged.

"Mom. I'm pregnant."

I stopped breathing. *The rash.* I should have known. Tanya always had always reacted to fake gold, but worse when she was pregnant. "Did that little shit get you that cross necklace because of this?"

She let out a long breath. "Yes."

"Oh, Tanya." I saw the flower shop sail right out the garage door—the water-logged tulips behind it. She would never make this work now.

"Please don't tell anyone. No one knows. And I don't want anyone to know. Ever."

"Ever? But… you'll be showing soon."

"I'm getting an abortion."

I choked. "You—what?"

"I told Curtis that if he didn't get the vasectomy checked and I got pregnant, he would be staying home with this baby. He's refusing. And so am I."

"But…" A gruesome image of my brand-new grandchild being ripped from my hands and thrown in the trash flickered through my mind.

"Mom, please don't." The pain in her voice was thick. "I need you on my side. I've been thinking about this for two weeks."

Curtis silently stomping through the house the day I went to help Tanya set up the garage came back to me. "That's why he's so mad you're going ahead with the flower shop."

"Yes. Mom—" Her voice broke on a sob. "I can't have another one. You know how much trouble I had with both the girls. Before, during, and *after*."

Violent nausea, depression, hard labours, a preemie, massive bleeding, blood transfusion, infection—twice—more depression. My mind skirted those stressful months, trying not to focus on the times I truly thought I was going to lose my daughter—physically and mentally.

"I don't want another baby." Her voice was so choked with grief I barely understood her.

I remained silent. I really didn't know what to say.

"And if he thinks that I'll just change my mind because I'm a *mother at heart*, he has another thing coming. I'm a human at heart, and I'm putting myself first. This should never have happened. This is not my fault. This is on him."

"Oh, Tanya."

"The appointment is a week Tuesday. I would love to have someone with me and since only two people know and one is refusing to come, I could use your support, but I'll understand if you can't give it."

I thought about how many times I'd joked about only having kids to get grandkids and I suddenly understood that was the dumbest thing I'd ever uttered. Wanting my children to sacrifice themselves and their lives so I could have a little joy, a little redemption from all the hard work I'd put in, was beyond selfish. Could I really turn my back on my daughter because she wanted to abort my grandchild? Now even I was putting pressure on her to have what I wanted.

I had just told myself that I would support Tanya in any way possible for her own personal success. It wasn't up to me to say what that looked like. It was up to her. I couldn't force her to carry a pregnancy she didn't ask for any more than she could ask me to live a life that wasn't mine. "Yes, I'll be there."

The breath she let out was long and hard. "Thank you, Mom." She started crying in earnest. "You understand that I do feel terrible? I'm not stupid. I know what this means. I'm getting rid of my girls' sibling, my husband's chance at a son, your next grandchild. And yes,

I know I would love it once it arrived, but at what cost? When does the mother become more important than that child? Babies are not a gift. That's what we've been conditioned to believe, so that when you don't want it, the guilt is on you. Babies are work. We are animals reproducing. There are no miracles involved. We need to take God out of this."

Her words were so sure. I fought back the urge to jump in and offer to babysit. *That's not what Tanya wants.* I reminded myself over and over. Stan would be beyond livid. "I'll be there," I whispered again, sealing myself as the family secret-keeper.

Whether I wanted to be or not.

DANA FOUND ME sitting on a long, curled piece of driftwood half an hour later. "Everything alright?" she asked as she joined me.

"Yes. No. I don't know." I threw up my hands.

She patted me on the knee. "I'm here to talk if you need." She sat for a moment longer, but when I didn't speak, she excused herself to get us packed up and moving.

As hard as I tried to see this from Tanya's perspective, I couldn't help but feel sad for what was being lost. Maybe if society didn't force women to choose between career and family, if raising children became a more integrated, community-based thing, it would be more feasible. Tanya could run a home-based business with a baby strapped to her, but she would come up against every difficulty possible, because the world still conspired against us at every turn. And I knew eventually she would be forced to give her dream up for the benefit of the family. I cursed Curtis for being such a selfish asshole.

I turned Tanya's words over and over in my mind. I hated that this was a decision being forced upon my daughter, but as I recalled what she said, it became clearer and clearer that the simple truth was, Tanya did not want another baby. That's exactly what she had said.

I don't want another baby. I fought against myself and the trap women fell into when it came to having children. Men were allowed to walk away from this situation every second of every day around the world—they were allowed to abandon a child they didn't want with not much more than a disapproving head shake from society.

But women? Women in the same situation were suddenly shunted to the lowest, most deplorable level of humanity. Because it's against our true nature? I shook my head.

A tiny part of me envied Tanya for being able to do this. I had not wanted my third baby, but there had been no other option.

Then I wouldn't have Jonathan. And on days like today, that seemed like a nice outcome.

I gasped at my own hateful thought.

Why was it all so goddamned complicated? I rose and slipped my phone into my pocket and walked over to Dana, my steps heavy. This was a bad way to start what was supposed to be a beautiful day.

DANA HAD US fed, packed, and ready to go by nine. "It's important to pace ourselves today." She clipped the top of her backpack. "The portion of the trail from Chin beach to Bear beach is rigorous."

I needed to turn myself around for Roxanne's sake. *Fake it 'till you make it.* I reached overhead, then swan dived, pretending I was able to get within a foot of touching my toes. Flexibility had never been my strong suit. "I feel great," I said to Roxanne, twisting this way and that to test out my guts, surprised there were no ill effects from last night's indulgences.

"Nope. No hangover with pot, that's part of the appeal." Roxanne hoisted her backpack on and followed Dana away from our campsite.

The air matched my mood, the morning ocean mist hanging low over the beach as we walked along, giving it a gloomy, isolated feel.

I shivered and zipped my coat up. Soon, the sun would be up and the fog would burn off. As we picked our way along the beach, my thoughts on Tanya transformed, as well. I wanted what was best for her, regardless of what *anyone* else lost. Settling into this realization helped lift my mood.

After twenty minutes, we veered off into the forest. Puffing up a steep incline, I thanked myself for not being a smoker. Slippery stairs covered in vines and moss appeared ahead of us.

"Be careful here, ladies!" Dana called back as she started up. Head down, I powered through until I'd reached the top, then turned back to see where Roxanne and Monique were. They had stopped mid-climb, Monique leaning over Roxanne.

"Are you okay?" I called back down, taking an automatic step toward them.

"Yup," Monique said, bending over Roxanne. "She just lost her breath. We'll be right up."

I watched them for a moment longer, but finally, the two made it up, Roxanne looking worn. I stayed back with her, going slow until she could find her groove again. We came to another steep ascent, and Roxanne stopped, hands on knees, appraising it through wary eyes, sweat shining on her forehead. "I don't know if I can do it. Maybe I'll stay here for the night." She laughed roughly, ending in a choking cough.

A tingle raced down my arms, my hands suddenly overheating. I knew we shouldn't have done this. "Dana!" I called, waving. "Roxanne needs a break."

I was shocked at how fast Dana turned and jogged back to us. She bent down and looked into Roxanne's eyes. "You okay?"

Roxanne nodded. "Just winded. I'll make it."

Dana frowned at her, but sat down along the edge of the path, pulling a bottle of electrolytes out of her bag and making Roxanne drink it.

Something moved to my left and I flinched. I looked harder, but only saw shadows. I turned back to Roxanne, unable to take my eyes off her—waiting for a wince or a grimace that would tell me the truth about her condition.

"Stop staring at me, wanker!" Roxanne barked, giving me the evil eye.

"Well, stop worrying me!" I shot back.

Roxanne popped up, swaying slightly. "There's nothing to worry about. Let's finish this mutha'." She focused on the top of the hill, steely determination in her eyes.

"You go first, Willie. I'll bring up the rear," Dana instructed, waving Monique and I forward.

Monique pulled my arm. "Let's go."

I dug deep and plowed up the hill, my thighs burning and chest heaving by the time I got to the top. Maybe I had bitten off more than I could chew. Maybe hiking the trail at sixty-three was a dumb idea. Panting and watching Dana help Roxanne up the hill, I gradually regained my normal pulse. Dana literally pulled Roxanne up the last couple of steps, where she fell to the forest floor, her chest rising and falling rapidly and shallowly.

"Roxanne!" I fell to the ground just in time to see my best friends' eyes roll into the back of her head.

"WATCH OUT!" DANA barked, shoving me aside. In one swift move, her pack was on the ground, and she had pulled out a small silver tank. Wildly, I thought for a moment Dana was going to give Roxanne the propane from the little stove. Dana hooked a plastic tube around Roxanne's ears and the cannula into her nose, turning the tank on. "You'll be okay. We'll get some oxygen into you, and it'll be alright," Dana soothed, pulling a strand of damp hair off her face.

"How come you have an oxygen tank?" I asked, a strong wind stirring the treetops above our heads. A raven took flight, cawing loudly as it went.

"I used to be an EMT," she said, not taking her eyes off Roxanne. "We're going to have to get you out of here.".

Roxanne pushed Dana's hand away. "I'll be fine," she rasped.

"No. You won't, and you know it."

I took in all of Roxanne in this moment—her pale face, her sunken eyes, her thin body, her rising and falling chest. This was the look of an extremely sick person. My eyes roved over her from top to bottom, again and again, desperate to find evidence that it wasn't as bad as it looked. I came up empty. My nose started running, tears coming to my eyes. I sniffed, finally settling on her face, searching those blue eyes for hope.

Everything fell away but the two of us. The trees stopped rustling; the birds went silent. Roxanne's chest lifted raggedly and shuddered its way down—my best friends' glassy eyes beseeching, silently apologizing. *Get her head up.* Lying flat must be bad for her lungs. I crawled to her head and crossed my legs, gently gabbing her armpits and pulling her onto my lap. Monique ran up the path, holding her cell up for signal. Straining my neck, I dropped my forehead onto the top of Roxanne's head and breathed as deeply and evenly as I could in hopes that her body would mimic mine as babies did to their mothers, my silent tears dripping into her hair.

My mind raced away from the truth I had suspected for days. The steroids, the painkillers. All the coughing fits. Years of smoking. There was only one thing she had, and it wasn't emphysema.

"Why didn't you tell me?" A tear plopped on her grey shirt.

"Because… I didn't want you… looking at me that way," she wheezed and closed her eyes.

- 20 -

LUNG CANCER. THE words stung every time I thought them. Monique had been able to get through to search and rescue, and they carried Roxanne out on a stretcher. Thankfully, we had been close to the access point at Port Renfrew. The rest of us had been shuttled back to Dana's car. Now we were sitting in the hospital in Victoria, waiting for a doctor to come talk to us.

My face and neck burned, my armpits drenched as I yanked off my coat and undid the top button of my polo shirt. I held back the anger I wanted to hurl at Dana and Monique for not telling me the truth earlier, but they insisted Roxanne made them promise and it wasn't their news to share. I refocused and internally raged at Stan from keeping me away from my best friend for so long. I could have had years with her before this happened. He literally stole that from me. From us.

Someone cleared their throat, and everyone looked up. The doctor took her glasses off, perching them on her braided hair, and came to sit next to Dana. "Hello. I can't say I'm surprised to see you back here. But I am surprised it's been almost a year. She's one tough cookie!" She reached out to shake my hand. "Hello, I'm Doctor Carver, but just call me Elise. You must be Willie. Roxanne's desperate to see you." Elise smiled grimly, deepening the parentheses on either side of her mouth.

"First, how does it look?" Dana asked, her normally composed voice faltering.

"Well, she's already six months past the six months I originally gave her, so on that front, pretty good." She pressed her lips into a line and frowned, pausing before speaking again. "But I'll be honest. When I see people holding out for something—or someone…" She paused briefly and glanced at me. "Once they've succeeded in their mission, they tend to go down downhill quickly."

I inhaled sharply. Hearing the actual words struck right down into the marrow of my bones.

"Let's just say, I would make the most of the time you have left together." She rose and smiled again. "In true Roxanne fashion, she's still declining treatment. I can't do anything about that—she knows her own mind and has consent on how this will go. I am going to send her home with oxygen and some pretty good pain meds. You'll be bringing her back soon enough, I suspect." She handed Dana a card. "Here's my cell. Please call or text if you're bringing her back."

Dana shook Elise's hand. "Thank you so much, Elise." The doctor nodded and left the room.

"Go to her," Dana nudged me.

"Shouldn't you go first?" I was baffled. "You've taken care of her all this time. It should be you."

"Maybe it *should* be me, but I think it *needs* to be you. I'm not going anywhere. Go." Dana waved toward the door.

I seized Dana, mumbling into her neck. "You have more grace in your pinky finger than I have in my whole body. Thank you."

"I think you need to get to know yourself a little better, Willie."

I STOOD OUTSIDE the door of Roxanne's room, twisting my hands, running through what I should say to her. This was not the time to be at a loss for words. I took a deep breath and then another. Setting my shoulders back, I pushed the door open and walked in, my heart instantly breaking.

Roxanne lay in bed, her body a small mound in the middle of a pile of white blankets. She looked so small as a huge pillow embraced her bald head. Still, she had the loveliest face.

"You're so beautiful." I sighed.

She smiled weakly as I sat on the edge of the bed. "Why didn't you tell me a year ago?" I asked. "It would have been a good excuse to finally make that trip out." Maybe then I would have found my voice, asked for what I wanted and not been forced into the situation that actually brought me here.

She shrugged. "It just… never seemed like the right time. And I'll be honest, I thought I was invincible."

"Now, I'm going to have to stay here forever, or until—" I clamped my mouth shut.

"No, you're not. You have to show back up in your own life. Plus, I promised my dad I would come home when I got really bad."

I let out a long breath, partially relieved that I didn't have to choose between taking care of my best friend and supporting Tanya. But Roxanne knew that. She knew it would tear me apart to have to decide, so she did it for me. "I'll cherish this time for the rest of my life. You'll never know how much you've helped me." I moved a strand of hair off her face.

"You've helped me too. I've been searching for years for the person I'd been when I was twenty, but I know now you can never really go back."

A smile grew on my lips. "But we sure had a lot of fun trying."

"Damn straight we did."

"I love you, Roxanne Hopkins."

"I love you too, Willie Bennet."

I shook my head. "Oh, yeah, I forgot about the last name thing."

"That's my dying wish, for you to change it."

"Please don't say that."

We sat silently for a minute, our eyes avoiding making full contact. Finally, I asked, "What do you need from me?"

Roxanne sat up and moved her legs to the edge of the bed. "To get me out of here."

I shook my head slowly. "That's a really dumb idea."

"Remember, we don't tell each other that what we truly want is dumb."

"Right."

"And… I'd like you to adopt Bo. He loves you and needs a good home."

I laughed. What a strange twist—coming home with a ferret. The grandkids would be delighted. "That, I can do."

I ENTERED THE waiting room an hour later, pushing Roxanne in a wheelchair. Dana's head dropped onto Monique's shoulder; her eyes squeezed tight against the tears. Monique watched us with a look of mixed irritation and resignation. I stopped to make sure the oxygen tank was secured to its little cart before we headed outside, into the unknown.

Monique and Dana loaded Roxanne into the car and my head swam. *This is too much.* "I need a minute." The sun was too bright, the air too devoid of oxygen. My hand shot out to the car to steady myself.

Dana tipped her head at me. "Of course."

I moved over to a bench before I fell over. My blood pressure hadn't bothered me at all since coming out here. I closed my eyes and focused on breathing. It took a long time for the feeling to pass. My phone vibrated and I squeezed my eyes even tighter. *Ignore it,* I coached myself. But what if it was Tanya or Annette? I pulled it out and gaped at the message from Jonathan that was obviously meant for Annette: *I was joking about moving mom into a nursing home, you stupid cunt, but thanks for making her probably hate me now. Your meddling work is never done, hey?*

I clenched my teeth. *I'll kill him.*

- 21 -

THE VIBRATION STARTED at the end of my toes—like someone was tickling them with a jackhammer. As I gripped my phone, reading the word over and over again, the tremor moved up and through my entire body, pure hot rage blurring the message.

He called his wife a cunt.

A maniacal cackle bubbled up my throat.

The memory of Stan dying swam back to mind, the way my back was pressed to the wall while watching him. *Cunt*, he had spat at me as the life left him, the word riding out on his last breath. He'd had his final, honest say. It hadn't been the first time I'd heard him call a woman that, but it had been the first time he'd directed it at me. And if I'd been honest with myself, I'd known that was what he truly thought about women as a whole. Every time he'd said it, he was really saying it to me as well. Stanley Alfred Copeland, King of the passive-aggressive criticisms designed solely to keep his wife in place. Calling other women fat cows, saying they were nagging bitches, stating with such venomous authority that women severely lacked brain cells, that their nattering voices gave him a headache. I'd always been so blindly proud that he wasn't saying these things to me—grateful that I was one of the good ones, the likeable ones, in his eyes.

I had been so wrong.

From a man's perspective, it made sense that they were getting more desperate. Surely, if I was born into a world that worked in my favour, I'd go to great lengths to hang on to my privilege. If I could loaf around and know I'd always be cleaned, fed, and jacked-off, surely I wouldn't change either.

I had conformed. Meanwhile, women like Vivian never had, and Annette and Tanya were hot on the heels of taking a stand. Stan knew I hadn't wanted a third child. But it didn't stop him from hounding me until I gave in, trying for the son he desperately craved, my vagina chaffing from his unwanted prodding. Stan got what he wanted in more ways than one. I knew now that his teary begging for that son was simply a production, a means to an end, that what he'd really wanted was to pull me back from the freedom I'd been inching toward as the girls got older and more independent.

I sat on the bench, shaking from head to toe. My daughter was in a no-win situation, my son was a pig, and my best friend was dying. What the fuck more could go wrong today?

I'll show you who's a cunt.

My toes curled, my thighs tightened, my stomach pulled in. By the time the tension got to my hands, I was ready to explode. I launched my new phone at the road and screamed—a wretched screech—causing every crow to lift from the nearby treetops in fright. The blue gadget bounced and rolled, coming to a stop a few feet behind Dana's car. Roxanne, Dana, and Monique turned to me from inside the car with wide eyes. I jumped up, my fingernails digging into my palms, chest heaving. I needed to do more, destroy something else. My eyes whipped back and forth, landing on a nearby garbage can. I pulled the aluminum can out of the wooden holder, lifted it back and swung it with all my might, throwing it as far and as hard as I could. The air rang with metallic clattering as it rolled down the sidewalk to a slow halt.

Now everyone outside the hospital was staring at me as I stood puffing on the sidewalk, litter strewn around me. Dana jumped out of the driver's seat and rushed to my side. "Willie." She gripped both of my shoulders tightly, almost painfully, in an attempt to bring me back from the edge. "I'm here."

My nostrils flared as I took in her dark brown eyes. In the bright afternoon light, they had an amber hue. Slowly, my breathing returned to normal. I blinked, taking in the mess I'd created.

And started to cry.

ROXANNE WOULDN'T STOP going on about how *epic* my fit had been. After Dana had ushered me back to the car, she and Monique had cleaned up the garbage, restored the can back to its holder, and rescued my phone—which had a shattered screen but shockingly still worked. Tanya's news wasn't mine to share, but Jonathan's misconduct was. As I told them about the text, the murderous rage I'd felt toward my son fizzled. Thank God.

But the feeling that was left in its place—a solid, hot lump so far beyond disappointment I didn't know what it was—settled into my stomach, making me ill.

I watched the trees fly by as we made our way back to Tofino. My tantrum seemed to have momentarily revived Roxanne. Her cheeks were bright pink, and her grip was strong as she clasped my hand in the backseat, telling me once again how the can had sailed majestically through the air, dropping used napkins and banana peels as it went. According to Roxanne, it was, "Literally, the best thing I've ever seen."

I tried to get behind her enthusiasm—see what she saw in the fit—a woman at the end of her rope, not giving a flying fuck about letting her emotions boil over in public. But she didn't seem to get it. *My own son.* Who also had a son.

We were dealing with generation after generation of men who

thought exactly the same. Things were never going to change.

I FELL INTO bed and didn't get out for two days. Time passed in a dull blur—a real-life vacuum. I could not let myself feel everything that was boiling inside me because I didn't know if I could survive such strong emotions. I knew this was the worst possible way to express my love for Roxanne—to crumble when the going got tough—but I could not muster the energy to move, let alone cook and clean for her.

Roxanne is dying and my son is a dick and my daughter's getting an abortion. The thoughts played on a loop, hour after hour. I had a nagging feeling at the back of my mind that I tried with all my strength to hold back: *This is what I get for not calling 9-1-1.* Karma or whatever you want to call it—this was what I deserved.

Every once in a while, my phone would buzz, but I continued to ignore it. Even the thought that something could be wrong with one of the grandkids didn't alarm me enough to make me check. I felt dead inside. My stomach hurt. My pulse swung from racing to almost non-existent. I started to wonder if, after surviving everything, this would be the end of me.

After nudging me a dozen times, even Bo gave up trying to rouse me and just curled up at my feet, joining me in a vegetative state.

Dana and Monique popped in repeatedly, checking on me and making sure Roxanne was cared for, once leaving soup and sandwiches by my bed only to have to remove them on their next visit. My body went into such a torpor, it didn't even want to poop, which left me feeling plugged and nauseous. Dana stopped by the evening of the second night and gently informed me that Roxanne's dad was coming to pack the apartment and take his daughter back to Vernon on Wednesday. Barry was almost ninety, but Dana assured me that he was in incredible shape and still drove daily and that he would be a good caretaker. I sobbed at the thought of a parent seeing their child to the grave.

"That's only a couple days," I whispered, sniffing hard, my voice gravelly from lack of use.

"Yes." Dana handed me a wad of tissues.

"What am I going to do?" I looked at her, more tears forming in my already soggy eyes. *I can't go home. I can't stay here. Maybe I'll book myself a one-way flight to Mexico.*

"You have to take all that you're feeling and act. And speak. Just plowing through life *hoping* things will get better is a sure-fire way for them to continue as they always have."

I dragged the tissues across my face. "I'm… I'm angry. Very angry." The words ironically lacked the emotion they were meant to convey. They felt flat, toneless. Maybe if I confessed the other third of my pain to Dana, that my son-in-law was a selfish prick who put my daughter in an impossible situation, heat would tinge the lifeless words.

Dana smiled. "The world doesn't like angry women. They're scary."

Scary. I thought back to the times we'd shot the men from the balcony and the way a few of them had skittered along, casting nervous glances over their shoulders. How for a second, Black Beard looked like he was going to wet himself as I pressed the blade to his neck. I had enjoyed giving them an ounce of their own medicine in those moments. "You know what I would like, Dana?"

"What?"

"I would like someone to fear me. Just once. I want them to finally see what we're fully capable of and I want it to scare them. Does that make me a monster?"

"Nope. That makes you fed up." Dana patted my hand and left me to work this out for myself.

- 22 -

I FINALLY ROSE the next morning, stiff and achy. The first thing I did was check on Roxanne, bringing her a cup of coffee doctored her way—all the sugar, none of the milk—choking back the realization that it would be one of the last times I did this.

I sat on the bed beside her, shocked all over again at how she seemed to have deflated so suddenly. And how I'd just lost two whole days with her. Now I was a shitty friend on top of being a failure as the mother of a son. My head swam. Things were happening too fast.

She propped herself on an elbow and took the drink, blowing on it and taking a tiny sip. "I was holding out, that's why. Just like Elise said."

"What?"

"The way you just looked at me. You were wondering how I'd gone downhill so quickly."

I dropped my head. I'd lost my ability to hide my emotions. It was a good and a bad thing. "Sorry."

"Don't ever be sorry."

"I know, but I have very limited time with you, and I just wasted two days moping in bed!" I threw my hands up.

"So? You needed it, obviously. You powered right through your husband dying. When were you ever going to take a moment and stop?" She watched me intensely.

I shrugged heavily, making the bed lift and dip. "I'm so mad," I blurted.

"You have every right to be."

"What am I supposed to do? With Jonathan? I can't just sit here and watch while he calls his wife the c-word." I'd read a frantic apology text from Jonathan earlier this morning, but I certainly didn't want to give him the forgiveness he was begging for. He'd sounded sincere, but this was not something that one could simply take back with even the most heartfelt words. It had created a deep gouge that was incapable of fully healing. I wondered if he had resent the original message to Annette or if seeing it sent to his mother had panicked him enough to just leave it. Maybe she didn't even know how nasty he really was.

"I can't tell you that, Willie-Millie. You have to ask yourself. You already know the answer, you just have to trust that." She grabbed my arm and squeezed, moving herself to the edge of the bed. "Help me up. We've got a lot to do today."

We spent the rest of the day packing. Roxanne ruthlessly directed me to put everything in bags and take it to the local Goodwill store. By five that evening I had made three trips—stopping once at the grocery store to buy all the chocolate. Roxanne proclaimed her last days were going to be fuelled by only her favourite foods. It was shocking how decisive she was with her belongings, but I guess when you know you have very little time left, you really only need a fresh pair of panties and a good book—the first being optional.

She arranged for the foster care of her animals to be over, the friend who stayed the other night coming to take the cats and dogs. I hid in my bedroom, holding Bo tightly to my chest while the young woman collected their things. Roxanne told a wild story about how she had opened the front door yesterday and Bo had dashed off into the night. *So uncharacteristic of him,* she'd proclaimed. There was such compelling sadness in her voice, I almost believed her. Now we just had to cross our fingers that paperwork wasn't required to fly a pet across the provincial border.

Dana and Monique stopped by, saying they would take care of the furniture and final walk-through of the apartment after we left. They really were the sweetest women I'd ever met.

By seven, Roxanne was exhausted. I tucked her back into bed and then returned to my room to pack. Once done, I paced the apartment for over an hour, a restless energy tingling through my legs every time I tried to sit down. *I hate them.* If it hadn't been for the confines of motherhood, the prison of marriage, I would have been out here years ago. Roxanne and I would have never been separated long enough to need a reunion. Stan had taken all of that from me. He had stolen everything I'd had at the beginning of our relationship—absorbed it for himself like Ursula from The Little Mermaid—while I withered. My confidence, my charm, my wit, my autonomy.

I tripped over the corner of the carpet in the living room, a pain shooting through my ankle. "For fuck's sake," I muttered, angrily pressing it back in place with my toe. It just curled back up again.

What I really wanted to do was take it out on someone. Passively watching my husband die hadn't been good enough. The rush I'd felt as I pressed the knife to Black Beard's throat returned to me. Maybe I could finish what I'd started. On a whim, I trotted to my room, grabbed a sweater, and returned to the kitchen to dig in Roxanne's purse for her car keys. My hand brushed something cold and hard. I smiled and slipped it into my pocket.

I PARKED THE car in the back corner of the parking lot facing the entrance of the pub and rolled the windows down. It was stupid to even put myself in this situation, but I was feeling reckless. Moods like this came and went over the past few days while I'd decayed in bed, where I oscillated wildly from rage to defeat, and less and less, to hope. But maybe Dana was right—hope was useless anyway, so there was no point in having it.

The sun had set, but the sky wasn't fully darkened yet and there was just enough orangish-blackness to cast a horror-movie hue over the scene. I pulled the knife out of the pocket of my cardigan. It had a beautiful cobalt handle that was almost pearly. I gripped it carefully, released the safety and, making sure my fingers were out of the way, pushed the silver button. The blade swung out with a satisfying click. The corner of my mouth twitched.

A streetlight came on, hissing as it warmed up. I twisted the blade, reflecting the light. Stan had a small collection of knives he took fishing. Several times over the years, I'd done this same thing, imagining what it would feel like to drive it into his soft belly. Or slice his saggy neck. Or even just hold it up in front of him and hiss, *Change, or else.*

But I wasn't a murderer. I was simply a woman who'd taken advantage of an opportunity that presented itself to her. Tell me that men hadn't been jumping on such luck all of their lives, believing they deserved everything that came to them?

I pressed the release bolster and used my other hand to gently press the blade back down. Then I held it out and opened it again. *Click*. A full grin spread across my face. I sat opening and closing the blade repeatedly until dark had fully descended and the door of the bar swung open and Black Beard tumbled out.

I knew he'd be here. I just had a feeling. My stomach rolled and bile rose up in my throat. What was I really going to do? Stab him? He was alone. And I'd already proven that I could be irresponsible when someone else's life was in my hands.

I pushed away all the alarms going off in my mind and body, got out of the car and strode toward him, knees shaking as I went. He was leaning against the wall, smoking.

My whole body thrummed with adrenaline. "Hey!" I shouted.

He glowered into the partial dark of the parking lot. His face blew up with delight when he realized who I was. "Come back for more, you ol' biddie?"

I swallowed. I knew I should just leave.

I took two steps forward and pressed the release. *Click*.

He dropped his cigarette on the ground and stepped on it. "You wanna play again?" He lunged for me, laughing and swiping at the air, but still several feet from me.

I shocked myself by not flinching but swinging back. His squeal was music to my ears as he clapped his hand across the slice in his forearm.

"You fucking—"

"Cunt. I know," I cut him off.

He took a silent step toward me. "You're going to regret that." His eyes bore into my chest as he licked his lips.

He's going to rape me. Suddenly, the courage that had brought me here drained out of me. "You should be scared of me," I said. My words lacked conviction. My rage had officially been replaced by fear. What the hell was I thinking? This guy had over half a foot and at least a hundred pounds on me. I took a step back.

He saw his opening. In one swift movement, I was on my back, head ringing from hitting the pavement, yet still somehow unable to believe that he had hit me. *They will always be able to physically overpower us.*

"Dude!" someone yelled from across the parking lot. "What the fuck are you doing?"

Black Beard looked at me quickly, his eyes flashing, telling me I got lucky, and then he disappeared into the night.

Someone rushed to my side. "Are you okay?"

The halo from the streetlight made it impossible to see his face clearly. I nodded and took his hand.

"Willie?"

My stomach dropped. I knew that voice. "Mark." My attempt to confront the enemy was foiled. And then I was rescued by another man? I dusted myself off, humiliated.

"Are you okay?" he repeated.

"Yes."

He bent down and pinched the knife between two fingers, carefully handing it back to me, an obscure look on his face. "Were you planning on being a little stabby tonight?" His attempt at lightheartedness did not mask the horror in his voice.

I suddenly saw myself in his eyes. A murderer. I'd gone full circle. "No," I lied.

He surveyed me silently for a second before finally saying, "He's not a good guy."

I nodded. But did he deserve death? That was not up to me to decide. I desperately needed the safety of Roxanne's house. I started walking back to my car, all the fight gone out of me. Instead of dealing with my real problem, I'd almost done something tragic. Instead of calling my son out, I'd almost taken someone's life. I didn't recognize myself.

"Do you… want to get a drink or a bite to eat?" Mark called after me.

I stopped, stunned. Even after what he'd just witnessed, he still wanted to be with me? My palm burned and I held it up to see it scraped and bleeding from the fall. I gingerly touched the small lump on the back of my head, thankful my fingertips came away with no blood. I could easily go home with Mark and find some more of those orgasms Fran had wanted so badly for me. But honestly, I didn't want to be ten feet from *any* man right now. I turned around to face him. "Thank you, but no."

He frowned, his lips turning down a bit. *Oh great,* I thought, *he's going to get all pissy at having been turned down.* I had to cut this off. "If you think I owe you anything for saving me, you've got another thing coming." My words were harsh. My eye twitched.

He held up his hands. "I didn't think that for a second. I just thought you looked like you could use someone to talk to."

I dropped my shoulders, turned, and got back in the car. Once inside, the tears started. *What's happened to me?* I used to know how to act like a proper lady. The old me would have practically fallen over this handsome man in gratitude for being saved. But in a way, it had almost pissed me off more.

I started the car, holding the key a second too long and causing the engine to grind, then pulled the shifter roughly into Drive and screeched out of the parking lot.

BARRY ARRIVED AT eight Wednesday morning. He looked just like I remembered—bald head, laughing blue eyes, hunched from years of being taller than everyone else. "Willie." He reached out and pulled me into a tight embrace, still on the threshold of the apartment. "It's so good to see you after all these years," he said into my hair. He smelled like a musty bachelor—cigarettes and processed meat, with aftershave to cover it all up. I liked him all the same.

"Barry." My voice broke and my shoulders bucked with a repressed sob. Seeing him had brought home the reality that this was it. That it was probably the last time I'd see my best friend.

He pulled back from me and took me in with bright, clear eyes. "Thank you for making this trip. It was all Roxanne wanted. Her final wish." He was prepared for this. I didn't know how it was possible, I couldn't even think of caring for a dying child—even after his beastly actions, losing Jonathan would still break my heart—but here Barry was, as stoic as ever.

"Please don't talk like that." I hated this sad truth, but also, a warmth bloomed in my chest to know that seeing me was someone's dying wish. I *was* special.

I made Roxanne's old favourite for supper. But as she picked at the lasagne, I could see the end was near and it was truly time for her to go home. She had gone downhill so quickly and as I nibbled my food—unable to look at her—a fat tear fell to my plate and leached into a noodle. Who needed to add salt when grief could season their food? I almost cry-laughed at the thought and wished I could tell Roxanne so we could laugh about it like the idiots we used to be only days ago.

Barry slept at Dana and Monique's, as they had a spare room. He and Roxanne were leaving first thing in the morning, and my flight home was scheduled for six the following evening.

At some point in the night, I was awakened by Roxanne having a coughing fit. I bolted upright, heart hammering, silently begging for it to stop. After several minutes, she was still going, so I crept into her room, slipped into her bed and curled myself around her. Her wheezing alarmed me. "Do you want me to get your oxygen?" I asked gently, wrapping my arm around her and pulling the blankets over both of us. Roxanne had always been bigger than me, but tonight, she felt diminished in my arms.

"No," she said, her voice a low whistle. She groped and found my hand on her stomach and clenched it, her fingers reflexively tightening with every deep hack.

I flinched and swallowed. I couldn't do this. I wasn't strong enough to lie here and listen to her die. I wanted to pull away, save myself the pain of this, but as Roxanne barked and coughed, I found my steel and pulled her as close to me as I could. Chest to back, I willed her pain to leach from her and into me. I could carry it. I was strong.

When she had settled down, I whispered over her bristly head, "I'm sorry I've been kind of out of it the past couple days. It's just finding out you're dying and then getting that text from Jonathan has really messed with my brain." *And Tanya.*

"That's alright. You're here now. Just give me tonight." I felt her body relax and sink into the mattress. She must be so tired.

I held her tight, willing my breathing to regulate hers like I had in the forest only days ago. Eventually she fell into a rhythm that eased my mind. Right before I drifted off, I said, "I love you so much. I'm sorry we didn't have more time together."

She didn't respond, but I felt her chest hitch slightly.

- 23 -

DANA CONVINCED ME to visit our favourite beach one more time before I left. I tried to refuse, knowing how hard it would be, but Dana would not stop bothering me until I gave in. After all she had done for me, I owed it to her to comply.

Roxanne and Barry had left early this morning in a flurry of tears and good-byes. As I held Roxanne, I felt like I was going to choke and had to leave Dana and Monique to finish up the parting words. It was so weak of me.

I wiggled around on our favourite piece of driftwood, Dana on my right side. I could not get comfortable. The same log I had sat on nearly every day for the past two weeks was now poking my behind. My lower back sagged with exhaustion. I shifted and squirmed, already feeling lost without Roxanne beside me. I had loved who I had become in the short time I'd been out here. There was no way I was going to be able to live the same without Roxanne—my bravado was already weakening, cracking, disintegrating, and she was barely gone. The bravery I'd developed since I came here was because of Roxanne, Dana, Monique, and the Island. Back home, I would be immersed in the old ways, and everyone would expect what they'd always expected of me, and I'd let it happen, like I always had. Stan being dead and me quitting my job were only tiny drops in the ocean of battle women still faced. I was not strong enough to stand up to *the man* by myself—every day, all day. One little woman could not take on a world that despised her. I didn't have it in me. Look what had just happened last night with Black Beard.

I could stay. I'd already ran from my problems; would it really be a stretch to stay hidden from them? I could take over Roxanne's apartment—Bo my companion—and continue where she'd left off. Walking the beach every day. Calling Mark when I felt the urge. Going on adventures with Dana when I pleased. Eating every delicious thing Monique prepared for me. I could picture it, feel it, practically taste it. Living moment to moment, day to day. With no one to worry about, no one to fight with. An easy life finally attained.

I settled into the idea, silently watching the waves, the dark grey sky, the air heavy between Dana and I. She picked up a beautiful pink and grey stones and turned them over in her hand. "There are many ways to nurture." Her voice sounded distant, as if she was talking to me while fading into the background. My fingers twitched. I didn't want her wisdom right now. I just wanted to linger in my new decision. I'd cancel my flight and never leave.

I swallowed hard. "What do you mean?"

Dana let out a long breath through her nose. "Kids aren't the only thing women are meant to care for. I nurture a lot of other things. Cats. The environment. *Other women.*" She smiled at me. "And I do it because I want to."

Women also needing nurturing was a new concept to me. We gave, the world took. "Yes, you do," I said absently, watching an insect scurrying across the sand, searching for a hiding place. Dana was so much stronger than me. I must be such a disappointment to women like her. A low rumble sounded over the water, a light mist reaching from a cloud down to the ocean. A few people on the beach started making their way back to their vehicles. I knew we should get going, but I couldn't take my eyes off the approaching storm, marvelling at the speed with which it moved. It appeared that the beautiful weather I'd experienced while out here had run out. The storm rolled and tumbled its way toward us with growing intensity, absorbing the horizon as it moved.

"You're not seeing it, are you? What I'm trying to say."

My brows furrowed as I watched the sky, trying to convey disinterest in her prodding.

"You're a nurturer too, Willie. But it's always been demanded of you. If you can set your boundaries and dictate what you give, then when you do give it's a joy, not a burden. It'll come from your heart and leave you fuller than before. When it comes from expectation, it leaves you drained."

I'd heard this before. I couldn't put my finger on it, but in the pit of my stomach, there was a truth that if I were to acknowledge would leave me with no more excuses. And that was the opposite of what I wanted right now. It would be so much more peaceful to just turtle and roll through the rest of my life. I recalled how completely exhausted I'd been the night I let Stan go. Drained was not an adequate word. There probably wasn't a word in the English language that could express how I'd felt that night.

I refused to go back to that.

"We're going to get walloped," Dana said, getting up and stretching.

"Good." I never took my eyes of the murky squall. Let's see what I was made of.

She touched my shoulder. "I'll wait for you in the car."

The rain hit like a thousand hammers, not bothering to start with delicate drops, but huge pelting discs. I hunched over, letting the sky dump its wrath on me, soaked within a minute. Looking up slightly, I could barely make out the pebbles at my feet, the grey dimness was so enveloping. Beside the slapping of the drops, it was strangely pleasant inside the storm, as if nothing mattered except surviving it.

For a few blissful minutes, I forgot my heart was a shattered ruin and I had run out of energy to fight.

It was over as abruptly as it started, the mist lifting, leaving a drenched beach—and human—in its wake, on to deluge the forest. *I survived the storm.* I thought I'd let Stan go so I could be myself. And what did that look like? I knew the answer in the pit of my stomach, but it would be the hardest thing I'd ever faced in my life. I lifted my head higher, the waves settling back down.

An eerie calm descended over the beach. The ocean had flattened, and the birds had moved on. I was alone. The couple that had left before it rained had not drifted back. The family with little kids running to and fro screaming as the chilly waves licked their toes had not reappeared. For the entire stretch of water and sand, I was truly alone. I was surprised by how terrible it felt. It dawned on me how lonely I would be out here, regardless of how many friends I made, how many lovers I took, how many facetime bedtime stories I read. There would still be no kids popping by to say hi, no grandkids baking by my side, no Mom's hand to hold.

After what seemed like an hour, I heaved myself up and made my way back to the car, Dana ever-so-patiently waiting for me, heat cranked up. I winced in apology for my soggy condition. "I guess it's time to go home," I said, my heart not fully committed to the statement.

"I suspect it is."

I HAD A couple quick errands to run before I left the island. I walked in full daylight to the graffiti on the fence that had been turned into *women only want to fuck men over*. I shook the spray can muttering, "You are so stupid." Everything women did was turned back on us, making us the bad ones. If only they would stop and just listen to what we were trying to say. There was plenty of room on the fence to add what I wanted. I thought of the *Jeopardy!* category

"What women want" as I wrote. My answers then had been mostly superficial. *For men to stop telling us to smile, to let our hair go grey, a bed to ourselves, to eat chocolate ice cream without thinking about our waistlines, to be able to go out at night without fearing rape, male birth control.* But I knew now there were deeper, yet simpler answers. Something they could maybe wrap their puny minds around.

The can hissed as I frantically wrote, the spray turning my hand black. I welcomed the evidence of my wrongdoings. *Go ahead. Take me to jail.* I was ready to stand up for what I believed in, regardless of the price.

A car slowed behind me and I glared at the driver, daring them to stop and confront me. But when it came to a halt near the curb and Max jumped out, I smiled.

She came to stand next to me, hands on her hips. *"Trust us. Value us. Hear us. Respect us. Honour us,"* she read, then reached out and motioned for the can. "May I?"

We stood back and admired her addition. *Empower us.* Another car passed and we didn't even bother to look.

I don't know how long we stood there staring at the mural, but at some point, this stranger reached over and took my hand in hers, which I grasped right back without thought, a silent determination and strength passing through the connection.

AT THE AIRPORT, Monique hugged me and then Dana, little Bo squished between us. They stood side by side facing me on the sidewalk, Dana rattling on about how much she was going to miss me. Monique watched me quietly. I appreciated her ability to sit back and observe, only speaking when she had something monumental to say.

"You've got to say something about the text, Willie. You can't let it go by silently." Dana beamed at me, the sun brightening her face. "Speak now or forever hold your truth, because there might be no coming back from this one. Are you going to stand letting any man call a woman a cunt, let alone your own son? If you let Jonathan get away with this, it'll fester inside of you. It will fuel your resentment and hate. Don't you want to have an active hand in letting that go?"

"If anything, you should hold him to a higher standard *because* he is your son." Monique added, touching my arm gently, leaning forward. "You need to show them how to treat you. Maya Angelou was a smart lady. It'll be hard for him, but if there's love, he'll come around."

We parted with the promise to stay in touch, everyone agreeing not to mention that it would be sooner rather than later at Roxanne's funeral.

Bo and I got through security easily. An old lady on the verge of tears over the abandoned pet she had rescued for her grandkids did the trick. I put him in the little carrier with a kiss and took a seat near my gate and waited.

As I waited for them to call my flight, a twitch started in my toes and worked its way up to my knees and right up to my hips. The lady sitting next to me scowled at me before moving to another seat because my bouncing legs were shaking the whole line of seats. I felt on the edge of something. And I knew if I could see myself now, the gleam in my eyes would be chilling.

A brick upside the head was the only thing Jonathan would listen to. There was no other choice. It was all I had left. I took a deep breath and texted Annette: *I get home tonight. Can you come over for a coffee tomorrow? We need to talk.*

Her response was an immediate *Yes.*

- 24 -

I STOOD OUTSIDE my house, smiling at the Onyx shingles. They looked good. There was a small oil stain in the driveway where Jonathan's big diesel truck had lingered. He hadn't balked at my early return, which shocked me. He was holed up in the spare room at his house right now, pouting, while the women in his life decided his fate. I didn't have to wonder how he felt because I knew all too well.

The second the plane had landed, I knew I'd made the right decision by returning. Staying away would have been a punishment for me, not a reprieve. I had been cowardly long enough and was prepared to do whatever was necessary to ensure joy in my twilight years.

I stepped over the threshold of my house, the old utilitarian aluminum door slapping shut behind me, and set my suitcase and Bo's carrier down. I stood for a moment; my chest puffed out in appreciation of how far I'd come. *The hero returns.* I smiled at my cheesy thought but couldn't deny it held some truth. In so many ways, I was finally my own hero.

I closed my eyes and breathed in deeply—searching myself for a feeling I knew I should have—coming up empty. "I don't miss you." I breathed the words out and let the guilt go.

I opened my eyes. Stan's rotten old blue chair was still here, Walleye Wendy on the wall, shades of brown everywhere. Where had I been in all of this? Where were traces of Willie?

Probably in the kitchen.

I could leave, turn around and never come back. Find myself a new place, let Jon have this one, claiming I couldn't bear to be here anymore. I'd never have to feel the traces of Stan again.

But.

I *was* here too, all these years. I was just buried under him. Just like my sewing machine that was buried under his fishing stuff. So much of me lived in the walls of this house. It wasn't too late. I could still make this place mine. I owned it. I could strip it down and build it back up, like I had done for myself. And I'd start with a nice, new wooden screen door, like I'd always wanted.

I collected Bo out of his carrier. There wasn't much of a setup for him here, so I tried to replicate what Roxanne had so he would feel at home. I went to the kitchen, stopping only briefly to take in the beautiful bouquet of flowers on the kitchen table. A pink envelope leaned against the glass vase, and I knew immediately it was from Jonathan, but I ignored it for now and focused on getting my friend settled.

I dug around in the cupboard under the kitchen sink and found a grey plastic tray that sat there to catch plumbing drips, then went back to the living room and retrieved an old newspaper from Stan's table and layered the pan with shreds. I put Bo into it, and he peed immediately. "Good boy." I fetched him a bowl of water and poured some food I'd brought with me from Roxanne's before returning to the kitchen for a glass of water for myself.

I gently touched the edges of a vibrant purple flower on the table. I wished I knew the names of these things. I definitely did not inherit my mother's green thumb. I picked up the card. *So glad you're back, stocked the fridge, love Jon.* "It'll take more than flowers and milk to undo what you've done," I whispered.

I knew I needed to actually talk to him. This slinking around through text was chicken shit. I read the card again. He was trying to make amends. I should at least be decent enough to try back.

I downed the glass of water, peeled a banana, and dialed his number.

"Mom! Welcome back." His voice was full of nervous energy and the sound of it bolstered the fight in me. He should be concerned.

"Hello, Jon. How are things?"

"Good. How was your trip?" His avoidance of my question annoyed me, but I gave him a few details before plowing into the bad news about Roxanne. "Oh, I'm so sorry. Mom. I know she's been a good friend for so long. Whatever you need, I'm here."

I smirked a little. He was trying *so* hard. There was a pause in the conversation before he finally said. "Mom?"

"Yes?"

"Look, about the text. I know you're upset with me and… I'm not too proud of myself, either. But I was mad she told you about the nursing home idea, and I just said something I shouldn't have."

"Yes, you did. She didn't do anything wrong by telling me. It was the truth."

"I know. Can you please forgive me?"

I scoffed. "Of course I forgive you, Jon. I don't hold grudges, and you're my son, I love you." I walked into the living room and could imagine Jonathan sitting in a chair just like Stan's—a throne of laziness—while Annette ran the house around him, listening to his stupid comments about her bringing her exhaustion on herself by giving in and doing his laundry years ago after a proclamation that she would never. I could let this go, taking his sincere apology to heart and give him another chance. But then what would everything I'd accomplished in the past few weeks mean? Where would letting Stan go really have gotten me? Because I knew in my guts, I would always be on guard with Jon. A deep trust had been eroded and it would take more than a couple of nice words and a bunch of flowers to re-establish it. And what about Annette? She'd never be able to be truly independent with him hanging on. "But just remember that won't stop me from doing the right thing."

"Which is?" His voice cracked.

"You'll see."

BY THE TIME Annette arrived with Tim's at ten the next morning, I had been up for hours, packing Stan's stuff and shoving it back into his fishing room, rescuing my sewing machine at the same time and restoring it to a useful place in the living room. I could barely close the door to the room by the time I was done. The kids could deal with his shit eventually. I took all of his knickknacks, magazines, and DVDs from the living room, all of his clothes from our bedroom, every single thing in the basement that was his—old high school memorabilia, electrician textbooks and manuals, and a strange little collection of animal stickers I had no idea about. Every animal imaginable, but a special emphasis seemed to be on African animals—lions, giraffes, elephants. Maybe Stan once had dreams of travelling there. It saddened me a little to think he'd had such huge aspirations that he'd never discussed with me. Not that I made small talk easy for him. I probably tuned him out more than I'd ever realized. I wondered at the idea that I'd never had much interest in what men had to say either. The divide between the sexes may be deep, but if *both* sides—and all the representations in between—were willing to have open, meaningful conversations, things could be moved beyond the Adam and Eve wound.

But this was my house now, and later today I was going to the furniture and hardware stores and getting to work on my little redecoration project.

I was throwing the new collection of condiments Jonathan had accumulated in the short time he was here into the trash when Annette showed up.

"Wow. Your hair looks even better in person." Annette leaned in and gave me a one-armed hug. The coverup beneath her eyes was obvious. I wanted to reach out and smooth the streaks it had left. I noticed a couple of greys in her lovely brunette hair—just a few veining away from her temples.

I rubbed her arm. "Jonathan with the boys?"

"Miraculously. Only six more days of quarantine to go." She smiled weakly and settled on the couch.

We sipped our coffees for a few minutes before I set mine down. Bo jumped up and curled into her lap. "Oh! You're so sweet." She stroked his back while giving me a questioning look. I told her the whole story of how I'd become an adoptive mom to an overgrown weasel.

Finally, I took a deep breath. "Listen, Annette, I have something to tell you." I exhaled fully. My throat tightened and tears sprang to my eyes. I was about to ruin a family. And I didn't like it one bit. As I told her about the text, her face remained neutral.

Finally, she spoke. "It's not the first time, Willie."

"What?" I bleated.

"There's been a couple other instances he's called me that… and a few other not-so-nice names."

I jabbed myself in the chest. "*My* son?"

"Well, I'm sorry, Willie, but if a dick raises you, you're bound to look like one eventually." There was a touch of mirth in her wince.

I shook my head in confusion. Who was she talking about? "Stan?"

Annette nodded. "When I first started coming around, Jonathan seemed like the nicest guy, but my first taste of his father was… unpleasant. Do you remember the first time I came over to meet you guys?"

"Yes." Easter dinner, 2012. Jonathan had moaned about us not having his favourite kind of IPA beer and Annette had socked him—not some light tap to indicate he was being rude, but a closed fist drive to his upper arm that had him rubbing it with an aggrieved look on his face for several minutes after. I had immediately fallen in love with Annette. A third girl in the family who reminded me of myself when I was young and feisty.

"Well, I was alone in the kitchen with Stan, and he said to me, *Well, if you aren't a fine piece of meat.*"

My nostrils flared. "He did not."

"And then he said, *but those child-bearing hips tell the real story.*"

I was seething. To know that Stan had talked to his future daughter-in-law like that made me ecstatic that I'd just shoved all his shit into a room and locked the door. "Like, you were built to have kids?"

She nodded. "Don't be too mad. It's not like I—*we*—haven't heard all this shit a million times. I do have a lot of junk in my trunk and men seem to like it, even if they don't know why themselves." She tapped her hip. "Fertility reigns supreme."

Here I thought I was going to swoop in and save Annette with my grand plan, but she did not need saving. She just needed help. I thought of Dana talking about being a nurturer. I thought of Max and what she had written on the fence. *Empower us.* But I'd never looked further, into my own marriage, to find the answer. And here I was now, looking into my son's marriage. I couldn't believe Jonathan had called Annette names. It was beyond childish and petty. It made me wonder if he'd ever loved her. And did he love me? "Do you think they actually love us?"

Annette's green eyes were suddenly tearful. Her hands twisted in her lap as she contemplated her answer.

"No. How can you really love someone but be content to sit there and watch them work themselves to death without offering to help? There's nothing that says I love you about deliberately offloading housework onto us to free yourself for more time in front of the boob tube." Her eyes slid to Stan's chair. "I haven't told you, but I have to go for a biopsy on my breast. I found a lump a couple weeks ago. Jon knows about it, and he still pulled that shit about not being able to stay home with the kids and then moving out. I swear that man has *given* me cancer." A tear fell onto her lap, but she didn't bother to wipe her face.

"Annette," I choked, feeling guilty that he had wormed his way back into her house. I'd had three lumps biopsied over the years and Stan barely lifted an eyebrow, just joked about my lumpy tits. None of them resulted in a full mastectomy, just lumpectomies, but I was suddenly certain it had only been a matter of time. "You need to finalize the divorce. I know I'm his mother, but I also know how this is going to go for you if you stay with him. No more chances."

She leaned back on the couch and rubbed her forehead. "Yeah."

I suddenly wished I could put the two sides of my life together, just for a day or even a couple hours. Roxanne, Dana, and Monique with Annette, Vivian, and Tanya. *Oh, the noise we would make.* Men would *hate* that. A small smile spread across my face.

I WAS JUST boxing up the last of Stan's toiletries to throw in the trash when the doorbell rang. Opening it, I was surprised to see Bruce. He was clad in his work uniform—a green polo shirt and dark jeans–so I assumed he was on his way home from the University. "Oh, hello, dear. Come in." Bo immediately circled his feet.

"A ferret?" He put his hands on his hips, a smile playing at the corners of his mouth.

I cringed, waiting to be admonished for doing something so rash and stupid. "Yes."

He bent down and scooped him up. "I don't know why, but I always wanted one." Bruce nuzzled his face in Bo's fur. "The kids are going to die." He laughed.

Relief washed over me, and I turned to the kitchen. "Would you like a drink?"

"No, thanks. I just thought I'd pop in on my way home from

work and see if you need anything."

"Vivian sent you?"

"Nope. She was busy running Ainsley to the dentist, but I know she'd want to welcome you back, so I thought I'd do it for her." He lifted an eyebrow, a little proud of himself. That was alright, he deserved the recognition. He was the best man in my life right now.

"That's very sweet of you." This was what real love looked like. Doing what you saw needed to be done without being told. Anticipating what your wife needed and doing it before it was demanded of you to simply make her life easier. *Before she got cancer.*

"Actually, while you're here, I could use some help."

He set Bo back on the floor. "Whatever you need."

"Did you bring your truck?"

"Yup."

I looked back at Stan's chair—his favourite place in the house—and crossed my arms over my chest. "It's time for some change around here."

BEFORE TURNING IN for the night, I texted Tanya: *I'm home and ready to come with you Tuesday. Tell me when to pick you up.* I would not ask questions of her or her decisions. I would only support her.

Bo jumped on the bed and spun in a tight circle before settling on Stan's side. I laughed at the realization that I had replaced my husband with a furry rat. Bo lifted his sleek little head and gazed at me. I reached out and patted him and he closed his eyes, the most minuscule smile pulling at his pink mouth. Even this non-verbal animal could convey more appreciation for me than a human male.

My phone lit up: *Thank you, Mom. I don't want to do this alone, so you don't know how much this means to me. 9 am works.*

Satisfaction spread across my chest as I turned off the light and settled into bed. I would not see another woman drown under the weight of unwanted motherhood ever again.

- 25 -

"TELL ME MORE about your island adventures." There was red lipstick on Fran's chin, so I reached over and rubbed it off with my thumb. She had been very upset when I told her about Roxanne. She had known her for as long as I had and was always happy to have her over when we were younger. "It's just not fair," she'd sighed, blowing her nose.

"Well, it might cheer you up to know that I found that orgasm you insisted I go looking for." My neck flushed, but I held my grin in place—I had nothing to be ashamed of. Before I left, I was mortified to talk about this with my own mother, but now it seemed to come up easily.

She leaned toward me, watery brown eyes glinting. "Tell me everything."

I laughed. "It was only a couple of times, but I have to say, you may be onto something." I tapped my finger on my chin in mock contemplation.

"Details," she sang.

I leaned back in my chair, both elbows on the armrest, hands clasped over my belly. I told her about how, immediately after finishing the mural with Max, I went straight to the whale watching centre looking for Mark. I had regretted not taking him up on his offer for a second sex-a-poloosa after he rescued me in the parking lot from that asshole. I'd apologized again for ditching him and then brushing him off, explaining that now I was in a rush to go back home. We were alone in his front office. "Well, I'm not going to miss my last chance," he'd breathed huskily. I'd leaned across the narrow counter and pulled his face toward me with both hands, kissing him, his stubble rough on my palms. I'd meant it to be a soft kiss, but it had immediately grown urgent. Within five minutes, Mark had locked the front door, turned the open sign around, and had me on the loveseat in his office.

Fran whistled. "I'm so proud of you, Wilhelmina. About the graffiti, too."

"I'm proud of me, too."

Fran looked at me intensely. "You know it wasn't ever about the actual sex, right? Why I wanted you to do this?"

I shook my head. "I know. It was about orgasms." I hadn't even muffled my moans as Mark's mouth expertly worked my clitoris into a frenzy. I literally couldn't remember ever being sexed like that—by anyone—but especially not by Stan.

"No. We can give ourselves orgasms." Fran waved her fingers in the air. "It was about tapping into that primal urge and going for it without thought. It was about trusting yourself to know what you want and seizing it. It was about learning to ignore all of the stupid things we've been fed over the years so we can turn the narrative around. *Old woman are gross, women who sleep around are sluts, sex is for procreating only, we don't deserve pleasure so raw and intense, it's immodest.* That bullshit spills over into all areas of our lives. All the things women are taught to hate about themselves, all the things we've been told are wrong for us to want, all the ways we've been taught to not trust ourselves." Her cheeks were rosy as she leaned back in her chair. "All the shame that keeps us from taking what we deserve—like men have been doing for eons."

My mother was *deep*. I nodded, watching a young man dressed in street clothes help an elderly woman from the kitchen. I seriously doubted Jonathan would do the same for me once I was here. The thought choked me up.

"And the real kicker is that women will still never take half of what men have taken all their lives. It's not in our natures."

"And that's bad." I nodded in agreement.

"No, it's not bad. In fact, that's what makes women, women. We know how to take what we need and leave some for others. Greed is a line I, personally, will never cross. Except with shortbread cookies. I'll take all of those."

I smiled at my mother, seeing her maybe for the first time as a true friend and ally. "I'm sorry you got to this place so late in life, Mom."

She waved me away. "It seems we're getting there a little earlier with every generation. Maybe you'll live to see your granddaughters stay the course right through until they're married and have their own kids."

Maybe I would. And if I helped their mothers as best I could, the chances were even higher.

A FEW DAYS later, as I was pushing my new gorgeous floral wing chair around the living room, trying to find the perfect spot, when my phone rang.

Annette. "Hello?" I chirped. Mags was coming to paint the day after tomorrow and the thought of a reinvigorated house had me on cloud nine. For the living room, I'd chosen a light sky blue that reminded me of the Island.

"Willie?" Her voice was tight, and my stomach dropped.

My breath caught in my chest. "No."

"I'm afraid yes. The biopsy came back as cancer. I'm scheduled for surgery in a week."

"So soon?" I fell onto my chair and wiped a bead of sweat off my forehead.

"They're being aggressive."

"That's good, I guess. Have you told Jonathan?"

"Yes." She scoffed. "And get this. He's still refusing to leave the house. I should have never let him back in."

That's on me for kicking him out. Bo jumped up on my lap and curled up. It suddenly occurred to me that Roxanne had never shown me Bo's ability to dance. Mr. Bo Jangles. A lump rose in my throat. Barry had called me yesterday and told me Roxanne had slipped into a coma and the end was in sight. A tear ran down my cheek. I was losing my best friend; I couldn't lose Annette too. She needed me. Now was the time to tell her my idea. "I don't want you to go through this alone. I'd like you to move in with me. And the kids of course. If we can't get Jon to move, then I think this will send the message that we won't take his crap anymore," I said, running my hand over Bo's soft fur.

Annette sobbed something. I was quite certain it was a heartfelt *thank you.*

- 26 -

HAVING ALL OF my girls in the same house for the day, even though it wasn't my house, and it wasn't for a good reason, almost brought me to tears. Tanya stood beside Jonathan and Annette's kitchen island with a placid look on her face, her eyes staring off into some faraway place that didn't involve the stress of what she was being forced to do. The abortion appointment was tomorrow, and a part of me wished she'd told Vivian as well so the three of us could go together. It was selfish of me, but I felt like I needed moral support too.

Annette and Mags emerged from the basement with a couple more empty suitcases, laughing about how easy it had been to lure Jonathan out of the house for the day. "Nothing like the promise of an afternoon away from his sick wife with eighteen holes of golf." Annette rolled her eyes.

It disgusted me how easy it had been to bribe Jonathan away so we could pack and move Annette and the kids without him knowing. "What time does Bruce need you home?" I asked Vivian.

She laughed as she folded clothes for Gabby and put them into a suitcase that was laying open on the couch. "Well, I'm assuming he'll call uncle around supper time. Five kids under five is almost more than even I could handle."

"He's a saint."

Vivian eyed me with her steely gaze. "No, he's not. He's a dad."

"You're right." It was going to take me a long time to unlearn everything that had been driven into me over the years. Men watching their children were not amazing. Got it.

"Let me help you pack your room," Tanya said to Annette, finally snapping out of it and moving to take one of the suitcases.

"Thank you." Annette disappeared down the hallway, Tanya following her.

I followed Mags to Connor's room. She was barely five feet, and I made a mental note to dig out the ladder from the garage for when she came to paint my house. She grabbed a packed suitcase and turned back to me. "I'm done with Connor's stuff. Whose car should I take it to?"

"Wherever you can find room, sweetie. We're all heading over to my place for pizza after we're done here."

I made one last sweep of Gabby's room, grabbing several of her favorite stuffies and jamming them into the duffle bag I was carrying. Laughter broke out in the master bedroom, and I smirked, knowing exactly what Annette and Tanya were laughing about.

"Mother!" Tanya called. "You are a scoundrel."

"Don't move it," I called back.

"What did you do?" Vivian appeared in the doorway of Gabby's room, drawing her words out suspiciously while gazing at me.

"Oh, nothing. Just gave your brother a new sleeping mate."

She pinched her lips into a smile and bolted from the room, desperate to see what I had done. She clapped her hands and squealed, "You put a *fish* in his bed!" She erupted in laughter.

I buttoned up the duffel bag and lugged it to the living room. Wendy Walleye had found a new home. I hoped Jonathan liked his wife's replacement. He was living his father's legacy, after all, so why not give him one of Stan's prized possessions?

THREE EMPTY PIZZA boxes and a couple of bottles of wine were the remnants of our celebration. We all sat back and sighed, content with the action we had taken today. When I'd found out that Jonathan refused to leave the house, I'd offered myself and my house to Annette. She had declined at first, saying my days of looking after kids were over and she wouldn't put that on me. I knew how much she wished her parents lived closer—Ontario was just too far away. But when I'd taken her by the hand and looked into her eyes, saying I *wanted* to do it, that it was about women supporting women, she had crumpled into my arms with relief at not having to do this alone. A few hours later, her mother called me in tears, thanking me for being there for her daughter when she couldn't.

It had been a bold move—choosing my daughter-in-law over my son—but I knew in my gut that it was the only way to show him how important it was to support women, particularly mothers, if you wanted a healthy family. It wasn't enough to *hope* that things were changing, and just talking about it wasn't enough, either. Action was required.

Yesterday, I'd asked Barry to hold the phone to Roxanne's ear so I could tell her my plans to upend Jonathan's life. Barry swore Roxanne's hand flinched as I spoke. I deeply hoped on some level she heard me. Before he hung up he told me something red and fast was about to show up on my doorstep as per Roxanne's request. I laughed long and hard, imagining myself ripping around on her bike.

Vivian lifted her head to speak. "My push for on-site childcare at the research centre has finally paid off." She lifted an eyebrow. "*And* they're actually paying the two childcare workers they hired what they're worth and it's not minimum wage."

Everyone nodded and murmured their approval as Annette saw Mags to the door. Vivian went to the washroom and, alone with Tanya, I saw a chance to ask her about her upcoming appointment. "Has Curtis come around?"

"He won't talk to me. All he does is stomp around the house and glare at me. I swear, that man wouldn't know how to have a constructive conversation if his life depended on it."

I glanced at the pictures on the mantle, which were some of the only things I hadn't touched in my Stan-free renovation. It was such a lovely collection of joy where Stan was allowed to persist. "So, he's for sure not coming?"

"He says he'll have no part in destroying a child."

"What does that mean for the future of your marriage?"

"I really don't know, Mom, but I can't believe it's good."

One death and two divorces. How had my life gone from whole to losing three men in a matter of weeks?

Tanya's brown eyes searched mine. "Mom, Annette told me what made you do this, inviting her to stay here."

"She did?"

"Yes. I'm disgusted with my brother." Her face darkened. "As much as I hate seeing this happen to my family, I think you did the right thing."

My eyes flicked to the mantel again. Maybe having only happy snapshots was the problem—that we only allowed the good aspects of life to be shown in public. These smiling faces didn't tell of Gabby's epic meltdown moments before the Christmas family photo. They didn't show the rage that had been simmering in me while I held a young Jonathan, knowing Stan had just told me it was stupid to consider going back to work while the kids were young. Maybe if we didn't cover all the bad stuff up, it wouldn't be such a disaster when it all came out.

Annette returned to her spot on the new burgundy couch and pulled a cream blanket over her legs. I sat quietly listening to the others talk, looking at the new ring on my finger. After I'd fished the old rock out from under the couch, I'd driven straight to the pawn shop. With the money, I'd bought a matching pair of silver bands with branches etched on them. In the store, I had laughed so hard at the memory of the snake stick attacking me that I wet myself a little.

The other band was on its way to Roxanne by courier. I let out a long sigh, hoping dearly she would get it before she passed and was able to understand the significance of it.

As happy as I was, I couldn't slough off the sense of doom settling over me, pushing out the bright victory of the day. It was a dark feeling, like I didn't know for sure if I had in fact done the right thing. It was easy to talk bravely in front of these women, but inside lurked the beast of doubt. I closed my eyes. *I'm so tired of second guessing myself.* How nice it would be to just decide shit and move forward? I had never seen Stan question himself. Even Bruce, who was a fantastic husband and father, never seemed unsure of anything. He even wore that ugly orange t-shirt with confidence, despite how it made his skin look sallow.

Something bad was going to happen before this was all over. I just knew it.

BRUCE SHOWED UP at seven with the kids. "Oh, you look exhausted." I chuckled, taking Mila from his arms. She snuggled into my neck, and I kissed the top of her still-bald head.

"I am." He set their other twin, Oscar, down, who ran to Vivian. Ainsley hugged my leg before going to her mom. "Okay, back to the car for the second load." Bruce returned a few minutes later with Connor and Gabby.

I escorted the two to their temporary bedroom with their mother. We'd taken the single mattresses and bedding from their house and put them right on the floor next the existing spare bed. It was a tight fit, but they didn't seem bothered as they both ran in and jumped on them. "This is only for a little while and soon you'll have your own bedroom, alright?" We had to clean out Stan's fishing room, and then that could become the kids' room so Annette could have her own space. This old ranch-style bungalow also had another spare room downstairs, but Connor was still too little to go down there by himself.

After a quick visit, Mila started yawning and resting her head on my shoulder. "That's our cue to go," Bruce said.

"Can we come back tomorrow to visit Bo, Gramma?" Ainsley asked.

"Of course you can, sweetie." It had taken him a minute to warm up, but Bo turned out to love the attention the kids gave him as long as they sat in a quiet circle and waited their turn to pet him as he made his rounds.

After Vivian and Bruce left, Tanya and I curled up on the couch, Annette joining us after tucking in the kids. I poured her the last of the wine.

I glanced at the clock and mused, "Jon should be home by now."

"Yeah." Annette swirled the red liquid in her glass before taking a sip.

Tanya lifted an eyebrow. "Think he'll come here?"

"I don't know. He'll either explode or pout. I'm really hoping for the pouting, because I don't have the energy to talk to him today." There was a hitch in Annette's deep sigh, and I knew she was nervous. I didn't blame her—I'd never had the taco to get this far from Stan. I smiled to myself, knowing Roxanne would be proud of my self-correction.

"They really just take every chance they can get to weaponize this shit against us, don't they?" Tanya shook her head. "Like, how hard is it just stop and listen and think instead of retaliating to defend your privilege?"

Annette sniffed. "I should have known."

"What do you mean?" I asked.

She looked at me with her glassy green eyes. "No offence, Willie, but there were warning signs in the beginning, when we first started dating, that I ignored."

I had a hand in this. The thought choked me up. "I'm sorry for how he was raised."

She waved a hand at me. "It's not your fault, it's the socialization into this bullshit that keeps being perpetuated. Literally, like a month after we started dating, he stopped taking care of his apartment. Dirty dishes would be piled up, piss on the floor of the bathroom. I think he knew my type A personality wouldn't be able to stand it, so I just cleaned here and there."

Tanya laughed. "Curtis tried that too, but I just refused to come over to his place anymore. And here I thought I had taught him something, but he was just biding his time, trying something new every once in a while to see if it would stick." Her eyes avoided mine. She would have to explain a breakdown to Annette if she let lose what she was holding in.

"Stan did the same thing." I thought back to that fateful night and the laundry comment. Had it all really started with the first time I threw one of his shirts in with my things? They knew how to survive as single men, but the second a woman came around, they unloaded anything and everything they could.

Annette leaned forward, elbows on knees. "I just kept ignoring the little things he stopped doing, telling myself it was minor. And then the kids were born. Did I ever tell you he went to McDonald's an hour after Connor was born, leaving me alone with him? Because he was *starving* from not eating for twelve hours. Like, I hadn't eaten for thirty-four hours! When he came back with the food and set a big mac beside me while I was fighting with Connor to latch, I threw it at him. The incomprehension on his face told me he truly didn't understand what he had done wrong."

"It's domestic abuse," Tanya blurted. Annette and I turned to stare at her.

"That's a bit of a stretch, no?" I asked.

"Well, we know not to stick around after the first hit now, right? That used to be acceptable, beating your wife, and now it's not. Think about it. If both parents are working the same hours, why is the wife still doing the majority of the chores and taking on most of the child-rearing tasks? How many times has my brother sat by and just watched you work yourself to death without lifting a finger to help?" Tanya's eyes blazed at Annette. "And now you have cancer."

"Marriage is bad for women and good for men," I muttered, half to myself.

"Exactly. It's actually been proven that marriage shortens women's life expectancy, erodes their quality of health, destroys careers, but it's wonderful for men in that it allows their careers to grow, allows them more free time, gives them free domestic labour, *and* they live longer. I think maybe I should reconsider my own marriage." Something worked over Tanya's face, and I thought for a second she was going to tell Annette about the pregnancy, but her lips pressed shut.

"And yet we're socialized into wanting marriage from the get-go," Annette agreed. "Or even worse, believing we have to earn marriage and fight to keep it, forcing us to think 'getting a man' is our only life goal. And I was not that girl who dreamed of her wedding day. Oh God, I went so wrong!"

A loud pounding on the front door made all of us jump. We looked at each other, eyes wide and lips pursed. The air around us came to life, buzzing with tension. No one moved.

The scorned man had arrived.

- 27 -

I PUT MY hand out to stop Annette from rising. "I helped create this monster." And I would end it.

I pulled on a sweater that had been draped over the back of my chair and stepped to the front door. My hand rested on the doorknob for a moment as I closed my eyes and tried to slow my racing heart. Finally, I opened it to see Jonathan's taunt face glaring at me. I moved forward, forcing him to step back as I closed the door behind me. I would not have the kids hear his rantings. The sun had just gone down, and a moth was already bumping up against the porch light.

"You're the one woman in the world who I trusted," he hissed. The pain in Jonathan's voice almost broke me as he stood there with his hands held out in front of him.

My heart almost tipped over from the sting of that comment, but I forced it upright. "And you're the one man in the world I had hope for," I countered.

"Don't turn this around on me."

"This is *all about you!*" I bit out through clenched teeth, feeling Roxanne's energy surging through me. "This whole thing"—I waved to the house behind me, indicating to his wife and kids inside—"is your fault."

"I never wanted a divorce!" he shouted incredulously.

"Of course you didn't. Then who would take care of your kids and clean up after you all day?"

"Oh, don't start on this 'inequality' thing. I work more hours than she does, so shouldn't more of the home stuff be her responsibility?"

"But she would work *more* hours if you were more helpful."

"Then she shouldn't have had kids. Aren't they the most important thing?"

Yes. No. This comment deflated me a little. I opened my mouth, but no retort would form.

"I work hard, give Annette and the kids everything I have, and this is the thanks I get?" His shoulders fell and I could tell he was tired too. "I know guys that literally do *nothing*. At least I come home every night."

I thought of people at the funeral gushing about how Stan at least came home every night. The bar for men was set so incredibly low. "It's not enough," I whispered to him.

"You'll never be happy, will you?"

"Who? Me?"

"You, Annette… women. You wanted it all and you got it all. You're allowed to have a family and a career. And you're still not happy. I could be Bruce and it still wouldn't be enough."

We were silent for a moment when the door opened behind me. "Just go, Jonathan," Annette said.

Seeing her tore away any softness I may have managed to instill in him. A hard nugget of hate settled into his eyes, as he clenched his fists and looked back to me, ignoring her.

"Mother. I know you're incapable of treating your son like this."

Incapable. There was that word again. "You'd think after all these years you'd be more capable," Stan had said over the failed mashed potatoes. My toes curled.

"You can't do this to me," Jonathan pressed in an authoritative tone that I did not like one bit.

"Oh, just *watch* what she can do." Annette's voice was full of venom. She was right. One of the things men hated about women was their 'incessant chatter.' They didn't listen to our words. Annette could ask until she was blue in the face for Jon to remember to take out the trash on Wednesday nights, but he would never learn to do it on his own unless we left him high and dry. It would take leaving the can until it was overflowing and stinking to high heaven before he'd notice and even then, he'd likely blame Annette for it. Men only paid attention to the thing they were known for: action. Annette's voice dropped to a whisper. "You have no idea what women are capable of without men. We don't *need* you, and that's what scares you the most."

I knew what his childish retort would be before he even said it. "You need my sperm." I could tell he believed his haughty reply sealed his victory over this argument.

"At this point, I'd rather see the human race end than see it continue the way it is." Annette's words slammed down between us—a concrete barricade that ended the conversation.

He turned and marched down the steps. With one leg in the car, he turned back to us. Even in the near dark, I could see the ice in his eyes. "Maybe I do know what women can do. I know what *you* did, Mother. Or rather, what you didn't do." He lifted an eyebrow. "When I said I thought you'd blanked out, it was because I didn't want to even think what the other reason would be for the time lapse."

Shit. I'd almost forgotten about this since I'd gotten home and been so busy creating a new life and Jonathan seemed to have dropped it. My ears buzzed as fear coursed through me. I crossed my arms across my chest to hide the shake in them.

He slowly moved the rest of himself into the car and closed the door. I could leave it at this, let Jonathan think what he wanted. But one little problem remained: he would never know the real me. My prison would never fully disappear until I accepted that I was worthy of love and respect *in spite* of my sins and shortcomings. I walked down the stairs, and he rolled his window to hear what I had to say.

I took a quick breath and blurted, "You're right. I waited to call."

Annette gasped behind me. I waited for Jonathan to pick up his cell phone, dial the police, and drive away and out of my life forever. He simply stared at me for what seemed like a year, eventually leaving without another word.

Once he was gone, Annette squeezed my arm a little tighter and looked at me. Her unspoken gesture and beseeching look assured me that we were in this together and that even if it was true, she'd take it to her grave. "Let's get some sleep," she finally said.

We gripped each other's hand as we stepped back over the threshold in unison.

- 28 -

I SAT SILENTLY in my car outside the abortion clinic, holding hands with Tanya. I'd pooped four times this morning—my sign that I was stressed to the max. The low, grey, windowless building was designed to blend in with its residential and commercial neighbours, but the picketers still knew it existed. A half-dozen women walked silently along the sidewalk, holding signs about how precious all life was. Images of tiny dead babies were taped to the signs. I tipped my head as they passed. Where were the men? Why weren't they protesting? Oh, that's right, they had more important shit to do, like advancing their careers and building their legacy.

They were also very busy controlling the women. They didn't actually give a shit about the babies.

I looked at Tanya and my heart plummeted. Her face was gaunt, making her look twenty years older, freshly shed tears glistening on her cheeks. I cursed Curtis once again for putting her in this situation. I pulled a clump of tissues from the box and stepped out of my car, ready to support my daughter.

We rejoined around the back of the car, where she crumpled into my arms. "Mom." Her voice was thick.

"Shh, shh, shh." I murmured into her hair. "It'll be okay." I held her until her shoulders stopped heaving. Finally, she pulled back and nodded, looking at me to keep focused as she wiped the tears off her cheeks. A sob rose in my throat, and I fought it back. But why? This was a sad situation and emotions were okay. I released a quick torrent of tears and Tanya reached out and wiped my face.

"This is," she started, but froze, shaking her head.

"I know."

There was nothing to say. I put my hand on the small of her back and guided her toward the entrance. I pulled the door open and let her walk ahead of me. A horn sounded from the entrance of the parking lot. I turned to see Curtis's blue Dodge Ram race into the parking lot, where it rocked to a halt.

His door swung open, hitting my car, and he jumped out. "Tan!" His keys clattered to the ground, his wallet slipping out of his shirt pocket as he leaned forward to retrieve them. "Wait!"

I looked back to see a tiny, beautiful smile on my daughter's face. "He was always such a klutz," she whispered as she began crying in earnest.

It was going to take tiny steps for them, interspersed with giant leaps forward. As Curtis pulled Tanya into his embrace, brushing her hair off her forehead, he whispered, "I'm so sorry." He reached up and unclasped the cross chain from her neck and threw it to the ground.

I had never, ever been so happy to see a man in my entire life. I smiled and shook my head as I followed them in, holstering my finger pistol.

- 29 -

three months later

I STOOD HOLDING a small box, the sound of the ocean bright in my ears. The sun was high and glinting off the water in a billion dazzling diamonds, the sky a clear blue. Not the striking pink and orange sunset that had been haunting my dreams lately, but still just as beautiful.

In the dream, Roxanne and I were on her motorbike, riding through the forest and into the surreal sunset, a pink ocean peeking out from behind the trees. It never changed. We just rode and rode, me clutching her waist, her glancing back to smile at me. A couple of old baddies, living their best life. I hoped the dream would stay with me for years.

I had just finished telling Dana and Monique how I'd applied to renew my nursing license, and they'd hugged me tightly in congratulations. I didn't tell them I'd also got my motorcycle license because I didn't want to worry them.

"She would have loved this day," Dana whispered from beside me.

I wiped the tears from my cheeks. "Yes. The afternoon was her favorite." Monique touched my arm gently from the other side of me.

"Are you ready?" Dana asked. I nodded and passed the box and flower to her so I could bend and roll up the cuffs of my pants. I stood again and secured the bright red scarf with the jewel-toned birds around my head. *Stan would have*—I cut myself off. No more Stan thoughts were allowed space in my heart.

I'd thought about growing my hair out, but one night about a month after I'd arrived home, I realized how much I loved not having to fuss with hair. So I'd dug Stan's clippers out from under the sink and buzzed the stubble off, laughing about the night Roxanne and I had done it for the first time. Tears had formed as I realized that Roxanne had known she was dying and didn't need the hair anyway. In the short time she had left, she'd shown me so much about seizing what I wanted.

I took the box back from Dana and stepped into the water. Dana and Monique had insisted I do this, that they would stand behind me for support, but that it was for me alone to do. I walked in up to my calves, the icy water giving me goosebumps. I took a few more steps and stopped, gently stroking the top of the box with my fingertips. "I'm sorry you can't see how far I've come, but I know you're watching over me." The tears renewed themselves. "But I wouldn't have gotten here without you. Give Stan a kick in the ass for me."

I bent and poured the little box of ashes into the water. It looked like sand on glass for a moment. And I set the white tulip I'd bought from Tanya's shop in the centre of the sheen. Soon the next wave rushed away and pulled her out to the ocean.

Tulips represented deep love. I was still so thankful that Curtis had stepped up for his wife when it was needed the most. The week after the abortion had been hard on both of them, but seeing the woman he loved most in the world so destroyed seemed to have turned over a new leaf in him. When I'd stopped by yesterday, Tanya had him in the corner of the garage, moving a shelving unit around and unpacking a shipment of flowers for a wedding, actually whistling as he worked, dropping things as he went.

I watched as the flower was pulled out to sea, knowing my dream that night on the beach with Tanya drowning, tulips swirling around her, had been a premonition of sorts. She had been drowning in her life, but the flowers had been trying to save her. Now, this tulip would escort my best friend to the great beyond. I stood and whispered, "I'm not leaving until you give me a sign."

Roxanne knew exactly what I was talking about, and it only took a minute for the Osprey to appear overhead. It's high, sharp chirp sent shivers down my spine.

FRAN HELD MY newly minted driver's license with tears in her eyes. "I don't know what to say, love. It's the best gift I've ever been given."

I smiled and reached out to wipe the wetness from her cheek. Roxanne had been right. I hated my married name. But when I'd gone into the registry to have it changed, an idea struck me. Who said lineage had to be patrilineal? I wasn't a Bennet any more than I'd been a Copeland.

As I stood frozen in front of the registry lady, a conversation with Roxanne had floated into my mind. *Maiden name,* she had said with disgust. *Why are women know by their marital status? Men are Mr. So-and-So their whole lives. We should be Ms. So-and-So our whole lives.* It had bothered me deeply. Something that I had never given a moment's thought to had suddenly angered me beyond reason. Every married woman that had gone before me had lost a part of herself. I looked at the registry woman and decided, on the spot, that the perfunctory succession of male authority had overstayed its welcome. I was my mother's daughter—a Hale. Tanya and Vivian had loved the idea so much, they were in the process of changing their last names as well. Matrilineal lineage was making a comeback, even if it was only within our little sphere.

I took the card back from her. *Wilhelmina Francis Hale.* "No more settling, Mom." I smiled as tears ran down my face, a legacy chosen.

"CONNOR!" I CALLED to the living room from the kitchen. "Get your little rump in here."

I heard thumping and then he appeared, black hair askew. He looked so much like his father. "What, Gramma?"

"First of all, please pick your shirt up off the ground and put it in the laundry basket. I'm not your slave." *Mommy martyrs no more.*

He picked up the smelly blue soccer jersey, ran to his room to deposit it and then returned. I smiled deeply at him. "Thank you. Now are you ready to learn how to make Grandma's famous hashbrown casserole?"

"Yes!" He pushed a kitchen chair up to the counter and hopped up. Annette popped her head in to check on us and I nodded to her that everything was under control. Gabby toddled in and I scooped her up and sat her on the edge of the counter, bracing her with my stomach.

"I'm just heading out to that showing. Should be back in a couple hours."

"You texted me the address?" There had been a female realtor who was killed at a showing a month ago and it worried me sick for Annette's safety. After two surgeries, she was declared cancer-free, and she didn't survive that just to be taken down by some women-hating asshole.

"Yes. And I've got my little friend." She patted her purse where I knew Roxanne's switchblade was concealed.

"Alright, stay safe." I turned back to Connor. "Okay, we start with this." I slid a bag of frozen hashbrowns over to him and a pair of scissors. "Just cut them open and pour them in the casserole dish."

I glanced at the clock. 4:30 p.m. I had a date tonight with a nice man I'd met at the gym. I was not in it for the long haul, but he seemed to be trying very hard to woo me, even agreeing the date had to happen in my living room as I was watching the grandkids tonight. He was a grandparent too and knew how important a relationship with the kids was. Maybe we'd sneak down to the basement to have a quickie before I sent him on his way.

I handed Connor an opened can of mushroom soup and instructed him to scoop out the contents into the dish. We worked silently, building the casserole step by step.

"Gramma, I did this with Dad the other night," Connor said as he clumsily scraped the can with a spatula.

"Oh, did you?" I tried to keep the shock out of my voice. Jonathan hadn't spoken to us for a solid month after our little blow-up on the front step, but he had slowly come back around for the kids' sake.

"Yes. He said it was his favourite as a kid that you made for him."

"Yes, he did love it."

Connor looked up at me and smiled. "He said you were the best mom ever and he owed you a lot."

Tears pricked at my eyes. Those words were honestly all a mom ever needed to hear from her kids for all she did. "That's really nice, sweetie. You remember to say that to your own mom, okay?"

He nodded aggressively. "And then he said he was trying to be a better dad than Grampa Stan had been."

Now a tear actually fell. I had driven past a *fuck men* graffiti on Sixtieth the other day and had cackled with joy to see two young men adding supportive phrases to it. It was a profound revelation to realize it was never me who had to change, but them. The truth was, I liked men. And I didn't truly want to see a world without them. They just needed to learn to do better.

I watched Connor with a smile. I also loved being a mother and grandmother. I didn't want women to have to refuse to have children to make a point.

"You don't know how happy that makes Gramma's heart." I nudged Connor's shoulder with my elbow.

Maybe all hope wasn't lost.

ACKNOWLEDGMENTS

I think the strangest, darkest things. Who in their right mind asks themselves; I wonder if there are women who would not call for help if their husbands died in front of them? But one of the beautiful things about being a writer is meeting other people who ask themselves similar questions. These ladies are my like-minded cheerleaders; Naomi K. Lewis, Natalie Budesa, Kelly Duran, and Maya Golden. Thank you for your time and friendship. I value your feedback, insights, and twisted minds greatly and am so happy we've met.

I'd like to thank Sam Bailey for the advice she gave me and the referral to my amazing editor, Michelle Meade. Also, I'm grateful to another editor, Lidija Hilje, who pointed out that this book is more than a tongue-in-cheek answer to a morbid question. It's about female camaraderie. And Rene Denfeld, who never ceases to inspire me with her generosity toward other authors. And to the unflappable Camille Pagan; if she can't make you believe in yourself, no one can.

Tons of gratitude goes to my first readers and mistake finders—Liz, Sabrina, Tara, and Jeanette—your continued belief in me gives me life. And a deep appreciation goes to my artistic consultant, Stacy.

I'm sure I would not be so passionate about equal rights if I weren't raising two firey daughters. Julia and Erica, you have turned me from a tomboy to a girls' girl and I'm not mad about it.

And finally, to the husband-who-lives, Jeremy. Thank you for supporting me to such lengths as to agree to move after nineteen years in our first home just so I could have a real office. I hope the bigger garage has eased your suffering.

ABOUT THE AUTHOR

Nicole Brooks has a Bachelor of Science and worked as an environmental consultant before staying home to raise her children. Her first novel, *Just Because We Can* (2018), inspired by her former career, was a Next Generation Indie Book Award Finalist. She lives with her husband and two daughters just outside Calgary. If you can't find Nicole, she's probably out driving around searching for bald eagles or playing pickleball.

Made in the USA
Monee, IL
26 September 2024

66582119R00148